Barbara Else is the author of four best-selling novels, two books for children, and has edited two collections of children's stories. Her first novel, *The Warrior Queen*, was shortlisted for the Montana New Zealand Book Awards and her second, *Gingerbread Husbands*, for the Booksellers BookData Award. She was born in Invercargill, and lived in Wellington, Auckland, Oamaru, Dunedin, Christchurch and San Diego before returning to Wellington where, with her husband, writer Chris Else, she runs the TFS Literary Agency and the TFS Assessment Service. In 1999 she was the Victoria University of Wellington Writer in Residence. Her favourite activities include walking, reading and gardening. She is a devoted cat-owner.

the CASE of the Missing Kitchen

BARBARA ELSE

VINTAGE

Acknowledgements

I am grateful for generous assistance from
members of the Police who helped with my enquiries.
I also have particular reasons for thanking
Jennifer Maxwell, Sarah Neale, Joan Ward and
Michael Easton. Emma Neale read the manuscript
at a crucial stage and gave warm encouragement.
As always, I have special gratitude for Chris Else's wisdom,
attention and perseverance.

This novel was written with the help of a grant from
Creative New Zealand.

Barbara's website is: www.elseware.co.nz

National Library of New Zealand Cataloguing-in-Publication Data

Else, Barbara.
The case of the missing kitchen / Barbara Else.
ISBN 1-86941-574-4
I. Title.
NZ823.2—dc 21

A VINTAGE BOOK
published by
Random House New Zealand
18 Poland Road, Glenfield, Auckland, New Zealand
www.randomhouse.co.nz

First published 2003
© 2003 Barbara Else
The moral rights of the author have been asserted
ISBN 1 86941 574 4

Text design: Elin Termannsen
Fried egg photograph on cover: gettyimages
Printed by Griffin Press, Austalia

Dedication
for Dorothy Jane and Lesley Gwenyth

part one

UGLY SISTERS

chapter one

Let me tell you right away, thirty-seven-year-old orphans are highly complicated creatures. A thirty-seven-year-old orphan who is the single mother of two children, is more complicated still. At the start of that week my life was already near to meltdown. Jarret, my lovely son, had left the house in a murky mood and I feared he was on track to screw up his second high school in less than twelve months. Tilda had her third attack of head lice. I was at the limit on both credit cards and had no work in sight. My boyfriend was starting to say we should move in together, but in the basement of my heart I suspected it was time to say goodbye. I'd no idea why this was so. Sometimes electricity works in a romance, other times the lighting flickers and dies out. As I used to say when I was small and living in the States, and trying to be nonchalant, *de nada.*

You want to hear my relationship history right away? You want more proof of how messed up I was? Briefly, at the age of twenty-one I married for love. Brief was the word. Later I found a new guy and that too was a mistake, though it resulted in my second child, Tilda. For some years I tried living alone — with two kids, you can still be alone — and now in this new relationship the inexplicable was making me uneasy. Such serial romantic disasters are normal for most women, and men. I call it *staggering towards the Zen of partnership*.

So: we're starting at nine-thirty Monday, the first day of a terrible week. I had been tricked into baby-sitting my best friend's ten-month-old daughter Zoe, who had emptied out my scruffy bag and thrown up over my wallet. To this point all the wallet had contained was those maxed-out cards, twenty dollars, coins for parking, and seven parking tickets. But that morning I had to see my personal banking adviser. It never makes a good impression if your wallet smells of anything but money.

I dragged the junk basket out of the hall closet and scrabbled through it. Among the snarls of string and stationery equipment were a calculator with no battery, a pair of rusty pliers, formica samples for the day I could afford a new kitchen, and bits of coloured plastic that had come from who knew where. I shoved it all back and hauled Tilda's toy box from behind the sofa. Under a pair of broken fairy wings was a Barbie doll with wrecked hair and the old wallet I had ditched two years before. I flipped it open. Tilda had stowed pickle slices in the plastic windows. She'd stored a mustard sachet too and it had burst. How many times had I yelled at Luke, her father, *don't you dare take her to McDonald's?* For heaven's sake, the child's mother — me — was an occasional chef, on call for cafés whose real chefs took occasional holidays or came down with minor illnesses.

Why I was a chef, I didn't know. Chefs are supposed to be curvaceous and cook with love. I am scrawny and attack food with irritation, very like my father's attitude to carpentry when he Did It Himself with a hammer. As well as being a chef I sometimes tried dressmaking. Now and then a little shop in Cuba Street sold my work but I had bad luck with customers in person, in my home. My friend Annie hinted this was because I was too truthful about their dress sizes.

I tossed the old wallet in the garbage and went to find Zoe. She was crawling to the kitchen, carrying the staple gun from the footstool I was trying to upholster. I rescued her and was sponging her breakfast off my driving licence when Bernard called from Thee Ultimate Café.

'Suzie, please Suzie, say you're free today.' As usual, his throaty growl reminded me of the engine on a snow-plough, perhaps because he looked like Santa Claus. 'Faludi has asthma. We're not too busy but I need you.'

'I am sad for Faludi, happy for me,' I told Bernard. 'I'll be there in an hour.' I checked what I was wearing: black jeans and sweater, okay for visiting the bank and for concealing with an apron later on.

Zoe threw up again and laughed. I phoned her mother's mobile. Over Zoe's hilarity, I shouted that her baby had been going to visit the bank with me but would not enjoy Thee Ultimate Café. I'd drop her back at Annie's in twenty minutes. If Annie was not home, I'd tie Zoe in her car seat to the letter box. Annie chuckled. She did not think I was serious. I was very serious, and also not sure how pleased I was with the haircut Annie had perpetrated on me the previous day. She'd promised to fix my fly-away hair to give me presence. Some fool I am. In the only complete sentence he had uttered in five days, Jarret said directly how he hated this new hair. Tilda had sneaked glances with an expression identical to the one she wore whenever I presented her with eggplant.

Our Burmese cat, the burly Nameless, sprang onto the kitchen windowsill and mewed through the glass. He wanted food. We had none. His black markings included a mask over the eyes. His teeth were buck, one of several reasons he couldn't be shown as a pedigree, which in turn was why my sister Philippa decided she didn't want him and cast him our way. He'd been a gift from her adoring husband, Roger. There's a saying about gift horses, not about cats, but cats aren't supposed to have buck teeth and look like thugs.

I'd pulled on my denim jacket and heaved Zoe in one arm, my old leather bag in the other, when I remembered I should have made a phone call. I nearly dropped the baby, but only nearly. In my rush to get ready, the cordless as well as the thriller I'd been reading had become hidden under Jarret's unwashed sports gear. Weird things were often happening in my house. But I couldn't get through to our older sister, Lara, down at Customs. I left a message with her secretary, to say I'd try to catch her from Thee Ultimate Café.

She had an interview today, a try at cracking the glass ceiling. Would those in charge — a representative of the minister, other big-boys including the head of her department who was leaving, consider her worth the extra fifteen thousand?

'That much?' It had popped out when she told me, I couldn't help it. At the nudge of jealousy I felt immediately unworthy. Capable my sister surely was. Family legend has it that for my first three years Lara saw me as an adorable pet to haul around. When I showed early signs of my own willpower, she set to work. The result was Suzie, doormat (you know, that prickly kind). Since then Lara had developed into a medium-powered person in Customs, early promise expanding towards full bloom. She would do a brilliant interview. She was already so successful. And Brick — her husband — was reliable and financially secure, loved her to bits, looked like a dressed-up bear in his Yves St Laurent suits. They had no kids. If there was a glass ceiling, many women in her situation wouldn't care. But the media is always ready to chew old dirt with its envious fangs, and I should have phoned her at the weekend, showed solidarity with my sister the bulldozer. There had been no basis for the journalistic beat-up two years back claiming Brick's security firm had inside running for a ministry contract — she and Brick were irreproachable. But public life can be tough on the blameless. How I wished I'd remembered to call her.

What power she had, to make me so guilt-ridden. *Families!*

Strangest organisms on the planet! Who needs families? That's what my mother would say when we were kids and my older sisters started up their double act of bossing (Lara) and hysterics (Philippa). She murmured it again each time my father was determined to go one way and she wanted to zoom along another. She muttered it when my sisters grew to become respected, adult members of the community and I remained a stubborn misfit. Sometimes she said it with biting humour and other times with blackest grit. But it was most often with a catchy chuckle after a puff on a hippie cigarette. My mother never spoke of her own family apart from what this expostulation might imply.

And here I was remembering *Families! Who needs families?* instead of being a good sister. The shame of it. I hadn't talked to either sister much lately. I'd dropped off a little present for Philippa's birthday a month back, then saw her briefly just last week. I had car keys to return when I could bear it. Would she be at home, or at Suite Three? — no, I couldn't spare a minute. I had given her enough time and attention collecting her car from its service and dropping it back at her place because she'd arranged too many meetings. I'd had to bus back across town to my own place. I still had her damn keys. She'd never even phoned to say thank you.

'Maybe Philippa can't use the phone because she's been torn to pieces by the bush rats in her well-to-do attic,' I joked to Zoe on this bad Monday morning. 'Oh, that is so low of me. Philippa is devoted to Suite Three. I couldn't do the kind of work she does. Animals in Asia need my sister. The world needs both my sisters.'

I juggled Zoe. Being a sister is an intricate condition. Trying not to fret, I closed the front door gently. A crack had appeared in the glass panel at the top. Had I more money, I'd have been better at household maintenance. The lock was shonky too. You'd imagine Lara, since her husband had the security firm, would have helped me out on this one. However, though Lara might talk about solidarity in her public life, as sisters we did not often copy *Little Women*.

I scooted a chewed back-end of mouse off the coir doormat and carried Zoe down my rickety front steps. In my elderly rusty car I drove carefully up the winding back road to Annie's suburb because I had the baby in her car seat, and left Zoe with her mother, who thanked me for giving her even a short time out.

'She wanted to staple my kitchen cupboards,' I told Annie. 'She thinks they need fixing. She is right. Please have no confidence in me with your baby ever again.'

Annie and Zoe both smiled as if they loved me, which made me feel bad.

'Your hair transforms you,' Annie said with pride.

Little clouds rushed across a bright sky as I drove into the hot bowl of the city. It was minimally consoling to consider most people probably felt as bad as this when they met their personal banking advisers. We talked about budgeting. I did not tell her about my parking fines.

As I climbed into my car again, family programming kicked in. I would phone Philippa and suggest I cook a celebration dinner at my house if Lara got the job. Would Philippa agree? She could be hard to read, that one. Three weeks ago Jarret had scrubbed her patio and she'd paid him only half of what she promised. Philippa and Roger had recently bought a tiny but expensive Frances Hodgkins, and she'd cheated my boy of fifteen dollars! I wasn't sure she cared enough about kids — about endangered animals in Asia, maybe, but not about kids. She didn't seem a scrap fazed that her own daughter was away as an American Field Service scholar. If one of mine left home, I'd be bereft. Maybe, like many of these things, the answer lay in family history. Till I was born, Philippa had been Lara's adorable pet. Another legend is that Philippa bashed me with a yellow plastic baseball bat as I nursed at mother's breast. What I say is, such behaviour in the young is understandable, and better than a two-year-old falling into a depression when an unexpected baby arrives and takes up centre stage.

But I should forget about my sisters, live my own life. After all, I had my worries about Tilda and Jarret and, once we were all home again late afternoon, hoped I wouldn't be too cranky to find out about their days.

As I drove towards Thee Ultimate Café I began to compose a personal mission statement:

To be selfish and look out for me and my own, which is Jarret and Tilda.

To sort out my own life (not anybody else's), which includes my financial situation and my love life.

To have a love life where love is the operative word . . .

This was indulgent and melodramatic.

To find the meaning of that awkward word with many facets: love.

And this was worse.

To maybe one day have a new kitchen or at least replace that missing cupboard door.

I had very little skill with mission statements. I was not even certain I knew what they were, apart from badly written in the main. My brothers-in-law would have told me the purpose of a mission statement at length, with great pomposity. I had soft spots for Brick and Roger, but in verbal flight they made me want to roll beneath the sofa and pretend I was a dust ball.

Though I whizzed along the waterfront I'd still be late for the café. No matter: once I had a skillet in one hand and a chef's knife in the other I'd be a miracle of helpfulness. Bernard would struggle on to his knees to show his gratitude.

I parked on the hilltop road outside Thee Ultimate Café. In summer this view of the harbour and hills ties balloons onto your heart. In winter it strikes bleakness through your soul. Today, the hills lay like animals wondering if they should pounce or roll over for a belly rub.

At street level, the shabby block of shops that held the café was one storey but at the rear extended several levels down the cliff like a jumble of boxes. Bernard had begun renovations to the café with a plate-glass window at the front some months ago, then stopped. A downturn in business. Poor Bernard.

As I locked my car I saw groups at every table. It was much busier than Bernard had predicted, two waiters moving fast in the open-plan kitchen. When Bernard saw me his sandy beard bristled like a huge cat's whiskers. I felt loved and wanted, also useful. For me, Bernard grew more kindly and appealing every season. It was so sad his wife had died those years ago, so very sad that this café had become his only solace. Years back, when he set up the café he had toyed with names like Wonton Delight and Thai One On, but my sisters had persuaded him that international would attract more clientele.

'Suzie — your hair! — we need two veal and mushroom, a Greek, one Spanish with orange, and a Thai. We have no desserts except the crème brulée and the damn thing's curdled.'

'It's Tilda's day for ballet,' I said, 'and Jarret has after-school sport. I'm yours till after four this afternoon. Bernard, your knee is sore, don't try to hide it from me. Please, slow down, I'm here.'

Bernard's throat gave that rumbling snow-plough sound. Before he'd finished welcoming me, my jacket was off, my apron tied. I scalded the biggest chef's knife and cracked eggs with my left hand while the other stirred the pot of veal to stop it catching. Together, Bernard and I and his little team (who that day seemed very waspish, but it's a common state with folk in service industries) made three tables of ladies who lunch very happy. Bernard chatted graciously with a journalist who was interested in cinnabar ware and had heard of his collection. We tiptoed around tables where couples were obviously having affairs. Clandestine? On a

Monday? Let she or he without sin even in their thoughts cast any aspersion. I cut their radishes into little heart shapes: that takes some practice.

While I ground up parsley pesto, Bernard and I joshed about Parmesan as we'd had done since I was a child bride with a child husband. Bernard always claimed I used too much, that the precarious life of a restaurateur meant a grain of Parmesan was more valuable than diamonds. I declared he was a miser, that now my brother-in-law Roger had moved from dentistry to importing food and gave him breathtakingly cheap rates, Bernard could afford to shake buckets of Parmesan. As he sharpened his boning knife, Bernard laughed. We had run out of carrot for a rapid carrot cake, so I mixed up pumpkin muffins. They rise like airy dreams and are superlative with sour cream. I invented them once when Tilda needed cheering up. It wasn't as much invention or good baking as a fluke — or Zen, the Zen of Muffins. One day I will write a *Cookbook For Those Who Loathe Cooking*. Cookbooks always sell the best, I guess you've noticed.

By now there were still three full tables but they were onto their coffees with only one dessert to come. I slapped all the chef's knives including the wicked boning knife on the magnetic holder — Thee Ultimate Café had a menacing array from paring knives to hatchets — and said triumphant things to one of the waiters about how well we had coped. Instead of being friendly, he whinged that Faludi always managed to skive off. But I had saved Faludi from working when he had asthma!

The woman who had wanted dessert sent her muffin back for low-fat yoghurt instead of sour cream. If she were dieting, why have a muffin at all? But I smiled. I swivelled to answer the phone, at the same time trying to open a new tub of yoghurt which spurted on the bench and up the window. The call was the weekly delivery of meat a whole day early: should it go to the entrance down the side?

'That one's too hard for me. Talk to Bernard when you get here.'

Bernard moved fast (big men, surprisingly, can do this even if they have bad knees) flashed his Father Christmas smile and scooped the phone but the meat man had hung up. When it rang again, Bernard answered. His smile shrank until his mouth looked like an acorn. He passed me the phone. I sneaked a spoon-tip of the pesto as Bernard limped away.

'Your sister told me where you'd be,' said a man's voice, a voice I recognised.

He'd called my sister? This man? It made no sense.

'I'm afraid that this is business, Suzie. Come down to Central. Be there in half an hour.' He hung up.

Okay, he was a detective. But did that mean he could order me around? It made my stomach feel peculiar. I grabbed a cloth, wiped the mess I'd made on the window, made the smear worse, and swiped it harder. There was a bang like a small explosion and a thud that went right up my arm. Far below, there was a crash and a tinkle. My right hand was through the glass. As I pulled it back I saw white flesh — or was it bone? — and red blood welling. I twisted the cloth around my hand, gawped at the jagged hole in the window, unwrapped the cloth to see if it was true — it was. A nasty cut that clearly needed stitches. A gush of bright red blood. I rewrapped the cloth, pressed hard, held it tight against my body.

There was flurry, a customer trying to look at my hand, me refusing, a waiter saying that Bernard should replace all the thin old glass in this place, it was well overdue for his revamp. Bernard changed the dirty cloth for a clean linen tea towel with pink checks and crimson edging. I glanced at the customers, apologised and hoped this hadn't unsettled any stomachs.

'Suzie, let Gavin take you to the medical centre. Get attended to, then I insist you come right back.' Bernard was gruff, concerned. 'You and I will have a mid-afternoon aperitif to help you relax.'

But if Bernard was going to pay me I could buy food for the cat, as well as some organic wash for Tilda's hair lice. And of course if you are summoned to the central police station on business, you need a good excuse if you decide not to go. I didn't think a cut thumb would be a big enough defence.

The waiter who had been so full of complaints drove me in my car to the nearby doctor. A nurse checked me over right away, said cheerful things, and inside twenty minutes I was cleaned up. A nasty flap on my thumb and a gash down to the wrist were sewn up with black silk. The doctor told me the good news: I hadn't cut a tendon. Even better, I hadn't cut a nerve. I should keep the hand elevated to help the circulation knit because the cut was against the normal flow (I believed him: that flap of skin had looked a sickly grey, close to dead already), and I must return in two days time to have the dressing checked. I was to go home and rest: it might seem a minor injury but it was a big shock to my system.

The nurse pinned my arm into a sling, told me to keep the hand dry and put no strain on it, and said I must find someone to drive me home at once or take a taxi. The whingeing Gavin had disappeared long since.

At my car, as I shoved the sling into my bag I remembered Bernard's linen towel, bloody and discarded on the surgery floor. A job for tomorrow, to fetch it. My hand had no strength and hurt like hell when I turned the ignition. But my car was automatic (old and rusty, but automatic) and I thought I'd be okay. I felt weird, and somehow snarky. How many people today had told me what I should do! The banking adviser! This nurse! That detective! As if I were second-class, something to be discounted, not completely human. This incident threw me back to when I turned seven.

On my seventh birthday — my birthday! — my sisters told me Mom and Dad had wanted a third child but couldn't have one. I was in fact an animatronic doll that had been rejected by the quality controllers at Disneyland. My parents had taken pity on me and salvaged me from the Anaheim trash. Lara told me that each time I burst into tears, my innards were at risk of shorting out. Philippa screamed and hissed like sparks to demonstrate.

'Liar, liar, pants on fire,' I whined. 'I'll go tell Mom. You'll both get busted.'

'Every night Dad opens a panel between your shoulder blades,' Lara insisted. 'So Mom can check your wiring.'

The story began to seem more likely. As many children do, I'd sometimes wondered if I really fitted into my family and, though both parents, especially Dad, were into Do It Yourself, Mom claimed to be the daughter of an electrician so was the only person in the household who could safely replace fuses.

My sisters stated our parents had sworn them to secrecy, but Lara and Philippa didn't think it fair to keep me ignorant now I was seven. They said the whole family was scared to death each time I had a bath. They said that now I was seven and therefore larger, I was no longer allowed to go in swimming pools in case everybody was electrocuted. They declared they had to watch my every move. For three days they called me Sparky. For three days I dealt with terror. For three days I sweltered in the Santa Barbara summer and dared not swim. Then I remembered our last trip down to Disneyland. We filed into a big theatre and there was Abraham Lincoln, the old guy who did the speech. He stood at a desk with wide blue sky behind him. He was so old he was in history books, and he was an animatronic doll. And there he was, still giving his big speech while behind him the sky turned rosy, white clouds appeared, slowly lengthened into stripes, and became the American flag.

However: back to my Monday. I knew Bernard would ask me to stand in for an indisposed chef again, even though I had shown such bad humour and been so clumsy. He'd paid me in cash as I had hoped. He had always understood about money, even lending some to my erratic ex-husband Gifford for an early get-rich venture. I doubted that Gifford had ever paid him back in full, although gratitude would have been expressed with exuberance, promises made with winning charm.

The dashboard clock said three-fifteen. Tilda's school teacher, nice lady, would be taking my daughter to ballet along with her own younger girl. I parked underneath the central library, found an old pay-and-display ticket from last week, shoved it on the dashboard upside down, and rushed round to do some shopping. Half an hour, that detective said? So what. I wished I could call him to find out what he wanted, but didn't own a mobile phone.

Once I'd found nit-busting wash and oil for Tilda, a roll of peppermints to keep my energy level up and other bits and pieces, I dithered over Petit Miaou or Chomp. Chomp was cheaper and came in larger cans. I bought two, shoved the shopping in my car and ran across to the police station. My hand was throbbing. I should have obeyed the nurse and worn the sling.

'Hello, Suzie,' said the motherly woman at the watch-house desk. 'How's the world turning for you this fine day?'

'Oh, Jane,' I said, 'too fast. I'm dizzy.'

She laughed, pressed the intercom and spoke into it. Cradling my hand beneath my jacket, I sat on a metal bench with a couple of complainants. Or maybe they were offenders, how would I know?

A man in plain clothes appeared through the security door. The skin over his cheekbones was stretched with tiredness. He glanced over me distractedly. Jane pointed, and he glanced back.

'Suzie! What happened to your hair?'

'I guess your clothes are that plain because you are a plain clothes cop,' I said. 'How was your weekend shift? Looks like it was a killer.'

'Suzie,' said the detective, who happened to be Caine, who also happened to be my boyfriend and the man I planned to dump that night, 'please come through.'

Though I had those plans for saying goodbye later, a tiny eel of sorrow moved in my stomach. Caine was always more closely shaven than seemed possible. I liked his sharp nose with the halfway crick where a criminal once hit it with a beer crate. And though I hate being ordered around, I have a curious thing for authoritarian tendencies. If you don't have to obey, they can be cute.

Caine swiped his security card, we entered the station and he rushed me up some stairs. Into a nasty room we went: carpet to halfway up the walls, spotty acoustic tiles and a Big Brother video camera and recorder trained on a table where he sat me. I developed an instant headache.

Caine took the chair opposite. 'Please bear with me.' He held up a clear plastic envelope, but lowered it when he saw my bandaged hand. I'd kept it under my jacket until now. 'What the hell have you done!'

'Nothing.'

'Let me see.'

I tucked it into my armpit.

He looked doubtful, but held up the plastic envelope again. In it was a business card smeared with mud. I moved to take it with my good hand but he kept it beyond my reach, held it just for me to see. The card was Philippa's, her personal one, not for the little charity she ran with that name she thought was such a pun, Suite Three.

'I tried to contact Philippa's husband, Roger,' Caine said.

I opened my mouth to say I knew who the members of my family were, but Caine kept right on talking.

'I tracked down your sister Lara — she was in a meeting and spared me less than thirty seconds. I also tried her husband, Brick, but no go. I don't want to do this to you, Suzie. But I am afraid we need you.'

I do not want to detail what happened next. It is still shadowy in my mind and I intend it stay so. Caine handed the business card to another detective who'd been lurking in the stairwell. I suspected something unorthodox was going on. Caine took me in a police Commodore to the public hospital and down into a place with a terrible name that begins with an 'm'.

By this time, I almost could not see straight and it had nothing to do with the aftershock of my hand smashing through that window. Caine, his invisible detective hat on, was very gentle at my shoulder, and there were people in hospital greens and whites. Someone pulled a sheet back from the top of a narrow bed in the place that begins with an 'm', and everyone waited for me to say, *Yes, that is my sister*.

One side of this poor woman's face was not a normal shape at all. She would have been difficult to recognise, whoever's sister she may have been. Otherwise, she was similar to any middle-class, middle-aged matron in any western city at that time. But her hair was mid-brown in an arty wedge-cut whereas Philippa's was blonde-brown in an arty wedge-cut. They also showed me some clothes: a black knit sweater (you could tell it was expensive), matching skirt, Italian high-heeled shoes, silver designer earrings very like my other sister Lara's, a heavy broken watch rather more like a man's than a woman's so I guessed she'd had some trouble with her eyesight.

Saying no would have been enough. Even shaking my head would probably have been enough. However I have this thing with authority so felt I ought to speak.

'No,' I whispered. 'It's not Philippa.'

Next thing I am sure of, the detective and I were in the unmarked car again and we'd stopped by the side of the road a mile or so around the bays. He lowered the windows. The waves seemed to be heaving up and down — seemed, I say, because the green scoop of lawn that led over to the beach chopped up and down for me as well. The hills on the far side of the harbour were blurred, looming closer and receding.

'What happened?' I asked.

'You needed fresh air,' Caine said. 'You fainted.'

'That much I know. Everybody in that . . .' That place. That awful room. 'They seemed used to people fainting.'

'I'm sorry you had to go there. Especially since it wasn't . . .' Caine's mouth twisted down as he must have realised it was far better for me that it was not my sister, dead.

'How come you had Philippa's card?'

He rubbed the crick on his nose. 'The woman was found under some bushes in a lay-by. No identifying marks on or around her except the usual empty Coke can and fast-food wrappers, and that card half under a rock, there by mistake or on purpose, connected or not, who knows? It may not be significant but it's the only lead we have at this time.'

The card could not have any relevance. I had dozens of cards in my bag from people and companies I could not remember. I think those cards must spawn in darkness like ball-point pens.

'But Caine, if you thought that woman may have been Philippa, you shouldn't be involved in this case given . . .' Our relationship, which he didn't know I planned to end that night.

'I'm not involved. It's not my case. You're right, I shouldn't have taken you there at all. But soon it won't matter because — this may be another shock to you — I'm getting out.'

He was dumping me? This had to be wrong. I was usually the dumper, not the dumpee. To be exact, fourteen years ago I'd marched off from my child-husband, and the second time, I'd thrown out a man much larger than myself, screaming invective that made me want to rinse my mouth with industrial cleanser. With Caine, I had planned things to be different, to be a decent human being and try to give reasons. I had not wanted to hurt this man. My stomach curled up around that little eel of sorrow.

Caine passed his hand over his eyes — oh, he was tired. He was a man made of wire stretched to its limit. 'I'm quitting the job. I'm fed up with villains. I am working on two big cases when it should be only one. I am working on several little cases as well. Enough's enough. I want a job where I have regular hours and a home life. I want to be married and have kids. Suzie, I want to start with your kids, an instant family. Then maybe we could have a kid of our own. Two of our own would be better. Three would be asking a lot, let's see how the first two turn out.'

The scent of his deodorant filled the car so tangibly, it smelled so clean, so (please don't laugh) right wing that it was tempting to crumple on him for protection. But good grief. Apart from any other consideration, I was thirty-seven. To have even one more kid, with Caine? And to think about such matters when I'd just seen that poor woman lying dead — those high heels, that heart-rending sweater, what use was the expensive garment to her now? Even the dashboard of Caine's car began chopping up and down like the scoop of grass, the ocean, the brown hills.

He leaned closer. 'We could honeymoon in Fiji. We could take the kids. I'd like that. Tilda would love it. What do you reckon about Jarret? Would it help lift his black mood?'

'This is a fine time to propose,' I told him, 'because I'm going to throw up.'

I opened the car door. Caine was compassionate, understanding, sympathetic. Believe me, he was all those things and more. He waited, then scooped dirt over the nasty puddle, reached a box of tissues from the back seat and said nothing while I wiped my eyes and blew my nose.

This would make it harder for me to dump him.

'I have to pick up Tilda. I'm late for fetching Tilda.'

'It's okay. While you'd fainted, I phoned the ballet teacher. I talked to Tilda. She's waiting through the next class. Tilda's fine.'

How come this man who had just put me through an ordeal in the 'm' room was being much too decent to be true? Why should anyone want to rescue me from my life between the minus and the plus of my bank account? Why should he want a wife with ready-made children, one of whom had head lice? And let's not mention Jarret, who refused to tell anyone his latest troubles.

Of course I had to dump Caine. But later on, that night. Not now in a public place where I had just thrown up.

chapter two

When I returned to the library car park after that needless ordeal Caine called police business, I found a forty-dollar fine on my windshield. *Stationary Vehicle Offence Infringement Notice, failure to display a current receipt in the manner required.* My own fault. Typical. Fingers wobbly, I shoved it in my still-damp wallet with the other infringement notices and scooted off to pick up Tilda.

Every little girl longs to do ballet. Back in California, how my little-girl soul had craved to take part in such beauty of movement, my skinny chest coveted the prideful encasement of a satin bodice sewn with sequins, my negligible hips the gather and froth of pink tulle.

Lara and Philippa learned ballet, and went through to Grade whatever, I don't know, but high. They were among the queens of our small ballet school in Santa Barbara and also later on in San Diego, long hair scraped in pony-tails from their porcelain-smooth temples. Their toes would *pointe*, their knees *plié*, their arms describe arcs of pure emotion while my younger heart wrenched with admiration and convulsed with jealous yearning.

I was not slender but scrawny, and knew the difference because my sisters told me. I possessed not sweetly rounded human knees and wrists but knobby insect joints. My hair was no sleek curtain but wisps so slippery that whenever Mom tried to give me a French pleat, the moment I moved my head hairclips pit-pattered to the floor like metal hail. Other little girls — boys also — in my class floated, skipped and polka-ed, as meticulous as dandelion seeds. I clumped and listed like a junior monster made by Dr Frankenstein on a day he had bad toothache. *Smile*, the ballet mistress cried each week, *Suzie, remember your smile!* My expression stayed a clench of jaw. Knees at tortured angles, I hop-hop-stepped instead of step-hop-skipped, whatever, I always got it wrong. Dad continued to fork out dollars for lessons. Mom mopped my tears and bought more hairpins. Philippa was the Sleeping Beauty in one production I remember, Lara was a most efficient Prince. I never wore a tutu. I wore a furry suit with fold-back paws. I was a dancing rabbit, one of ten. Dancing? Here is the truth that hurts: it was my job to peer around a *papier mâché* mushroom.

By now I knew this plight was typical of little girls no matter what country they grew up in. My heart wrenched again whenever I saw Tilda, seven years old, floating with the grace of a bundle of newspapers dumped out the back of a truck. She resembled not Princess Thumbelina, but a Cabbage Patch doll.

My annoyance about the parking fine still burned as I braked the car outside the hall where Tilda learned ballet. With my bad hand I found it hard to push the door into the hall, and the hinges gave a horror movie graunch. At first I was dazzled by the maze of light shining through the high windows, then made out some of the smaller children running in and out from the den beneath the stage. Madame Avril was demonstrating high kicks. She was seventy-six years old and very tiny. She could kick a beret off your shoulder. Till she turned seventy-four, she would kick it off your head. When she had ended her demonstration and stood like a fragile goddess barking out orders, I nodded my apology. Tilda, my ballet-struck girl, jumped off the bench where she had been watching ethereal twelve-year-olds pose, *jeté* and high-kick, each hoping for a significant role in the mid-year concert coming up. She ran towards me still in her pink tights and pink leotard, her pink exercise cardigan tied around her. Her school clothes bulked out her *Hello Kitty* bag.

'Your hand!' she cried. 'What did you do?'

'Don't fuss. Tilda, change out of your ballet shoes.' Each week I had this tussle with my daughter.

She has a stubborn jaw. She showed it to me. Madame turned her exquisite tiny head and regarded my child. Tilda grinned, plumped down and untied her slippers at once.

As we drove home, and thank goodness it was not far, Tilda confirmed she'd talked to Caine on Madame Avril's mobile. 'Caine says he's coming over for his dinner.'

That was right. He'd said he'd cook because I shouldn't with this bandage. I was eroded by how nice he was, and wondering how to dump him.

'Will he sleep at our house too?'

'How was your lesson?' I countered.

'Madam Avril shouted at me.'

'That doesn't sound like her.'

Tilda seemed smug. 'It was when I kicked Cormac. I don't think boys should do ballet.'

We had work to do on my daughter's ideas of gender roles. 'Tilda, some of the greatest dancers of all time have been men.'

'I think my own opinion. So can you,' Tilda replied, and there was not much answer to that. I was relieved I would not have to sing The Song to cheer her up. I was in no mood for singing. Also, The Song is very embarrassing. We try never to sing it in public.

We parked in my run-down garage, dark and gloomy because

it was overgrown by tree ferns. I gathered up the organic products I hoped would smother my daughter's nits but not affect her general health, and jostled my bag and packages up the front steps. Jarret's bike was propped on the veranda. He was home before I'd expected. As I entered, the house smelled especially male.

The afternoon had shaken me. My arm pulsed, deep and heavy. I dumped my bag beside the hall stand and began searching in it for the sling. In the kitchen, the blender whirred at full pitch: Jarret mixed a gunky sports drink each afternoon when he came in.

Tilda ran on before me to the kitchen. 'What a dreadful mess,' she screamed.

I stopped trying to figure out how to wear the sling and hooked it over the kitchen door handle as I dragged myself and the groceries to see what was the matter. Tilda stood with hands on hips, a little fishwife. She learned that from her government official Auntie Lara, not from me.

Jarret chug-a-lugged his disgusting mixture at the sink, and on the bench was the bag of stuff I knew was his school project . . . All the kitchen cupboards were open, the shelf of the one where the door had disappeared a few months back was now broken in half. The pantry double doors were open wide, with one shelf wrecked there too. Rice was strewn along the bench. Seashell pasta littered the floor. Dry goods, cans, bottles of sauce, spices, were scattered everywhere. The cat, our hungry Nameless, crouched on the sill as he had this morning, staring through his bandit mask.

'Jarret! What's going on?' Though I tried not to yell, my voice was not as calm as custard.

His wiry shoulders lowered as he turned. He looked guilty, as boys do. 'I shut the fridge when I came in.' His tone implied that you should expect no more of a preoccupied boy. 'Hey, Mum. Cool bandage.'

My brain, which had momentarily stayed out on the front porch, pulled up next to me. I looked over the dividing bench into

the dining area and living room. The footstool I'd been uphol-
stering was upside down although it had been right side up. Books
had been hauled off the shelves. The toy box was upended — but
I had left it like that. I went back along the corridor and glanced
in every bedroom. The only thing not overturned was the junk
basket. Drawers and cupboards had been dumped out. Poltergeist?
Earthquake? A disappointed burglar? I didn't worry that anything
had been stolen — we had nothing worth nicking. The TV was
still there, and the old stereo. Jarret's ghetto blaster was under his
desk. Tilda's first most precious thing, her fairy princess doll, lay
half under her pillow. Her second most precious thing, the ballerina music box her father had given her, was upside down on her
duvet. In my room, the dressing table had all the drawers emptied,
books shoved off the bedside cabinet, my lacquer jewellery box
tipped out on my bed — necklaces, old earrings, the out-of-date
guarantee for my watch. Everything seemed to be there. The few
bits of make up I owned were spread across the carpet. I picked up
the bottle of Anaïs Anaïs that Caine had given me for Christmas.
The stopper was tight and none had spilled. Tears smarted in my
nose, as sharp as lemon. Jarret had followed. 'I thought it was just
that you'd freaked, Mum.'

I gave him what the three of us term The Look.

'Junkies looking for drugs?' he asked, off-hand.

I try never to swear at my kids. This time I managed it as well.
Drugs is something I would never do, have never done, not even
the little cigarettes my mother liked, and Jarret knew it. Nor are
drugs what caused Jarret to leave his old school, let me make that
clear right now.

I realised I should call Caine — I realised I certainly should not
call Caine and take advantage of a man I meant to dump. Therefore
I dialled emergency as a member of the public ought to do and
reported the break-in. The dispatcher took the address but recognised my name and voice. He said a car was on its way, and he'd

make certain Caine heard, too. This is the trouble with socialising with your boyfriend's workmates. Ten-pin bowling has a lot to answer for.

Caine was on the phone to me almost at once. 'Is the intruder still on the premises?'

'I have no idea. He'll be stupid if he is. Though it may have been a she. Or several shes and hes, who knows? I'll go and check.'

'Stay where you are!' Caine snapped. 'Grab Tilda and get out of the house. This minute. Jarret too.'

'I can't stay where I am and get out of the house at the same . . .'

'Don't be pedantic! Leave the house.'

Anger gave me strength to heave Tilda up and give her to Jarret. 'Wait on the street,' I ordered.

'I still haven't found my keys, Mum.' Jarret had been using the spare set. 'The burglar must have found my keys, that's how he broke in, the bastard.'

'Get out with Tilda!'

But Jarret carted Tilda back into the kitchen. I was about to yell good and loud when he grabbed his school project and carried that as well as Tilda down the steps. She draped her arms around his neck like a cartoon heroine.

I fetched both kids' bags and despite — or because of — Caine's dictatorial behaviour, checked every room for the burglar or for signs left by him or her, beneath the beds, in the wardrobes, the broom closet, and in the laundry room out back. I nipped over the raised brick patio where Dad had set a rotary clothesline, and checked the sloping path down the side of the house. No burglar. No signs. Nothing missing.

As I left the house with our bags and an overnight case another dark blue Commodore and a patrol car pulled up. Caine leapt out of the Commodore with the energy of a dog released for a run — he was an Alsatian in plain clothes and I confess the sight made my insides go into a tangle. I should mention I am terrified of dogs, so please, go figure that one.

'You are a very stupid female.' He may have meant this to be a whisper but it was a penetrating stage whisper and he obviously wanted to shake me. 'What did I tell you to do?'

'Why are you here? You should declare your interest!' I stated. 'You should take a step backwards from this!' That's the way they talk in the police. On a good day it used to make me smile.

Jarret scowled and did not look at Caine. Tilda was a wide-eyed grin. The two constables from the patrol car grinned as well. One was a dinky policewoman as pretty and tough as you could wish to see. Even though I was angry and afraid, I wanted to set her in icing on top of a cake.

Caine apologised, hand to chest. My knees turned mushy for a second. He whispered — a genuine whisper — that his behaviour showed he must indeed resign as soon as possible. I nearly said I thought he'd handed a resignation in already, but limited myself to apologies as well. My behaviour showed I was nearly freaking out and no wonder, I'd had a bad day.

'Of course, Suzie. Forget it. Let's check inside.' He seemed eager to get on with the job. Before today I'd never seen him in work mode. My head did not like it, but those knees were still a problem.

The trio of police persons looked inside and quickly established, as they told us when they were back out, that someone broke into the house between the time I left and the time that Jarret came home just a few moments ahead of Tilda and myself. Such genius. I did not comment. But if Jarret had just arrived, the house had smelled too much of male. The male perpetrator had either been there a very long time, had an extreme odour problem or I had a most sensitive nose.

Caine, rubbing his own nose, interrupted my thoughts. 'Suzie, those other occasions when things happened . . .'

The crack in my front door, he meant. The cupboard door that vanished. 'It's hardly odd. One's wear and tear, the other is the children not confessing. I do my best on upkeep and with parenting.'

The kids rolled their eyes and said nothing.

'You're certain nothing's missing?' Caine asked. 'You'll have to get new locks. You can't sleep here tonight. Let's see — I'm meant to be on a call-out now. Can you stay with your sisters? Either one?'

Tilda batted her eyelashes. 'Auntie Lara doesn't want me around until my scalp is fixed. Mum bought organic wash for me today. But Auntie Lara really means she doesn't like it when I hit her gong.'

'Gong?' Caine asked.

'I don't like it either. Jarret dared me.'

Jarret looked darker by the minute. 'I did not dare you. It's just that show-offs can't resist.'

'You did so dare me!' Tilda cried.

'Be quiet.' I fished the roll of peppermints from my bag and gave them a couple each to shut them up. The kids were fascinated by the huge brass gong in Lara's hallway. It was purpose-built to summon Tibetan monks across Himalayan divides. 'Tilda is right, we may not be welcome at Lara's tonight. I could phone Philippa . . .' My jaw wobbled. 'You thought Philippa was . . .' I didn't want to say 'dead' in front of Tilda.

Caine glanced at Tilda as if he too had words he did not want to say in front of seven-year-old girls.

'Can we stay at your house?' Tilda's eyes gleamed.

'Now you'll definitely forget to ask me how my day went,' Jarret mumbled.

I had a realisation such as only mothers can experience and turned The Look on him again. His skinny shoulders shrugged. Once more, that guilty attitude, and this time I suspected . . .

'You've blown your second chance? Oh, Jarret. Say I'm wrong.'

His eyes looked near me, not straight at me. Jarret was in a scrape again. For the second time in a year? My boy and I needed a quiet talk, or even just to be in silence.

Caine didn't ask what was going on. He was a man with intuition. It would be a profound loss to the police force if he did indeed resign. He'd disentangled the mystery of a murder in a national park. He had explained the disappearance of the deputy PM's press secretary (the guy had simply had enough, went AWOL, and nobody blamed him), and lately solved the riddle of the abduction of a troupe of Russian acrobats: Caine revealed them to be five agile and enterprising university students who fooled people by talking in fake accents. Praise caused Caine's mouth to become a wiggly line of shyness. A fan had built a website in his honour. It had caused jealousy in the ranks before it was dismantled.

Caine hunkered down beside my daughter. 'Tilda, here is the key to my place. Why don't you and your mum deal to your hair in my bathroom and I'll bring pizza home for dinner by, say, seventhirty? I think this call-out will be short but I'd better scramble.'

'Do you have a night light?' Tilda asked.

Caine hammed it up. 'For you, Tilda, there will always be a night light.'

'Ah, spew,' Jarret muttered.

'Shut up,' I hissed.

Caine ignored this mother-son exchange, another sign he was far too much a good guy. 'You lot can spend a day or so with me until we get your place cleaned up. Suzie, give me your keys.'

'I will hang on to my keys!'

Something like anger wrestled in Caine's face before he once again looked clean and in control.

'Okay, Suzie. The constables will pull the door to. They will leave everything locked up. But promise you won't come back here tonight.'

'How many beds at your house?' Tilda asked. 'I don't like to share with Mum because she wriggles.'

The muscles in Caine's face turned crisp. The constables grinned harder.

'Enough,' he said to them and to me, more quietly, 'You're very stressed. No wonder. We need that holiday in Fiji.'

Jarret glowered at us. 'Who's going to Fiji?'

'Jarret, shut up,' I said.

'Yeah, shut up, you!' cried Tilda.

The kids began that universal sibling routine of silent punching. I gestured to the policemen to overlook this mild domestic violence. The uniforms climbed back up the steps to my house. Caine led me around to my garage. Still mutual-punching, Jarret and Tilda jostled for the front seat. Caine took Tilda gently by the shoulder, sat her in the back and told her to fasten her seatbelt. She smiled at him again, the gap-toothed minx. It's the way all little girls smile when they are in ballet costume, which she still was, my pink sausage.

'Nameless!' I cried. 'I didn't put down any Chomp!'

'Cats survive.' Caine tried to shut my driver's door.

'I have to talk to you,' I said in a low voice. 'Without the kids.'

Caine nodded. 'Later. Are you all right to drive? Are you certain?'

I did not trust myself to say another word. My arm and hand were throbbing. I wanted to lie down with painkillers and strong coffee.

'Well — okay. Look after your mother,' Caine told Jarret, who was still glowering. 'Wash your hair,' he said to Tilda.

He took an uneasy glance at my new style but all he said, looking far too weary for a man who had not yet finished his day's work, was not to do anything stupid till he managed to get home.

I controlled myself and only said, 'As if.'

chapter three

The kids had not been to Caine's before. His place was one of a row of modern pseudo-terrace houses, the elbows-in, one-room-wide houses that made me imagine the early settlers must have been terrified to death of the spacious new world they had arrived in. They could not bear the size of the sky. All that enormous space to spread their lives in, and they built rows of tiny hutches. Caine's hutch was utilitarian in the modern way, subdued lighting in the hall, a lot of chrome.

How could I dump Caine in his own house, when I was unable to return to mine and also had my children with me?

Jarret — my goodness, I was weary of his glower — turned on Caine's TV and I left him to it. Tilda ignored my request to change into the clothes in her *Hello Kitty* bag and stayed in her leotard. What the heck — the rules had already turned to smoke today. I found a plastic bag to keep my bandage dry and we washed her hair in Caine's bathroom upstairs. Tilda was impressed no end by his stack of fluffy towels in shades of military green and air force blue. The tiles gave me a flash of the hospital whites and greens

I'd seen that afternoon. I shuddered.

As Tilda moulded her lathered-up hair into peaks she promised for the umpteenth time that she would not wear anyone else's hat at school, nor use someone else's comb, nor even hug her friends until this latest infestation was cleared up with everyone in her class and out of it. We rinsed her hair.

'That is a serious promise, now.' My good hand deep in a fluffy towel, I gave her head a tiny shake. 'What is a promise, Tilda?'

'It's what kids say to make their mothers happy.'

Beneath the towel I caught another glint in those eyes. I was not convinced her mother's happiness came before the temptations of playing hairdressers with her friends. I had been trying for many weeks not to say what I said next because it had elements of black-mail. However for every parent, single or paired-up, the time for blackmail comes repeatedly.

'You cannot be a ballerina if you have hair lice.'

'Why not?'

'Those pirouettes make the lice fall out and other ballet dancers slip in them.'

Though I didn't expect her to believe it for a second and Tilda had the grace to laugh, she turned thoughtful as if she realised for the first time nits held no glamour. I combed the organic oil through her hair, and she sat in front of Caine's TV downstairs with Jarret and didn't say another word.

I wanted to phone my sisters now and tell them all about it. But Lara had that interview this afternoon — and here was my chance to talk to my boy. I beckoned him into the kitchen and propped him against Caine's fridge.

'What went wrong?'

'Wrong?'

'At school today.'

Jarret looked away from me and took a breath.

When you are a parent there is always one of your kids for

whom your heart breaks every day. Jarret was this kid for me. 'You're not a bad boy. You're honest, gentle and intelligent. You are my much-loved son.'

He gave a single laugh that would do a gangster proud.

'Do you have a letter for me from your teacher? Or the principal?'

He moved his head two centimetres to the left, which I took to be a negative.

A sigh began in the pit of my belly. 'Jarret, I know I'm not a great example, but I have such hopes for you.'

Jarret held himself motionless. At last he glanced at me again. In his eyes I saw this skinny, snub-nosed kid knew his mum loved him, but that was not much help to him. Somewhere at the bottom of all this was the fact that I walked out on his dad when Jarret was one year old. Somewhere in all this was the fact that his father was hot-tempered and erratic, charming, generous with words and promises, but a miser with what counts — honest words and keeping promises. I had loved Gifford so much, believed in his schemes. I'd been twenty-three years old — however, I had known what was important. Love drives us to extremities. Love can be misguided. It is never to be trusted, unless it is the love of a mother for her kids, and even then a mother sadly, badly, can mess up.

'Whatever it is, we'll sort it out,' I told Jarret. 'Get yourself some sports gunk out of that cupboard. Ace detectives drink it too.'

'Top cop — top drop,' Jarret said with sarcasm that surprised me, accompanied by an excellent imitation of Caine that did not. My son had been a mimic since the age of nine months when the neighbour's cat taught him to mew. This made me think of our own cat. I hoped Nameless would soon snare another mouse.

After I checked on Tilda, still quiet in front of mayhem on TV, I climbed the stairs to fix the fold-out sofa bed in Caine's study for Tilda, then into the loft to unroll a camping mattress for Jarret. No way did I intend to sleep in the loft and as Tilda had made public she did not like to sleep with me. Nor would I sleep on the sofa downstairs, and could not expect Caine to do so. So was it one more night for me in this man's bed? I would appreciate strong arms around me tonight, but planned to keep it chaste.

I entered the main bedroom to pick up the phone. Caine and I had spent good times in this bed. Weekends when Tilda was with her father and Jarret with friends (because his father could never be counted on to keep arrangements), Caine had prepared a tray of cheese and dips and champagne, and we used this bed as if it were an ark to float us off from real life into safety. Oh, making love with Caine — his moves were strong and slow, methodical as you'd expect from a detective, until I'd feel myself dissolve around his clean, crisp-muscled flanks. He'd bring me to a prolonged burn of sweetness, and then he'd turn into a wild man while the sweetness peaked and pitched . . .

And I was going to say goodbye to that? Why did the thought of settling down and being happy make me hurt so? It was odd to be in this bedroom now, Jarret and Tilda downstairs as if it were a family home. I found a packet of painkillers on Caine's dresser, swallowed two dry and nursed my hand. His wish to have a baby stole round in my belly. Each time I'd been pregnant, I'd carried my growing size with such contentment. I'd even enjoyed labour because I felt constructive and important for a change.

But these were thoughts I had to let slip by. Here was real life, and I should get in touch with Philippa and Lara. Today had made me feel as powerless and bewildered as when I was small, when my sisters knew things that I did not and I could not unlock their secrets.

I called Philippa with no success, then checked the time and tried Roger's Asian import office though I thought it would be closed by now. It was. Roger was one of those dangerous people who use cellphones in their car, but he didn't answer when I dialled that number either. Where could Roger be on a Monday evening, if not home and not in the office? A meeting? Had he and Philippa had an argument? This notion was so unlikely that I laughed with disbelief. As a couple, Philippa and Roger were so tight it made you wince.

Okay, I would try Lara. The phone was picked up right away and Brick said hello. He was older than the rest of us, just fifty. He remembered something called the *Friday Sports Post*, which had pink pages. His dad used to arrive home on Friday nights with the pink *Sports Post* and a pack of lemon drops in his suit pocket for little Brick to hunt out. The paper, apparently, contained a comic strip called *Brick Bradford* about a guy who had a space ship and adventures. Our Brick was content with large contracts from government departments, tartan slippers in the evening, and good whisky. This Monday night, the way he said hello, I knew it was a night for Brick and whisky.

'What a terrible day I've had,' I said.

There was a growly noise that I interpreted as *Me too*.

'Is Lara there?'

'She's in bed with a migraine.' Brick's voice was muffled. 'Let me clarify that. The bedroom curtains are drawn, someone is lying in there with a herbal pillow over her eyes and she hisses at me to stay away. All indicators are that it's your older sister after an unusually tough interview, the results of which will not be known till later on this week. She only has a long shot, as you know.'

'Oh, surely . . .'

'Indeed, after that unpleasant media attention in — um. When. Then. You know.'

'I'm sorry about Lara's bad day. Mine's still a shocker. Brick — the police thought Philippa might be in the 'm' room.'

There was another growly noise tipped up at the end like a question.

I explained. 'The police thought Philippa might be dead. A woman is dead. I had to identify a body, but it was nobody that I knew.' I heard the pun as I said it and the inside of my head turned dark and buzzy. I'd reached another stage of realising what appalling things had happened today, what I had seen, that dead woman who looked like a portmanteau version of my sisters. 'And, Brick, my house was broken into but I don't think anything was stolen. I have nothing worth stealing, as you know. I ought to say my house was only ransacked.'

'Burgled,' Brick said. For a second I thought 'Burgled' was a brand of whisky I'd not heard of, short for Glen Burgled or some such. Down the phone I heard the sound of something liquid. 'Suzie, where do you keep your passport?'

'I don't have one.'

'Surely.'

'No.' So much for Fiji, I could tell Caine.

'Share certificates?' said Brick.

I laughed. I knew how his pale blue eyes would look, all creased around with concern. This was the security system whizz trying to think through the backwash of whisky.

'Key to your safety deposit? You should check.' There was the sound again of something liquid.

'But I'm at . . .' The key was in my lacquer jewellery box. Or it should be. Though I had nothing worth stealing even tucked up in the bank, I swallowed and wished it were whisky, not an uncomfortable lump of dread. Someone had snooped around in my house, turned my cupboards and jewellery box upside down. If nothing had been stolen, perhaps they had been searching for something. But what? 'Brick, I'm not at home now. I can't check.'

The liquid sound again. 'We must change your keys. Double locks on all your windows. I knew I should have insisted you get an alarm. You must come and stay here. With the kids. Come here at once.'

'Brick, thanks, but we're okay. Tell Lara I will be in touch tomorrow.'

As I downed the phone I heard him shout, 'Where are you?' but it was too late to answer and didn't matter.

I sat on the edge of the duvet for a while, rested my injured hand upon my shoulder and chewed the nails on my good hand. (I never bite them off, I just chew. It used to drive my mother nuts. She would threaten me with oil of cloves.) Then I crept halfway down the stairs and checked on the kids, still watching TV, side by side like babes in the wood. Tilda had her ballet slippers back on and Jarret was helping her tie the ribbons. They had a give-and-take relationship, those two: sometimes they gave each other grief, other times they took real care of each other.

They glanced up as they heard my keys jangle.

'Where are you going?' Jarret asked.

'I'll be back soon,' I promised.

As I drove towards home, the last dark blue of daylight edged the hills around the city. Caine could not keep me out of my house, and the kids were safe at his place. Brick's comment about the safe deposit key had niggled me. The entire day was niggling me. My sisters and their husbands — was something going on? Brick was usually a restrained man, but now and then he could get very drunk indeed. This in itself was not a worry and had probably happened because Lara thought she had messed up the interview. But the other brother-in-law was not usually hard to get hold of . . . it could mean nothing. But where was Philippa? Though it hadn't been her in the 'm' room, still I was worried. It was impossible that Roger had left her or vice versa, but they may have had a minor falling-out over Philippa's passion for Suite Three's profile (any man can be pushed to his limits), or Roger's import-export business may have struck a sticky patch. Philippa may have got so snotted-off she'd pretended to run away as she used to do when she was pre-adolescent, hiding in the bee-tree down the back of the house till Mom and Dad were sick with worry.

These thoughts were petty. I was ashamed. As I urged my rusty car past Central Park, I sighed again from the pit of my stomach. The only way to stop getting involved with my sisters would be to leave this country and never again use a telephone. I could send them Christmas cards with promises to write at length when I had time, as so many people promise and you thank God when their words are proven empty.

Trouble is, if you want to escape your unpleasant reality you either have to go insane, or have the money. Lara and Philippa received their share of the family inheritance in cash. I got my house. Okay, when we moved back from the States Dad had thrown botany over for real estate, and he got a spectacular deal on my place. But it made my sisters and me feel weird that he hadn't treated us the same. *For the sake of the children*, said my father when he told us about his will. *It's for the best. Suzie will thank me in years to come*. He meant that since my life did not include a permanent man, some other such as himself must take control. My thoughts on that were complex outrage. He'd seemed outraged as well. Before I moved in, he had Done It Himself in the kitchen, his tongue stuck out between his teeth as he hammered, his sandy hair curled with sweat, his jeans tugged down over his backside as they're supposed to if you're a builder. He installed the rotary clothesline, laid the patio, braced the front steps (not efficiently), whacked his own forehead accidentally with the mallet, took as little notice of me as a bull takes of a gnat. He bashed each nail with a religious vehemence and I wanted to bash him too. When he'd finished at last, he wiped his face with a filthy hand that left more grime than he rubbed off, and grinned humourlessly at my mother. *God, families*, she slurred as she waved a ragged cigarette, *Who in the world needs families?*

Oh, spare me. Dad's problem was he felt somehow responsible for my marriage to Gifford not working out. He and Gifford had spent manly times together, tinkering with engines and hammering their thumbs. Like many scientists, Dad could be autistic about relationships. To him, you set them up like automatic payments and they should take care of themselves.

I tried complaining to my mother. All she said was, *Hush up. Worry about something serious.* Which, to her, meant zucchini relish. There was a surfeit of the damned things so no matter that everyone loathed it, she still made enough for a battalion. Or she was organising a march to save the whale, or her airy-fairy side was in the ascendant — finding a green Indian cotton skirt identical to one she'd worn in Boston when I was a baby and being maudlin about it to the sound of Joni Mitchell. At least she didn't care as much as Dad about my messing up with men. She seemed to expect good karma would come skipping out of nowhere, somewhere, else-where. I loved her, the hippie leftover, but oh boy.

Those parents. I would have felt guilty about selling my place after the effort Dad put into it, though as a carpenter he made a better botanist. My sisters, to give them credit, still felt bad we had not all been treated the same. So I owned a house and had no cash for maintenance. I tried not to let it fester, and sometimes succeeded.

I pulled into my garage as usual, then wished I hadn't. The car was hidden from view of the road. In the thickening dusk the tree ferns stroked the air like big dark wings. I should have installed security lights as a neighbour had done, but it was another of those expenses I couldn't be bothered with (like professional haircuts). I whisked myself out of the garage in case the ransacker had returned to the scene of the crime and was waiting to mug me. A dark sedan cruised by just like they do at ominous moments in B movies.

The house was all locked up as Caine had promised. I opened the door but when I flicked the light switch nothing happened. I tried the light in the living room. Still nothing. I rummaged in my bag for a pocket torch. Its batteries were so weak the light was a ghostly poached egg.

In my bedroom, I sorted through the contents of the jewellery box still heaped in the middle of the duvet, and found the safe deposit key. I slipped it into my wallet and began to place everything else back in the box: the watch guarantee, a bracelet of fake coins, the necklace and earrings, a birthstone ring I'd never liked, a little silver cat brooch with sparkles on its tail that Gifford gave me when Jarret was born. I found tears trickling down my face. This was not like me. But I'd never been burgled before. Not even only ransacked.

I was down to the last things from the jewellery box — an old amber brooch, the motto from a fortune cookie that I could recite from memory — *Life to you is a dashing and bold adventure* — when I noticed a small box sitting next to the lamp on the bedside cabinet. What was this? I picked it up. It was wrapped in dark blue tissue paper and had a small memo tag stuck on it. On the tag, teeny capital letters in my mother's skew-whiff printing said, *REMEMBER TO GIVE TO SUZIE.* In another hand was scrawled a jagged 'G'.

I prised the box open and found another safe deposit key — at least that's what it looked like. The phantom torchlight showed the inside of my wallet. I pulled out the first key and puzzled over them, side by side. The heads and necks were identical, but the teeth to stick in the keyhole were very different. Did they come from the same bank? I knew I'd only ever had one deposit box. But now I had two keys. Burgled — ransacked — what do you call it when someone breaks in, creates a mess, then you find you have more than you had? But of course, I just hadn't noticed it earlier. The box must have been dropped round before this all happened. Gifford. It seemed too small a mystery to bother about right now.

It would be a good idea to call the kids and check they were okay — but I found the phone was dead. The lights were out and now my phone as well. I tried following the cord to the jack point but the end was loose in my hand and it was too dark to find the socket. By now, the torch was useless. I don't want to tell you how bizarre I had started to feel.

The kids were sure to be fine. They were at Caine's house. Nobody would hurt my kids when they were in the house of a top detective, so admired he'd had a website built for him. A man who had proposed to me today.

What was wrong with getting married and living happily ever after? What was wrong with me that it hadn't happened already? Still crying and still hating it, I scrabbled in my jewellery box again for the silver and sparkle brooch Gifford gave me, enthusiasm and lack of self-knowledge shining in his eyes, as I guess my naiveté had shone in mine. I fastened it on my sweater. Pathetic, sentimental, and so what.

I picked up a pillow and wiped my face on it. There would be enough light through the kitchen window for me to sweep some of the mess while I composed myself. That is, if Caine and his two sidekicks had not swept the mess already. I doubted they had: everything would be even dirtier because of fingerprint powder. I should also put down that Chomp for poor Nameless.

There was no point in unpacking all the groceries before I'd cleared some space to walk around but I set the cans of catfood on the bench. Pale shapes of rice and pasta showed in the glow from the neighbour's security lights as I piled the sweepings against the side of the closed pantry. There was a tomato and basil smell, like pasta sauce. Something in the pantry seemed to be leaking out. The double doors were not properly shut. I nudged them with the broom thinking I'd clean up whatever puddled there tomorrow, in daylight. Something inside still blocked them. I pulled one open and did a stumble on the spot.

A human shape was in my pantry, half-crouching, an arm stuck in the vegetable rack. It was frozen-looking — waxy. It wore a blouse like an artwork that Philippa might purchase. The hairstyle was similar to Lara's tidy big hair. It had one tiny bare foot, the other in a well-made flat-soled shoe that glinted purple in the moonlight. It had to be a mannequin. A clothes mannequin. This dummy was a scary Lara-Philippa, *The Girls* condensed in one volume.

The leak had spread under the dummy. A dark leak like pasta sauce. I wanted very badly for the puddle to be pasta sauce. I still gasped with shock, my heart jittered. Then in the fitful light I took in the bulbous little toe, the slight twist of the nail on the big one.

This was not a mannequin. This, crouching in my pantry, was a real woman, not moving because she was dead.

part two

SO MANY COOKS

chapter four

Like most youngest girls — as well as many boys, no doubt — I'd daydreamed that I was an orphan separated from my true family, that in fact I was of aristocratic birth. Do kids who grow up in republics dream this too? Yes, and I'm the example, though I didn't go so far as to believe I was a princess. Being daughter of a duke would have suited me fine, though it was Philippa and Lara who behaved like aristocracy. One day I imagined I would be restored to my rightful place: somewhere I was not bossed by a bigger sister (Lara) or had my things trashed (Philippa) or was ignored (the pair of them), somewhere my talents (I had no idea what they might be) would be acknowledged, somewhere I would be valued.

Now I don't want this to be a tear-jerker. I grew up in a nice family and wanted for nothing except kinder sisters now and then, and I am sure I behaved like a brat myself on numberless occasions. My mother was a princess in her way, pretty and tough beneath that flower-child air. She kept telling me I had a brain. She took me to those ballet lessons and never once seemed disappointed I was clumsy. *You were a perfect rabbit. That's exactly what a surprised little rabbit would do*, she reassured me after that calamitous junior performance when I knocked the mushroom, it rolled across the stage and bounced over Sleeping Beauty. This, you'll recall, was Philippa, and you'd have thought she was contending for the Oscars. Sleeping Beauty was convinced I'd done it on purpose. It was an accident, I swear. My giggles on stage were pure panic. Back stage, she convulsed with hysterics and didn't stop till Lara punched her. But in the back seat of our mustard-coloured VW bus as we drove home in the dark, Sleeping Beauty grabbed my arm and bit down hard. She was ten and I was eight. I refused to cry. I didn't tell our mother, not even next day when she noticed the bite-shaped bruise with its red tooth marks, guessed who had done it and was furious that I refused to say a word. She screamed at my father, he yelled back, they paced around the kitchen till he flapped his arms once, twice, and grabbed a hammer. *It's too late at night for Doing It Yourself*, Mom shrieked, so he disappeared up to the botanical research centre to turn off a big switch. Mom packed us all to bed and filled the livid silence with the slicing of her scissors, making patchwork.

Children are supposed to be much more aware of things around them than most adults realise. If this is true, I can only judge that I was abnormal. I remember worrying that I might not have the right-sized heart. I didn't think I loved *The Girls* enough, and I didn't think that Philippa loved me. You might ask what was lovable about either of them after the episode of the animatronic doll, but I say most older siblings enjoy inflicting mental torment, and I was always eager to spend time with Lara if she let me. You might ask what was lovable about Philippa, after the vicious bite? You've got me there. I thought it might all be different, if she loved me. I wanted her to love me, and I wanted to love her. However, this is not a tear-jerker. As far as those sisters were concerned my too-small heart did bother me, but I knew I had a heart that loved my mom and topsy-turvied for my dad. That father. He used to make up goodnight stories. None of them were any fun. I would beg, *Dad, read to me. Read a book!* His reply was always, *You can read to yourself once you learn how*, and he'd continue with some saga about the smallest chicken in the barnyard settling down with a cute little skunk. Oh no! I knew the rules of children's stories, that the chicken was supposed to find some hens, to make it feel okay to be its own kind of animal. Or on-and-on my dad would ramble about a prince dressed in a boiler suit who went by helicopter, instead of wearing shiny armour on a war horse. I'd grow incensed beyond all reason. *Your story's wrong!* I'd holler. I still have no high opinion of the imaginative powers of anyone in botany or in real estate.

When it came to reading, I was known as a slow learner. For a long time I suffered Dad's stories. To my mind, stubborn was a more appropriate label than slow-learner. Why should a child do what is expected? What is wrong with being independent? It didn't worry me that I was slow because I knew I'd speed up when I decided.

Why am I telling you this now? To leave you dangling after that discovery in the pantry? Truth is, to think about it still heaves me over the cliff and into terror. I am trying to calm down.

Dad may not have read to me, but Mom did. Her airy-fairy social conscience was grounded in the concrete of common sense, as firmly as Dad had set my clothesline in that circle of concrete and bricks. Her choice of books was often the *Little Black Sambo* series now deemed politically incorrect by tight-assed spoilers. To me, as well as to Mom, they were simply good stories. Many of those books contain tigers who threaten to eat the small child. *There will not be enough of the child to go around*, a frog protested to many tigers in one book. The tigers smiled their scary smiles and in memory I still hear my mother saying in a special deep and funny tone: *'We're sisters.' The tigers smiled. 'We share.'*

A dubious statement. Some sisters may have shared. From me, Lara and Philippa confiscated toys and Philippa sold them to her classmates (though once, when Lara insisted, she did give me a modest commission). Those two excelled at performance, ballet, theatre, sports such as softball, skiing, tennis. Later on they had a series of boyfriends with good career potential, they married and bought nice houses in the same suburb, one with a plethora of fake Tudor and many automatic double garage doors. What did I have? Intelligence I defiantly refused to use, according to my mom, who nevertheless loved me.

I still worried now and then that I did not love my sisters as I should, that jealousy had withered my heart's growth. But when I stood in my darkened kitchen staring at the body of the second dead woman I had seen that dreadful Monday, it was clear I had a heart. It pounded in my chest as if it would gallop away.

A daze of time passed while I stood, heart panicking, the kitchen still redolent of basil and tomato. I had to do something — tell the police. The phone was out of order — so I must find a neighbour. But I'd lived in this house for four years, and hadn't met the neighbour on the left with the security lights. He worked on night shift and I doubted he'd be home now. On the right was a woman in her eighties. She'd taken to collecting cardboard and visits from community service workers who stood knocking on her porch while she shouted through the door they were not welcome. Across the street was a houseful of skateboarding students. Music thumped from their windows now, as it did most nights. Thank God! I'd use their phone. I picked up my bag, fumbled the door tight behind me — to preserve the crime scene, I suppose — and somehow reached my gate.

As I stepped onto the road a large car appeared from nowhere and nearly winged me. It was black, silent and disappeared again into the night almost as if I had dreamed it. I had gained the other side of the road, holding onto my bag like grim death (I didn't mean to use that phrase, it just leaped out), when another car came slinking round the corner, a Commodore, dark blue. Maybe it was the police without my having to call them. Too limp with shock to raise an arm and wave, I leaned against the students' fence.

Their front door was open wide. I saw through to their living area: some had beers in their hands, a few held mugs of coffee. Music thumped more loudly — it was rock — if that was what they called it nowadays. In fact I think it was boogie. I was not so old I would not know, but all I'd heard in my house over recent months was Jarret with his angry rap, Tilda with the Dance of the Sugar Plum Fairy (^{ting!}). The loudness of their music reminded me of when I was that age. For a moment I felt safe again, surrounded by normality though still tremulous.

The Commodore's lights switched off before it stopped a couple of doors down from my gate and a man — it was Caine! — slipped out of it like the shadow of a shadow and disappeared up my steps beneath the tree fern. Now you see him, now you don't. He entered my house.

But I had never given Caine a key. Did detectives carry skeleton keys with them?

One of the students, a young woman, had spotted me and strolled out to the porch. She was scrawny like me though much shorter, and looked as if she had been on the receiving end of a freckle-sprinkler.

'Hi. Your new hair is amazing.' She grinned.

I wouldn't have thought she'd noticed me before.

'How're your kids?' she continued. 'Your little girl's such a toughie.'

I mumbled a maternal thank you — such pride can buoy you even at these stranded moments.

She indicated the ridiculous large bandage on my hand. 'Hey, that looks serious. Maybe you need a beer. Or — ?' She cupped a ragged little tube that Caine would not like to see.

'Ah. My boyfriend, who I want to dump, is a cop.' I took the beer.

She laughed and hid the tube behind her back. 'It's a small city, but there's room for all sorts.' In the normal soft night air she peered more closely. 'Hey — are you okay?'

I glanced at my house. A shape, the shape of Caine, sidled carefully from my door, down the side of the rickety steps into the gloom of the shrubbery. My knees were still not strong enough to cross the road. After a moment or so there came the snick of a car door, and Caine was in his driver's seat. He drove away so naturally that the student didn't seem aware of him at all. The car lights didn't come on until he reached the corner.

Maybe Caine hadn't seen my car in the unlit garage off the street. But surely he had seen what was in my pantry — had I left the pantry open or had I shut it? Had he phoned for help on his mobile? If so, why drive away? Why wasn't he waiting for a back-up team, an ambulance? I liked this evening less and less each minute.

'Please, my phone's out. So are my lights. May I . . .?'

The young woman shrugged *of course*. I had another pull of beer and let me say there is nothing like fright and bewilderment to add flavour to social drugs. Then, in the safety of the students' flat, surrounded by skateboards and a number of backpacks with metal frames that might carry a new-born elephant with ease, I began to dial 111 but felt so worried, so strange that I phoned Caine's home first to check the kids.

The phone rang and rang. The answerphone did not click on. I counted at least twenty rings. Were Tilda there, she would answer. She was curious, interested, determined. She was seven years old. She would never leave a phone to ring.

Jarret and Tilda sometimes behaved like a pair of rats, as I had shouted at them many times — but I did not know what I'd do if I should lose them. Where could they be? Had they skipped out for a minute? Had they skipped out for the night, to stay with friends? I made myself calm down. They had done this before.

They'd been told not to. I'd strangle them.

The woman student was beside me again, buckling on a little bum bag. 'Hey, what's the matter?'

I tried to find my car keys and came up with Philippa's spare set. My bag fell to the ground and the student seemed to realise I could not speak except to say in little choking sounds, 'My kids.' I guess I hadn't calmed down one bit.

She retrieved my bag. 'My name's Beth. I know you're Suzie Emmett. I don't reckon you should try to drive right now. Where are your kids? I can drive you.'

I thought this was a freckled guardian angel.

Up till then my assumption would have been that you could tell your guardian angel anything. But this one was maybe fifteen years younger than me. She had those freckles on her cheeks. I didn't think I should tell her about the dead body.

She slung a skateboard into the back seat of my car, I found the right keys and she climbed in the driver's side.

'Hey, great,' she said. 'Automatic.'

'I thought only boys were skaties,' I managed to say with some coherence.

'Wrong grammar,' she told me. 'They *skate*. Lots of girls skate too. I'll take you where you need to be, then I'll skate on. I have a rehearsal at a lecturer's apartment down town. *The Duchess of Malfi*. You know it?'

Jacobean drama. Gore and passion.

I told her Caine's address and that it was too far for her to skate back from there. She waved the equivalent of *de nada*. I felt it polite to make more conversation so asked what she was studying. My words came out oddly, like balls of polystyrene from my throat.

She gave me a swift look. 'Asian studies and economic history. Hey, it's okay, catch your breath. You don't have to make small talk, and you don't have to tell me what's the problem.' She swung my car round the difficult bend at the foot of the hill. This city is known for its difficult bends. Trucks regularly get stuck in hairpins. Cars regularly dive off steep banks and land half inside someone's bedroom, the headlights nudging the duvet.

'It's nice to meet someone who's such a good driver.' I was still numb and quivery. 'I won't tell you my problem because it's hard to believe it myself. And good grief, you're just — so young.'

Beth flashed a grin. 'Yeah, well, at our house we're not ageist. We had a vote last night on the woman we'd all most like to sleep with. I won't embarrass you by saying you were favourite, but you scored two votes.' She grinned again. 'Don't worry. We know where fantasy begins and real life stops.'

Real life or fantasy, this was too much. I wished myself back in my little bed of thirty years ago, another of my father's stories making me escape from aggravation into sleep.

The windows of Caine's house were lit top and bottom, though the units on either side were dark. Beth stopped the car and handed me the keys.

'Thank you,' I said. 'But it's a very long skate back. I should give you taxi money.' I was amazed that I was such a nice person. I'd just come upon a corpse in my pantry, and I was fretting about this young stranger.

'Don't worry about me.' She hesitated as she looked at me. 'Maybe I should come in too. Just to see it's all okay.' She lifted the skateboard out with the grace of a long-time expert and carried it up Caine's steps. I knocked and called to the kids.

I heard the TV. I knocked and called out louder. I rattled the knob. All that happened was an advertisement for a bank with a warm heart.

'He never gave you a key?' Beth asked. 'Some boyfriend.'

I called Jarret and Tilda again and beat the door with the back of my hand.

Beth propped the skateboard against her thigh and removed a

credit card from her little bag. 'Stand aside.' She slid the card into the door jamb.

Prickles of fright raced up my arms. Caine had taught me this. It's the sort of show-off thing guys do when they're in the first flush of a romance. They usually regret it later on. 'You can't do that. This house belongs to a detective.'

'Your kids are either in there, or they're not. You need to know.' Beth manoeuvred the card until the door snicked open.

I dropped my bag in the little hall and looked into the living room. Beth followed, the front door left ajar. The bank advertisement was in its final heart-warming and unconvincing moment. No kids. I found I tiptoed as I went into the kitchen. There were signs of kid-sized rats having been into Caine's fridge, a knife with butter smeared on the blade, a pack of unwrapped cheese, but no actual real-life kids.

From the foot of the stairs in Caine's carefully subdued lighting, I called, 'Hey, guys? I'm here.'

Still no reply. I glanced back at Beth, framed against the street outside, ran up and checked the study, Caine's bedroom, the bathroom, even climbed into the loft. When I reached the top of the stairs again, Beth was still at the door, skateboard tucked under her arm. My ears were full of roaring like the sea.

'I can't see their stuff — Jarret's school bag. The oil for hair lice. *Hello Kitty*.'

'Hello who?' Beth asked. 'Oh, gag-city Kitty. Suzie, have they left a note?'

Her sensible question quieted me until we searched the kitchen bench, the dining table, the pad beside the phone, and found not one scrap of paper hinting what had happened. Little demons — what were they up to? Why had they done this to me tonight? I saw one of Tilda's sneakers under a chair and picked it up.

'I hate to tell you,' Beth said in a low voice, 'but life has suddenly turned even more depressing.'

I swung around. Caine was just inside the open door, a shoulder pressed hard against the wall. He held a gun, aimed right at me.

I was not worried. I had other things to worry about, and besides I knew this was like a split second in a movie. You know: the audience gasps with fright before the hero drops the arm holding the gun, mops his brow and says *Goddam, Suzie, I could'a killed ya, don't sneak up on me like that, goddam it, woman, I love ya.*

And that is what might'a happened except Beth pitched the skateboard at Caine. He yelled and ducked aside. Beth dashed after the board, somehow hopped on it and skated down the front steps. The *fddddrrrrr* of wheels faded into the night.

Clutching Tilda's sneaker, I gestured at the gun. I am not ashamed to say my hand shook. I'd known he was on a call out, but I'd never seen him with a gun. 'Whatever happened to *Hi, honey, I'm home?*'

Caine scowled and gasped — I doubt it's easy to do both things at once. 'Don't try to be hard-boiled. Who the hell was that?'

Should I tell him Beth was my neighbour? Why not? 'My neighbour. She called around with some mail. Where's the pizza you promised? More to the point, Caine, where are my kids? And why did you come in with a gun out?'

Caine tucked the gun into a holster at his waist. 'I didn't recognise your silhouette. It's the new hairstyle.'

I believed him.

'Why are you here with a gun at all?' I asked.

He seemed miffed as if I ought to get it right. 'This is a Glock.'

I gave a version of The Look.

'I should've turned it in down at the station, but I nipped back to check on you. I'm sorry I haven't got the pizza yet. Suzie, what do you mean, where are the kids?'

'They've gone.'

Did I trust this man or not? Did I tell him I left his house, went back to my own and saw him sneak in? Should I yell what the hell was he doing entering my house when I'd never given him a key? I might not have been suspicious, if it hadn't been for the body in the pantry. A body in your pantry definitely throws you. I guess I needed time to think.

Because I didn't have a lot of choice, I decided a smidge of trust might be okay. 'I went out for half an hour to the chemist.' Men don't ask questions about what women buy in chemist shops. 'When I got back, Beth was here. She helped me get in.'

Caine frowned, and again looked stretched and weary. I realised he might have seen me drive up with Beth. But that would mean he had been spying on his own house . . . This was too difficult to think through on the spot. My priority was to find where the kids had gone — but what was the best way to discover it?

I have always wondered why, in books and movies, when people find something disturbing — like a corpse in their pantry, for instance — they don't go straight to the police. Of course, in books and movies, this is just an excuse to set the story scooting down its track. If you find a body in your pantry, call the police immediately, they come and clear it all away and — immediately again — they understand it was nothing to do with you because you are as innocent as a day-old baby flexing its teeny fingers to the amazement of its parents, then the story is finished in a jiffy. A person in a book or movie must have an excellent reason for not calling the police, despite that person's obvious virtue.

Though I may not be strong on virtue, I had several excellent reasons for not calling the police. They were:

a) my boyfriend, who I had plans to dump, was the police;

b) my boyfriend, who I had plans to dump and was the police had entered my house using a key or other means I did not give him;

c) when my boyfriend entered my house using means I

did not give him, in all likelihood he saw the body in my pantry and I was not sure that he had called the police even though he was the police himself, and that seemed awry to me;

d) about two hours ago my boyfriend told me not to do anything foolish;

e) my boyfriend would think my returning to my own home in the circumstances of it having just been ransacked was a foolish thing to do even if I excused myself by saying I wanted to feed the cat, for he had told me cats survive and anyway I'd forgotten the cat again until this minute;

f) I have always resented it when anyone tells me not to do anything foolish;

g) I still wished my boyfriend had not wanted me to identify that poor woman in the 'm' room, and two dead women in one day seemed far too many; and when it came right down to it —

h) why should I tell him anything?

Eight reasons for not calling the police seemed a sturdy raft on which to make my stand although I realise by number six (or rather, 'f') it had begun to slide sideways into petulance. Mind you, my sisters would both claim I had cornered the market in petulance years back. And to that I would answer, it takes one petulant to know another.

But I was not myself tonight. For excellent cause, I was not myself. I'd had fifteen stitches in my hand and it was painful. I had visited the morgue (I said the word!). My house had been ransacked and on the same afternoon my ex-husband had, it seemed, brought around a mysterious key to — perhaps — a second safe deposit box. I had found a dead woman in my kitchen who, like the first dead woman, resembled my sisters but was not either of my sisters. I had no idea where my kids were, and my boyfriend had aimed a gun at me.

Caine had begun to rub that broken nose. I didn't think I was handling this well. I had been standing in the living room chewing my nails, not letting him know what I was thinking. Men like to know what their women are thinking. I think this is because they think we may not be thinking about them. Right now, my thinking refused to settle down and focus. This was bad. First and foremost, I was a mother. My kids. I had to find the kids. I said this to Caine and moved to the front door.

'I guess they followed me to the corner shops —' Even to me this sounded feeble, unconvincing. 'Maybe they got hungry waiting for pizza. I'll nip down there again. Tilda's still in her ballet shoes — oh boy, is she in trouble.'

Caine pressed his fingers on the crease between his eyebrows. 'I have lots on my mind. I realise I have stuff to learn about how to be a family man.'

That was a sneaky thing to say. *Goddam it, Caine, don't sneak phrases like family man up on me.* My heart, that in my dark kitchen half an hour ago longed to leap out of my chest and run away, now wanted to nestle against this narrow-nosed broad-shouldered police detective who had said he'd like to marry me. My skinny body hankered to slump against this detective. My bony shoulders ached to have him pat them, I wanted him to *there-there* and *shush* me, promise me all I needed was to go to bed, make love to that pitch of sweetness and dissolve. Then when I awoke it would be tomorrow and we'd start living in our happy-ever-after. I could have fancied having a family with this man. I could have fancied grumbling because he would not get up at 2 a.m. to change the baby.

I admit, my body slumped towards him. He picked up my bandaged hand, kissed it gently on the inside of the wrist. His arm came round my shoulders. He took a deep exhausted breath and rested his head against mine. His free hand cupped my face — then dropped to near my collar bone.

'What's this?' he asked.

I touched my sweater. It was the silver cat my ex-husband gave me when we were still in love and only children. I'd forgotten I'd put the brooch on when I'd returned to the house, the foolish thing I did not want to reveal to Caine. 'It's nothing.'

'You weren't wearing it this afternoon.'

I dislike observant men. So why did I take up with a detective in the first place? I was thirty-seven years old.

'I decided to tidy my bag, and there it was.'

Caine's frown became highly corrugated even though he knew how much paraphernalia I carried in that bag.

There was only one thing to do. I put Tilda's sneaker down, took up the phone and began to call the central police station. I knew the number off by heart because I'd used it many times to call my boyfriend.

Caine gave the groan of a man who'd had a nightmare day. He slid his jacket off (I saw the holster with the Glock) and slumped in an armchair. 'Order one with peppers and black olives,' he said. 'I expect the kids will want Hawaiian. Most kids do.'

Tilda, Jarret and I were a happy family, by and large. One thing we agreed on was Hawaiian pizza is an abomination in the sight of whoever looks on it. No matter the breadth of Caine's shoulders or the closeness of his shave, no matter how much my sense of self was disestablished by that crick in his nose, a man who imagined my kids would like Hawaiian pizza, who by now had not learnt otherwise, was a man I did not want to trust. I do not blame myself for this, and nor should you. He may have been one of this nation's finest, but do not blame me one bit.

By now, I was hearing the operator down at Central. She would have been astonished to hear me order pizza. I eased my finger on the button that ends the call then, veins fluttering, asked in a normal voice for two large pizzas, one with mushrooms, green peppers and black olives, another with bacon and pineapple.

'I hear the kids outside,' I lied to Caine. 'I'll growl at them on the step. You've had a terrible day, you still have to nip down to Central to return your Glock or you'll be in trouble, and you don't want to listen to me scolding. I'll turn the TV up to drown me out.'

He had his head back, eyes closed. He grunted, as men do when they've had a busy day and do not wish to listen to a woman chiding kids. My bag was still by the front door where I dropped it. I slipped Tilda's sneaker into it and crept outside.

Misty pools of lamplight — a big dog nosing under a hedge — far-off another *burr* of skateboards — but no Jarret, no Tilda. Hoping the TV was loud enough to conceal the sound of my engine starting up, hoping I could manage the ignition without more painkillers, I slid into my car as quietly as Caine had entered the police Commodore outside my house.

My car, the smallest and possibly oldest four-door automatic on the market, cruised slowly towards the shops around the corner. I slowed down even more to check inside the takeaways and dairy in case Tilda even now might be persuading Jarret to shell out for an ice cream. He would have money. He did odd jobs for Madame Avril at the ballet school as well as his Auntie Philippa, and Madame always paid more than she promised (unlike Philippa).

The kids were not in either shop. I sped up and headed for Lara's.

Why? Brick had told me earlier that Lara was laid out with a headache and Brick himself would be sodden drunk by now. But they were family. I could use their phone to call my children's friends' parents, find out if Jarret and Tilda had arrived on the doorstep and charmed a bed though they'd been told never to do that again. I'd call Tilda's father. I'd consider phoning Jarret's father, Gifford.

First, of course, I would call the police for real and offer them the crisis of my pantry.

chapter five

The security lights snapped on as I beetled up the drive of Lara and Brick's elegant two-storey town house. With ineffectual subtlety, then plain requests, Lara had tried to encourage me always to park out on the street. If she threw her migraine off, she would instantly suffer another to see my heap dropping oil on the pavers.

When I knocked, it took Brick a whole minute to answer. I heard him moving inside, the *huff whoof* of another weary man after a hard day. The *huff* and *whoof* of a large man after too many whiskies early in the evening, and no food.

A chain rattled. The door opened a hand's-breadth and Brick peered down through the gap. 'Suzie? For goodness . . . something's happened to your hair.' He unlatched the security chain. 'Come in at once.'

The hair again. For the first time in my life I had hair with weight and self-assertion. It was bemusing to be told that two people had voted me a woman they'd most like to sleep with, because that must have been before the new style. Mind you, when my hair was self-effacing other people had not merely wanted to sleep with me but had done so. Gifford, the father of intense, tormented Jarret. Luke, the father of ballet-crazy Tilda (my time with Luke was such a fiery mistake). The clean-cut and methodical Caine who always at the right moment became a horizontal wild man. Not to mention the one-night oddities you learn to forget — I'm digressing. I should move on.

Brick stumbled in his slippers to the kitchen and I followed. Oh boy, he was unsteady. Though I was worried and confused to hell and back, I could still put first things first. It was likely that the kids were just acting up. And if I mentioned the body in the pantry to Brick, he would be onto the police in a flash. They'd arrive to question me. Should they see Brick steeped in whisky so early in the week, his reputation for stability would tilt sideways. Therefore, because I like my brother-in-law, I decided I had better cook an omelette.

As I'd done in Caine's bathroom, I pulled a plastic bag over the injured hand. Brick stared then looked away. It seemed weeks since I last cracked an egg (I told you already I can do this with one hand), in truth it was only about six hours since last I held one. I worked out how to use a knife again with only one hand, sautéed onion and mushroom, warmed plates. Brick had consumed so much whisky since I had called him from Caine's that there would be no sensible support and guidance here till he was stuffed with carbo-hydrate so, with the magic of the microwave and other tricks I won't take the time to tell you, I created potato wedges.

He held a bottle of something Scottish under my nose. It smelled like car tyres.

'No thanks.' I checked the amount of garlic, parsley and Parmesan on the wedges. I didn't know how I could cook so well right now, forgive my boasting. Mind you, most people could cook with brilliance in a kitchen as expertly designed and modern as Lara's. It even has a cupboard with a glass door for her recipe books.

Though Brick wore his slippers, he was still in an Yves St

Laurent suit. It was rumpled. This was normal. If Brick walks by racks of suits in a department store, they need pressing right away. His tie was draped over the antique brass telescope they keep at the foot of the staircase. Beside it hung the monk-summoning Tibetan gong my Tilda loved and feared. Lara hated the gong too, but Philippa gave it to her once so she was stuck with it. Philippa had moved from brass to a brief interest in jade, and now seemed to be moving to art of the twentieth century. She'd never offered me her excess brass, but I wasn't peeved. Lara was the one stuck with the brass.

Brick tipped the bottle to and fro. A trickle left. He dribbled it into his glass and polished it off.

'Will Lara want a bite to eat?' I asked.

'She'll be ravenous when she wakes.' Brick opened a cupboard, brought out a bottle of another whisky with Bunna-something on the label, opened it and sat at the rimu breakfast bar. My brothers-in-law never drink a moderately-priced whisky. Whisky, for Brick and Roger, must have a name that evokes misty centuries of clannish pride. For them whisky must smell as if it has — strode? stridden? — been striding in tweed over heather-dotted highlands while wolfhounds snapped at quail, curlews cried across a loch and, to the far-off sound of bagpipes, Burns's poetry was recited in a choking-on-oatmeal Scots accent.

I put an omelette and a bowl of spicy wedges in front of Brick, and sat with him at the breakfast bar. The last food I'd eaten was that spoon-tip of pesto at Thee Ultimate Café. Without food I would be a frail vessel that keeled over. The antique telescope must have put these nautical images in mind. I didn't usually think nautically. So I nibbled a wedge or two, and it is true what my mother always said — you feel better once there's food in you. It doesn't solve problems, but a little food is strengthening.

Tears welled in Brick's bloodshot eyes. 'This is kind, coming to cook for me when Lara's out of action. You're a marvel to be doing it one-handed. I am a lucky bloke to have a sister-in-law like you.

I haven't used that word for years — bloke. Bloke.' He brushed his eyes and kept stabbing his fork into wedges, putting them into his mouth. 'Roger's a good bloke too. We're a lucky family, Suzie. We're a family.'

'That's why I've come . . .' I began.

'When someone you care about goes wrong,' he said, slurring, 'your whole world view goes *phut*! I've seen it happen. But this is just a minor slipper. Up. Slip-up.'

'Who's gone wrong? Who's slipped?'

All he did was chew more wedges, leaking tears. Some drunks grow rowdy, others weep. They all become unintelligible.

'Brick, I'm going to make coffee. You must drink coffee.'

He waved his fork towards the Bunna'thist'loch but I shoved the bottle in a cupboard.

'Please sober up. I've come for help. To stay the night. Brick, I don't know where the kids have gone.'

He raised his head, as I imagine wolfhounds might stare if they saw a mutant rabbit in the highlands.

'I told you earlier on the phone, Brick, I've been burgled.'

After a moment, he nodded.

'Then . . .' No, I could not tell him what I discovered in my pantry. By now, I hoped I'd been hallucinating. A clone-like version of my sisters, what could it be but an illusion? And Caine's sneaking around my house — maybe he was making sure it was locked up. But *maybe* means *maybe not*.

'Brick, I went to stay at Caine's with my kids, popped out for half an hour. When I got back the kids were gone. Then Caine came in and nearly shot me . . .'

'He shot your hand! He did? We'll call the police! No. Caine is the police. The bloke's a police.'

'No, this was a silly accident . . .' Would you buy a security system from this man? I dialled Caine's number and passed the phone to Brick.

'As you say, Caine is the police. Ask if Jarret and Tilda have come back. Don't tell him I am here.'

It was a powerful sensation, seeing such a large man obey me once he'd eaten of my omelette. Brick asked Caine about the kids, then looked at me. 'Suzie, he wants to know who I am.'

I think I rolled my eyes. Brick looked ashamed.

'Ah — you've guessed,' he said to Caine. 'The kids aren't there? Ah — where's Suzie? Sitting next to me.'

I snatched the phone and put it down.

'I didn't give you away altogether,' Brick said with pride. 'I didn't say exactly where we were. Oh, he has a brilliant reputation. He might figure it out. He pointed a gun at you? Really? It would have been a Glock. Suzie, do you think it wise to take up with yet another man who has — what's the way to put this — a short fuse?'

At this point, Brick's vagaries were such I could have detonated my own fuse, but there was movement in the kitchen window — a reflection. Lara stood in the doorway, wrapped in the purple dressing gown that made her resemble a duchess (as do most things). She looked not the least as if she suffered from migraine. No bluish nose, no pinched and whitened lips, no squint of pain. You work as a servant of the state, you must recover at speed from any set-backs.

'Hello, Suzie.' She glanced at my hair. The flare of Lara's nostrils always says more than words although she often uses words too, to ensure you have the full translation and the small print. The flare right now said that although my hairstyle claimed assertive things, the face beneath was still the mouse of yesterday. She glanced at my hand as well. 'God, Suzie. What have you done this time?'

'I thought you had a headache,' I said.

Her forehead pleated up like a Roman blind. 'The foulest day of my whole life. Why do ministers of the Crown only comprehend words of less than two syllables?' She sank onto the remaining kitchen stool. 'It didn't help that Roger tried to barrel in on a meeting . . .'

'Minor slipper!' Brick put in. 'Decent bloke!'

'Or that your detective friend actually succeeded in interrupting when he'd already talked to my secretary. I'm afraid I was short with them both. I apologise if it affects this latest romance of yours, Suzie.'

'Darling.' Brick waved his hands to make her pay attention. It looked like palsy. 'Lara, there are worser things . . .'

'Brick!' She looked incredulous that anything could be worse than her day, though perhaps it was amazement at his grammar.

'The children,' Brick explained. 'Suzie's kids.'

She looked at me more sharply. 'What about them? And why have you got that on?' Her tartness made me think a spider crawled on my collar-bone. I lifted my hand and touched Gifford's cat brooch. 'Suzie, don't tell me you are cheating on your detective friend with your ex-husband.'

This flashback to teenage scorn was irrelevant. It made me perverse. 'Why not? The man's always fun when he has money.'

'That man has broken Jarret's heart.' My sister slammed around the kitchen, making herself a plate of crackers and sliced tomato. 'Don't get sucked in by him again. Gifford had the nerve to come to my office recently as well as Roger, and suggest I squeeze some rules apart. Families! Who needs families, especially hangers-on who won't let go?'

I didn't care to hear details but Lara bored on anyway.

'His latest venture is importing earthmoving equipment from Japan. Used earthmoving equipment! Gifford expects regulations bent for that! My God, and our father had a soft spot for him. He has such bare-faced arrogance. He is nothing but manipulative and — and . . .' Lara gasped for the right word but ended up with 'off with the fairies!' (That is one reason I am fond of her. Her bossiness has the occasional sprinkle of ditz just like our mom's.) 'Keep your distance from him, Suzie.'

Tears leaked down beside Brick's nose again. 'His charm. I wish I had a fragment of his charm. Gifford may not have charmed you, Lara, but my goodness it can be money in the bank. He gets it from his mother, delightful woman, it's the Welsh in her. What a loss it's going to be when she retires.' He buried his face in one hand. 'The National Library will become a lesser place.'

In fact Gifford's mother scared the dickens out of me. I ignored Lara's needless warning about getting involved with my ex-husband again after more than a dozen years, each year an egg of pain that I do not wish to crack open and exhibit to you. I ignored my brother-in-law's tears. I took an old recipe book out of the special cupboard, found a pencil in a pottery holder on the windowsill, opened the book to a blank space at the end and began to write a plan of what to do. Our family has always done this. The backs of recipe books are scribbled with old Christmas card lists, notes on what money was owed to which business, ideas of jobs for rainy days. This particular one had been our mom's — jotted under the last entries in the index were the names of deceased family pets. It went something like: Stuffed Marrow, Vegetable Pie, then Fuzz-pants, Pigoletto, Alcatraz, and on for fifteen names, also listing species and causes of death but I won't itemise except to say there were no dogs, and Alcatraz was a much-loved neurotic part-Persian who died of euthanasia.

My writing was shaky because of the bandage. First on the list I made (I should have done this back at Caine's but you will remember that he came in with that Glock) was *call the police*. I added, *after calling the kid's friends* then *and calling Luke and Gifford*.

I started, therefore, with the friends. I am a responsible mother and carry the surnames and numbers of crucial friends in a notebook in my capacious bag. More parents should be as respon-sible as I am (and we'll forget the fact that I left Jarret and Tilda on their own and they disappeared, thank you). By now Lara wore her stuffed duck look — a duchess aghast, by a taxidermal Beatrix Potter. I called Jarret's friends and spoke to their parents. I did the same with Tilda's friends. I called Tilda's father. A young female answered. She sounded high on something illegal, and also as paranoid as Luke used to make me feel. I said I'd call back. I made sixteen phone calls while Brick focused on his empty plate as though it would vanish if he blinked. Lara continued to look like a shocked stuffed duck though she'd discarded her crackers and tomato, and was on her cellphone working with me through my notebook. Her peremptory efficiency is often a virtue. I hoped she would get the department head job despite the spoiled interview, crack the transparent ceiling at Customs. I called my friend Annie. I phoned Bernard but couldn't reach him. I phoned Tilda's ballet teacher. I still hadn't called Gifford's charming scary mother, Jarret's grandma: of course the kids would not be there. I phoned Luke again and insisted on speaking to him this time. A big mistake. I ended up screaming that he was as useful as a spare wheel on a fart. To be coarse is unlike me except when I talk to Tilda's father.

When I put the phone down, I was dizzy. This had been a day of picking up phones and putting them down, up, down, up, down, up, enough to make a person very dizzy, let alone all these surprises, like my ex-husband with his propensity for borrowing large sums and having grand schemes annoying my older sister at work, nearly being shot with a Glock, before that nearly run over by a big flash car outside my house, before that finding something dismaying with a bare foot in my pantry.

I had Gifford's number off by heart. You do, after calling as many times as I had to ask why he hadn't collected Jarret as promised, whether he'd forgotten his son's birthday, and so on. Gifford's mother tried to make up for it when she had time but even a charming grandma is no proxy for a dad. My boy's heart was trodden in the mud rather than broken.

Gifford's answering machine beeped at me. 'I don't suppose the kids are with you, but you have to know this,' I said to it. 'They skipped out of Caine's about seven tonight, and they know not to go back home because we were burgled this afternoon. I am worried. Call me at Lara's. Please.' It paid to be succinct as well as polite when dealing with Gifford.

And last, I phoned the police. I said I knew they didn't have the manpower to hunt for missing kids at the drop of a hat but I'd done my usual rounds and now I would like official help as soon as possible. I decided to keep the pantry to myself a little longer. Given who I was, if I told them over the phone they might think it was a hoax and stay laughing in the muster room.

Brick pressed a tumbler of B'Tullo'M'Wha'Snick into my hands. It smelled like the sweat of Loch Ness monster.

Lara swept her dressing gown around herself. 'That's enough to fell a horse. Just sip it, Suzie, it's potent. I'm going up to change. You should never face emergencies in your dressing gown if you can help it.' She left the kitchen and ascended the staircase. Lara cannot merely go upstairs, she always *ascends*.

How come her kindness and concern racked me off, even though I had come here to seek it? The pain in my hand had made me crabby. I took a gulp of the whisky and coughed like a walrus. I noticed Brick had poured himself another. He patted my shoulder gently, but in my state it was enough for me to stagger against the bench. I did not drop the whisky. I drank more. Brick was proud of me for that. I was the sister-in-law for him. I was almost as good as a bloke.

'There is no more you can do, my dear,' he said. 'Just wait for somewhere to . . .' He squinted into his glass. 'Some-*one* to arrive? Yes. One. Someone.'

I sipped more of this marvellous whisky. I finished the tumbler. It took ten minutes and I feared that was too fast because Lara was right, it was powerful stuff. But ten minutes was time enough, it seemed, for somebody I had phoned to leap in a car, drive like the clappers and swerve up the tasteful driveway. Brakes graunched. We heard fast footsteps and a beating on the door.

I assumed it was the police and lurched again at the marvellous whisky but, though he held onto his new glassful, Brick placed the bottle on top of the kitchen cabinets behind the rimu trim. This was good, both of us playing *hide the whisky*. I needed my wits: first find your wits, then keep them close about you — I wished I'd thought of that before. I could not afford to be squiffy, I needed to trace my children, and to decide how to tell these cops about my pantry, offer them the dilemma of whether or not the corpse was an illusion.

'Answer the door,' I told Brick.

'You're right. Door, door.' Carrying his whisky, he shambled to the hall in those down-at-heel slippers.

I tried to corral a sensible thought while out of sight Brick erupted with a welcoming roar and began a dialogue punctuated with whisky this and whisky that.

'Good God,' Brick bellowed, 'where is your nose tonight? The smoke, man. The burnt match note. The hint of rubber.'

Roger? We hadn't phoned him. That single malt — just one glass of it — on top of my dreadful afternoon — I clasped my hands over my eyes for a moment of sweet darkness.

'Lagavulin?' said Roger at last. He sounded less full of enthusiasm for the game than usual.

'Completely wrong!' Brick shouted. 'You must be getting 'flu. It's Bunnahabhain! But come in anyway, come in.'

'Is Lara here?' Roger asked.

From the top of the stairs, Lara answered herself in a tone fit to pickle pork. I could see her — she'd changed into sensible trousers. 'Glad you've dropped in, Roger. We have things to straighten out.'

'My timing was way off. I'm very sorry.' Roger came into my

view. Though both he and Brick are large men, their styles are very different, Brick smudgy round the edges, Roger always looking crisp and shiny new. But tonight, though his suit and shoes were admirable as usual, he had a poached egg glaze about the eyes as if he hadn't slept for days. 'Look, I know this will sound odd — I don't suppose Philippa is here?'

'I haven't heard from her for over a week,' Lara said as she descended.

Bits and pieces spiralled in my mind, still affected by that glass of Bumbly'moggagh: the body thought to be Philippa's in the 'm' room, that illusion on pasta sauce in my ransacked kitchen.

'Oh, Roger,' I said out loud. 'You should'a seen what I seen. Oh Roger, it was terrible. Roger — Tilda and Jarret have gone missing.'

As he stared at me, thoughts chased across his face and none of them seemed nice ones.

'The children!' Brick gave a single clap of his big hands. 'Roger, rack your brain. Brains! Brain.'

More thoughts chased over Roger's face and it seemed that he grew paler.

'The police thought Philippa . . .' I said no more, and wasn't even sure I'd said that much though Roger spoke as if I had.

'Yes, I've just come from — oh God, I've been at the morgue. They thought it might be Philippa.'

'Here's a man that needs a whisky.' Brick waved towards the bottle up on the cupboard.

A car pulled up in the street. The police this time? I stumbled a little as I moved to the front door. Yes, it was a police car and it seemed the in-house police-vine never slept, for close behind it was Caine's personal car, his old white Laser. Lara stepped beside me and gave me a hug. Her hugs were rare, and the more sincere for that. I hugged her back as we waited for those two policemen and that ace detective to approach.

They milled in the large hallway till Lara swept us, *grande dame*, into the living room where we sat down. She told Brick to shut the front door.

He said of course but, frowning at Caine and with a protective wink at me, sat down instead. Over Lara's face passed that look of endurance that appears now and then on the faces of all married people.

Caine took a seat at my side. I jiggled and stood up. Caine started to describe my kids. I gave him a Look and took over.

Jarret dresses like any fifteen-year-old boy, I said, so I did not need to detail his clothes: the police should already have the picture. I mentioned his dark hair, dark eyes. I talked about his expression, sometimes sullen, but how underneath was a soul jam-packed with angst over things that did not concern the police. I described Tilda, articulate for her age, winsome in her ballet clothes and with her *Hello Kitty* bag. All the time I wondered how to bring the conversation, in an artless manner, to what I thought I had seen in my kitchen and to what Caine, the snooping ace detective, might well have seen too if it were real and if the pantry had been open. I sympathised with characters in crime stories who, as they talk to the police, must have *what-ifs* spiralling in their heads like moths around a lamp. *What-if* Caine were on a secret case for truth and justice? *What-if* he had hidden the kids to keep them safe? *What-if* the kids had run from Caine because they discovered he was on a secret mission not for justice, but for evil?

In the street there was a screech of tyres, a bang of a car door, some noisy loping up the drive. I knew it was Luke, my Tilda's dad. I was right. He barged on in.

Never trust the name of Luke. It may be the name of the calmest and kindest of the holy apostles, and also means *not quite* as in only partly warm. This, for a man with a hair-trigger temper and, for me, an aroma with an undertone of brimstone.

'Suzie, what in hell is going on? What the . . .'

'Oh Luke, don't start,' I said. 'Wait till . . .' I nearly said *till I tell you the whole story*, but that's exactly what you can't say in front of the police at times like these. Luke glared. He said no more but his glare made a racket. He also glared at Caine, which in other circumstances might have been flattering to me but I couldn't stop to consider that right now.

'Ms Emmett,' said a constable, 'have you checked back home? Your children may have simply gone back home.'

Roger began to stammer something too but Caine held a hand up to still this line of questioning. 'I just drove by Suzie's place — no lights. Tilda always has a light on, right?' He smiled at me. Luke scowled like a thunderous midnight.

'The kids knew we had to stay away from home tonight. They trust the police.' I jittered into the hall away from Caine.

Luke followed: I sniffed him before I saw him, and caught him staring at my hair.

'Another mistake,' I said. 'Don't comment.'

'You look like Michael Jackson, only prettier.'

I gave a shout of unexpected laughter and flung a hand out. My bad hand. It struck the gong. Just one small tap. Just one! It hurt like hell, but the noise it made hurt more.

The air swelled in and out, and on and on. It was musical, oh, sure. And resonating? — you hardly know the meaning of that word. The police, Caine, the others, hands clamped over their ears and eyes squeezed up, tumbled out into the hallway. As the sound waves travelled round the globe even those monks in Tibet would have lifted their heads. At last the vibration diminished. There was movement in the driveway, out in the street. Neighbours clustered agog. One held a golf club. I saw at least one umbrella: the Neighbourhood Watch. There was a dog or two as well, and far-off howling.

Another vehicle pulled up, a big black four-wheel drive, and out of it jumped Gifford.

I will not repeat what Luke said at that point.

Gifford reached the steps. 'Suzie, I just got your message. Please forgive me.' Gifford had an enviable voice, like maple syrup. Every man, woman, child and dog turned towards him as he spoke, then were doubly mesmerised by his clear angelic eyes. I was reminded of that crowd that gathers around the spaceship in *Close Encounters*. 'There is no problem. The kids are at my mum's.'

A load of fear fell off me. I floated with surprise and with relief.

'Jarret called me from Caine's and I fetched them. I wrote a note for you Suzie, but I shoved it in my pocket.' With an appealing show of guilt, Gifford pulled a crumpled paper from his jacket.

Luke's face was murderous. Caine seemed guarded. Roger, skulking in the background, still looked drawn and anxious.

'At your mother's?' he asked. 'Why would they — Gifford, is that so?'

Stuffing the note back in his pocket, Gifford dismissed Roger with a little gesture of his other hand, but seemed cagey as he spoke to Caine. 'It's best to say this, Caine. Jarret has a problem with you. But that's kids for you, he's sure to get over it.'

My relief began to bubble through with anger. Those little rats! How could they put me through this, particularly Jarret, not telling me how he felt about Caine! But Gifford was right, that's just kids. And I had phoned everyone except Gifford's mum. I wouldn't have thought Tilda keen to go there. I'd disturbed my friends, the kids' friends and their parents — even the police were here now. I felt so goddam stupid. There was still something I had to tell the police of course, but not with this crowd listening.

Lara gave me a poisonous look — I'd embarrassed her in front of neighbours. 'Phone Gifford's mother now, Suzie. If you don't, I will.'

Gifford shook his head. 'Lara, you can trust me this once. It's perfectly safe for Suzie to go back to Caine's tonight. Okay, girl?'

Everyone was staring. Inside my head I saw the mannequin in the pantry. I saw Caine snooping up my steps, well in the shadows. I saw him sidling down again and driving away with the lights off.

Caine reached out. 'Come on. Let's leave your sister to some peace and quiet.'

I tucked my hands behind my back.

'What's wrong, girl?' Gifford asked.

'For goodness' sake. Go with your boyfriend,' Lara muttered.

My head was like a balloon from the whisky. My ears still rang from the gong. I saw only one way through the tangle of who to trust and what to do.

'I can't go with him,' I declared before that crowd. 'I've decided to dump him. I don't know why, but this is it. I'm sorry, he's not my boyfriend.'

Gifford glanced at Caine who turned aside, face stony as a mask. Luke's glare was as loud as the gong. Then Gifford grinned and held his own hand out towards me. God knows why, I took it.

chapter six

In Gifford's car, we took the road that led from the hills down to the highway into town. Isn't this the way it's meant to be, sitting next to the man in your life in times of trouble? The problem was, my life had three men in it: this particular one had proved untrustworthy too often in the past, Luke was much enraged as usual, and my son had no high opinion of the ace detective I'd just dumped in public.

Gifford's car, you may recall, was a four-wheel drive. Expensive. Smelling new. If you have ever sat beside an ex-marriage partner several difficult years later, you will imagine how false it seemed to make small talk. Since I'd walked out on him our dialogue had mainly concerned broken promises, blame, requests for child support that came to zero. I felt nauseous: probably the whisky. And still nobody but me knew how much trouble there might be waiting in that pantry. But I ought to call in on Gifford's mum. Gifford could drop me at her place, I'd check on the kids, and maybe have a word about the wider situation with that charming, scary, but undoubtedly sensible woman.

Over the smell of new leather I caught a whiff of spicy after-shave, and snuck a look at Gifford. How did he seem these days? In some ways, not one minute older than when we married. His dark hair was slicked back as if he'd just come out of the shower before dabbing on that drop too much of aftershave. Chunky shoulders, flat stomach, the way of sitting with his short legs tensed as if he'd spring up any second. But the triangle of lines that appeared on his left cheek when he smiled was deeper now. Patches of sun damage on his forehead showed too much outdoors, too little SP30. That tension round the eyes meant not enough REM sleep, doubtless caused by the cash-flow problems that had made him ask Lara to put leverage on some rules. The wear and tear increased his charm. Some men are like that. I was still able to understand why I had married him. But I did not wish to recall my wedding day. My parents had a dreadful fight in a side room at the reception: whispered hissing, beetling brows and all the trappings. Elizabethan melodrama in the wings. I never knew why. Perhaps it was just my tricky mother, who made fun of the romantic ideal now and then. One time when we lived in San Diego I tagged along with her to collect my father from the airport. He'd been in New Orleans at a conference and another botanist came off the plane with him. Arms out, she ran up and kissed the other guy, calling *How I have missed you, darling*. My dad was bewildered but the other guy and I cracked up entirely. Mom was a great one for jokes.

Anyway, as Lara had said only tonight, Dad and Gifford got on well. Gifford had even visited Dad in hospital before the poor man died, deluded, thinking it meant Gifford and I were getting back together. At least this misconception helped Dad die happy. And when Mom died just a few months later, Gifford sent on stuff from her estate that went to him by accident — an early draft of her will, copies of deeds to her house, nothing important, but nice of him to bother. In some moods, he would have binned it, as might I had the situation been reversed.

'Oh, thanks for that key,' I said, 'that little box. From Mom.'

'You got it? No problem.'

We passed the pet store with the huge plaster dog outside, the document security depot (which I always misread, not as Archives' Security, but as Archie's, good old Archie), the liquor store and the paint shop. When we spoke again, we did it simultaneously — an awkward cliché, but a flutter in my viscera told me it was because at least a little chemistry still simmered in the gulf between us.

'Just drop me at your mum's . . .'

'What say we . . .'

We laughed and he went first.

'It's a little late to visit Mum, girl. She was making hot milk and packed the kids off to bed as soon they arrived. She has a conference tomorrow.'

I pictured how Jarret would respond to hot milk offered by his grandma. From me, it would be seen as maternal brutality. From Gifford's mum the boy would take it like a lamb stunned into courtesy. Though she was a nice woman and would cope with Tilda and the hair lice, I still had an inward flinch. But I was glad at least one of my kids still had a grandparent, something I had never known myself.

By now we'd whizzed by the stadium and were passing the Museum of City and Sea: Tilda loved to visit the hologram rat in there and exclaim at the fake rat poop. My hands twisted together (small ouch). Rather than disturb Gifford's mother so I could see for myself the kids were okay, I would hold on till morning.

'Why do I have bad luck with men?' The words sprang out, surprising me. 'That was not meant to be tactless, more a . . .' How to end my sentence nicely? 'It's not fair on my poor kids and I guess it's my fault.'

'Same here, girl. I might even be ashamed if I had the bones for it.'

Wow — honesty? Maybe, as I had, Gifford had begun to

realise when you neared forty years of age, you could not rely on charm and a sporadic cash flow. Don't get me wrong — he had both, I only had the jerky cash flow.

'What I intended to . . .' Now I sounded too formal. 'I meant, if I had to take up with a detective, why did it turn out to be one I can't trust?'

Gifford grinned, turned up the charm full throttle. 'So, you have no strings tonight, girl. It seems we're on a date.'

This didn't seem a good idea. And how I wished he wouldn't call me girl. But by now he was pulling into the Courtenay Central parking building. I stayed politely silent while we walked along to a little Italian restaurant. Monday night. Pretty quiet. Gifford ordered a bottle of merlot and suggested cannelloni because it would be easy for me to manage one-handed. I said I'd eaten. It had only been a few wedges, but I couldn't face more.

'Can you call your mother for me on your cellphone? I just want . . .'

'Girl, she has to be up at 6.30. Wait till tomorrow. It sounds like the kids have had a rough day. We'll let them sleep.' His voice was soothing as honey. Sometimes that man could be considerate. He was right, it was close to ten now, I didn't want Tilda to wake.

Gifford sipped his wine, and I took a sip of mine to be polite. Polite again: yes, I was fussed about being courteous with this man. Now I was so much older, I felt that when we married we'd been more in love with the dream of it than the reality. Maybe we'd confused the physical urge with true love. Oh that urge when you are young and still have your clothes on, pressed together, that sensation of climbing, building to reach that point where you know you must break through to a new experience . . . I shouldn't get personal, but back then it had been a constant riddle to me how a wave of desire could end up just a damp patch. The one time I'd mentioned this incomprehension had not had a jovial ending. I'd had to insist to Gifford I knew precisely the meaning of orgasm. I did too, I'd looked it up. *Immoderate excitement or action* said one dictionary. *The height of venereal excitement in coition*, said another. There was a song my dad liked, by Peggy Lee — *So that's all there is, to a fire?* I had never mentioned that song to my young husband.

But Gifford's magnetic voice still did things to my insides. 'So tell me about this afternoon, Suzie. The burglary.'

I went through it all again, except going back home tonight and so of course not mentioning the pantry.

He looked at me over a refill of merlot. 'Nothing taken at all? Lucky. But as soon as you're allowed back in the house, check everything. Like — I don't know, your jewellery box.' He glanced at the little cat brooch.

The extra key in the box on my bedside cabinet came to my mind again. 'When you came around today, what time was it?'

Gifford tilted his glass but didn't sip. 'Oh, I gave it to Jarret this afternoon. I found it when I was clearing out some stuff. I was sorry to miss you. That boy of ours.' Gifford fixed his blue Welsh eyes on me and smiled. 'He's a great mimic, girl. It could get him into trouble. He does a good imitation of your ex-boyfriend.'

'He does. The boy's a star. Did he mention school to you, tonight?'

When Gifford shrugged, I felt relief and guilt. I didn't want my boy to confide his problems in his father and not to me. What an unpleasant person I was. Today had been too hard. I wanted to fall sleep, wake up, find out it had all been a dream.

'It'll be safe to clean up your house tomorrow.' Gifford indicated my bandage. 'You want help? You'll need it, girl.'

He was offering to do housework? I stared. He looked self-conscious. The waitress brought his dinner and asked if we'd like two forks, to share. My turn to flush. She thought we were really together, like romantic. But where was I going to sleep this night?

One of Gifford's charms used to be that he could often read my mind. He still could. 'I guess you won't go back to Lara's tonight after that little kerfuffle.'

A guilty laugh popped from me. 'You are not her favourite person. Nor will I be, making all that fuss for nothing and then scooting off with you. I'll pick my car up tomorrow while she's at work so she can't scold.'

He laughed too. 'So, how about Philippa's?'

I shook my head.

He smiled and oh, those deep blue eyes. 'But you can't go home, girl. You're not meant to go back home. So what will you do?'

I had no answer.

He smiled again. 'I've plenty of blankets.'

That voice was honey, the kind that is active manuka, guaranteed to soothe and heal. The drop too much of Paco Rabane showed his vulnerability. The way his hairline had receded made his scalp seem tighter, the way an animal's does when it's alert and ready to hunt — or run away.

'No.'

I had said it too abruptly. It could seem impolite. Alternatively, it could mean I longed to be in bed with him again, to see if this time everything worked. Complicated bubbles seethed inside — whether they were caused by chemistry or fright, they still spelled out *bad idea*. 'Gifford, that's nice of you, but I'll call tomorrow if I want help with the house.'

I emptied my glass and he poured us each some more. What should I do? Given the state of my house (a danger zone) and wallet (anorexic) I had two choices for accommodation, Annie or Bernard, the only friends who would be nice this late in the evening if I woke them.

Gifford brought out his wallet. 'Not to be intrusive, or presumptuous. But you've had a bad time. Let me help out. There are cheap hotels round here.'

I felt very uncomfortable indeed. I shouldn't have had any wine at all on top of Brick's excellent Bun'toch'sic. I really should have had a better Monday. I really should have talked to the police.

chapter seven

As I hurried to grab a bus down to the railway station, a breeze sifted up from the harbour and gave me goose bumps. Gifford had let me leave after I promised I'd go straight to Annie's. I cradled my aching hand as the bus bowled along Willis and Lambton. Though the ride was short, I almost fell asleep. What stopped me was how stale I smelled as I warmed up: wine, whisky, garlic from Lara's, a whiff of Thai rice salad from Thee Ultimate Café.

At the station I didn't have to wait long for a train to Annie's suburb. The carriage seemed strewn with young potheads, hopheads, skinheads — even on Monday? What would they think, if they knew what I'd been going through? I doubted they'd care a button. It was too easy to flirt with self-pity: I consoled myself it was the usual effect of late-night public transport.

At Annie's station I set off up the public steps. I had forgotten they were so steep, thick bush on either hand. It is only natural these days for a woman to be nervous late at night if she's out walking — forget late night, we can be nervous any time. Someone was behind me. I was afraid it might be a skinhead but it was a guy carrying a briefcase and wearing a suit. Even so, I kept climbing with my head down. Don't look anyone in the eye, my parents said the one time I remember being in New York.

He could climb faster than me. I glanced around. He smiled. I didn't.

I tried to climb more quickly but the guy in the suit caught up.

'It's tough, working late.' His teeth flashed as he smiled again. 'You too? Hard day?'

'Back off!' I yelled. 'I've just been ransacked! My boyfriend's turned out dodgy and he's a cop! I gashed my hand, it hurts like hell! I'm exhausted and confused! Where's some consideration!'

'Sorry, sorry.' He loped on up the steps into the dark.

Real life smelled bad to me. I did not need that episode.

By the time I reached Annie's house I was puffing. Too little food, too many shocks, too much over-reaction, too many steps to climb, it does that to a woman. I knocked on my friend's door.

Her hallway light came on, then the outside light. 'Who is it?' Annie called.

'Only me. Only Suzie.' I heard the security lock rattle as she unchained. 'Check through your peephole! Don't let me in until you're sure it's me!'

Annie threw the door wide. She was in her yellow dressing gown. 'Who could imitate your voice? Come in, sit down. You look awful.'

'I woke you. Annie, I'm sorry.'

She hauled me into her living room, sat me in a chair and perched on its arm. 'Are Jarret and Tilda still missing?'

'No, no, they're safe at Jarret's grandma's.'

'I tried to phone you, but your line is dead.'

And that was not all . . . My heartbeat stuttered.

From the baby's room came a whimper, a coo, the tinkle of a tiny bell, then silence. Annie cocked her head to listen like a bright little animal on a phone ad.

'Oh, Annie — I have to talk to the police. I shouldn't have come.'

Annie's hand came over mine. 'Just tell me what's wrong.'

Her dressing gown was quilted like my mother's, patterned with tiny flowers, the kind of robe that says you have to go make pancakes. I tried not to cry, searched for the muscle to climb out of this chair and leave my best friend and her Zoe to the peaceful life Annie's accountant husband was earning for them while he was off on contract in Peru. Why was it only now, in this scene of comfort, that I properly realised the ransacking and the discovery in the pantry (if it were real) might mean serious danger for me and my kids?

'What do you need, Suzie?' Annie coaxed in her motherly way.

Some trusty sidekicks would have been nice but it was too dangerous a role for Annie and Zoe.

She ruffled my hair when I still didn't answer. 'A good night's sleep is what I think.' She ruffled my hair a second time, muttering *hmm* as if she'd like to get her scissors there again.

'Actually, I'm starving.' All I'd had to eat since breakfast was that pesto and three wedges. No wonder I was weepy. 'A cracker and cheese maybe, and then I'll leave.'

'Minestrone, then my spare bed,' she replied. Annie hauled me into her kitchen and microwaved a bowl of homemade soup while we sat at her old oak table. She also made toast and cheese, which I gobbled like a pig, beginning to tell her between mouthfuls some of what had happened, like the broken window, my summons to see Caine, the ransacking, but not about the second key — which was just a very minor puzzle — nor about the pantry (why mention what you hope is an illusion?) and not about dumping Caine. Women are reputed to share all manner of personal stuff about their boyfriends but I was still mentally chewing over his un-cop-like behaviour earlier at my house. Even so, in my complicated way, I was ashamed I'd dumped him like that, in front of my sister, her neighbours, both my ex-es and Caine's colleagues. My face burned.

'Gifford made a pass at you!' Annie's hands curled over her mouth, just like a squirrel.

'No, he didn't — I don't think so. But it felt weird.'

'Ouch.' Her eyes were full of sympathy. 'You stick with Caine. He has such a confident voice. It's not as syrupy as Gifford's. I like it better.'

After half a bowl of her marvellous soup I felt calmer. Tomorrow morning, I would simply slip away while she was changing Zoe.

'You need a bath.' You could see Annie made a good mother.

'A shower's quicker,' I said.

'You're too tired, you'd fall over.'

She found a plastic bag to tape over my bandage, ran a bath, shook lavender salts in it and lit a candle that sent out soothing perfume while I soaked. After ten minutes Annie returned, helped me into a long white nightie that made me feel like a child on a Christmas card, tumbled me into her spare bed and whispered to have peaceful dreams. She turned off my light.

The warming minestrone and relaxing bath conspired to tug me into a cocoon from which I would, I hoped, emerge tomorrow full of drive and fire. Like a phoenix from the ashes — though I felt more like the budgie I briefly owned when I was twelve, soft grey Peggy Lee who died of moult.

I dreamt I was in Times Square. That trip my family made to New York when I was ten was a quick one, and Mom said no way would she take us near Times Square. Dad's agreement was a one-word shout before he pored over the map and his red hair curled tight and darkened with sweat, the way it did when he concentrated. But as I began dreaming, I remembered this weird scene came to me each time I was upset. Then I forgot it again, until — uh-oh — here it comes, the Times Square dream . . . *I must be about two years old, not ten, because I am sitting on the shoulders of a man who is my father. I can't see his bald head underneath the hat he wears. He decided to shave his head but not his moustache. My hands are in pink mittens with gold bells: they're clutching my dad's fur collar. I don't like the hat he wears. It's fur too. The top of it is all I see of him except his hands, also in mittens, holding my legs. I can't see his fascinating shiny new bald head. It's evening, and all around is a crowd of people, and on my dad's shoulders I am up so tall that I am looking down on most of them. The hats, the hair, the noise of people yelling, some awful music, lots of banners. The neon signs that all the world knows mean* Times Square, Times Square — *the Coke bottle and the other stuff — all blink and glow and dazzle. My mother is there too. I really hate Times Square. My mother is upset. She tugs my father's sleeve. All I see of her is her hand tugging and the top of her fur hat.*

'We shouldn't have come,' she whispers, a fierce whisper. I think she's scared of some bad people.

I know what I am going to do next. I'm going to pull Dad's hat off. In my dream I know I'm about to spit on his bald head.

I woke in the dark. My heart raced as my brain sorted out the dream of neon Coke bottles and fur hats from Annie's spare room and silvery curtains in the moonlight. I didn't know why that dream scared me so. It had no sisters in it. How can anybody figure out a dream? We'd lived in Boston when I was tiny, before we moved to California. I asked my mother, once, when it was that we'd been to hear music in Times Square. *Dear, you've seen it on TV.* She bustled about. *It is always on TV. Tomorrow, let's go to the zoo.* That made me happy. We were in San Diego by this time. I'd throw a cookie to Chester the brown bear who showed off by skating on wet rocks. I was certain he recognised me though I never let on to my sisters. He gave a special wave as he slid and enjoyed all the attention. Lara would boss us, about the best order in which to see the animals. Philippa would be in a paddy because she'd rather be at the Wild Animal Park. I loved the Animal Park too, though I hated going with my sisters because they scoffed at me for being crazy about the white pelicans. I loved seeing them up close, as you could at the flamingo pond — white pelicans from Africa, with pink faces, not the ordinary ones we saw around the rocks at La Jolla or freeloading at Sea World. I used to wonder whether the princess pelicans, as I called them in my youngest sister thoughts, could make friends with the ordinary kind, if they'd like to be free, living on the coast, able to fly. You have to see pelicans flying before you appreciate their strange determination. Sturdy things — they seem too ungainly to leave the ground, yet I still see them in my mind sometimes, the family groups with their raggedy wing-tips, arrowing in the evening across the bay of La Jolla Shores. Ordinary brown pelicans going about their business as a family should.

I fretted the rest of the night, unable to stop wringing my hands even though the wound ached. When I heard Annie moving at last, I found she had thrown all my smelly garments into her washing machine. I showered, shampooed my hair, combed it flat, borrowed Annie's yellow dressing gown (too short) and set about making pancakes. A good Californian breakfast such as my dad refused to cook when we lived there, though sometimes Mom did. Bacon. Syrup. Blueberries. An accountant who earned danger money in Peru earned more than enough to keep bacon in the fridge. Annie missed him, but I enjoyed her bacon, usually. This morning I was queasy and anxious. I cooked but couldn't eat.

Annie handed Zoe a morsel of bacon to suck, spread olive tapenade (debate this with the infant's mother, it was none of my doing) on toast, cut it into soldiers and lined them along the tray of the high chair. Zoe worked tapenade into her hair. *Nyum,* she said but at her stage of language development *nyum* signifies *how creamy this food feels as I stuff it in my earhole.*

On the clothesline outside Annie's window, tea towels shimmied in the breeze. I checked the kitchen clock — after eight — and phoned Gifford's mother.

'No answer?' Annie asked.

'The machine.' I was annoyed. She must be dropping the kids at their schools before she hurried to her conference. I'd call her early evening and, if I didn't catch her then, at least leave a message to say thank you for stepping in when the kids wanted her.

Now, what about the police?

'Suzie, you look a little crazy.' Annie poured me more coffee. 'Want me to come to your place, help tidy up?'

I thought about my house.

'You're looking even crazier,' she said.

Annie had to help me fasten the strap of the bra I borrowed from her. It fitted, more or less. I chose a long-sleeved tee from her closet, and a pair of stretch trousers. They were too short as well, of course, so Annie folded them up to look like three-quarter pants. She insisted on using gel to style my hair again, and assured me I looked fine. I love her, but some friends you cannot trust about the small things. I pinned Gifford's cat brooch onto my bag and swallowed some painkillers. Annie made me borrow her denim and lace jacket too, then sweetly drove me to Lara's to pick up my car. Thank goodness, nobody was home so I did not have to excuse my behaviour of last night. Annie made me promise I would phone her later on.

What I intended was to visit the police station in person, by myself. I should talk to a detective who was not Caine. But given the camaraderie in that workplace, given everyone knew me by now, how could that work?

I had to let my unconscious side make this decision about what I ought to do: left brain-right brain stuff. I started singing.

chapter eight

I sang old Olivia Newton John songs. She was a big star when I was in my adolescence, the age those things imprint themselves. The deceased Pigoletto (guinea pig, kidney failure) used to sing along when I played tapes to her. *Totally hot! Ee-eee.* I remembered reading somewhere that the noise guinea pigs make is referred to as pinking. I didn't know if that was true. I just kept singing.

My song sent me scooting down the hill, along the main road into town past all the places from last night. Archie's Security. The paint shop. When I checked the rear-vision mirror there was a big dark sedan trying to overtake a red courier van. I was so hyped up I kept ahead of them, and reached the clogged chariot race that is Featherston Street any time on a business day. Just ahead, a car pulled out of a parking space. This was a rare occurrence in the mid-city one-way system on Tuesday morning. I could hardly refuse, though wished I could — the central police station would be a mere minute's walk around the corner. I edged my rusty heap into the space and found coins for the pay and display.

Across the road and down a block or two from where I'd

parked, I passed my bank.

This time I made a conscious decision. I ducked on in.

It had been so long since I used the safe custody service that I'd forgotten how. I checked the signs. One, above a set of going-down stairs with a chain strung across them, announced *Safe Custodies*. I queued at Customer Services and hoped to wait forever, anything to delay going on to the police. But the line fed quickly through. The bank clerk beckoned another bank clerk who beckoned me to follow her, the stairwell was unchained and I was down in the bowels of the bank. There was the unlocking of the security gate, the clerk went through, relocked it and from the other side of the safety window asked my name so she could verify my signature, so on, so forth.

I fumbled both keys from my wallet. 'I can't remember which is which.' This was true.

She was a good employee, combining warmth and efficiency: were I a personnel manager, I'd hire her at once. I hoped she'd take long minutes turning through a heavy faded register like something from a musty Dickens novel, but she flipped plastic pages in a shiny red folder, said the first key was mine, and after a few more seconds said with an efficient smile that the second key was listed as belonging to my mother and myself. Goodness knows how she interpreted my vacant look. I peered through the security window at the place she had her finger in the folder. A signature like mine was there beside Mom's. My mother was indeed a tricky creature. Anyway, I was entitled to look in both boxes.

I endeavoured to seem un-astonished. Who had been paying for this second box these last few months? At this point I was a clever detective, and asked how many ways people could pay for such things.

'A regular deduction from their account,' the bank clerk said.

'And arrangements can be made to cover costs in advance?'

How clever I was being: this surprised me.

'No. It must come from an operative account.'

The right brain-left brain interface still worked. My mom had seemed to have no money, had not left much in her will. There must still be a bank account managed by Mom's lawyer and not revealed to me. Her lawyer had done a few dumb things after she died, like sending that stuff to Gifford although we'd been divorced for years. But that had been the fault of his new assistant who should not be criticised for some unimportant slip-ups, especially in the confusion of Mom dying just a few months after Dad.

Something wobbled in my gullet. I doubt I will ever be over not having my mother any more. I guess many human beings are like this. And oh boy, I guess by now you're wondering, as I was — had Gifford searched through that stuff of my mother's and held onto this second key because he always found it fun to be obstructive? No, it must have been a straightforward oversight. But I wished it hadn't been returned on the day my house was ransacked and my pantry filled with . . . Jarret hadn't mentioned that his father had come round, either.

I scolded myself for this mistrust of Gifford. Okay, mistrusting him was often fully justified. But last night the man had offered me money for a hotel. He'd taken my kids to his mother's. He was the father of my son.

The warm but impersonal bank person watched me sign for both boxes with my injured hand, found the bank's keys to the safe custodies, let me through the security gate. We entered another part of the bowels lined with tiny metal doors, she led me to my tiny door and we unlocked it. I slid out my box: the smallest size available. I followed her into another room where we used the keys to unlock a metal door two sizes bigger. The model employee asked if I would like to use a private room. I would. She carried the larger box for me: it looked like a strain.

In the very small space that is called a private room although it is hardly bigger than a box itself, I closed the door and was alone. As I looked at both boxes on the transparent bench that for some reason is lit from below, I felt not a little weird. I sat on the green swivel chair.

Which box to open first? I nearly let my subconscious decide again but an Olivia Newton John song in this small space would have been an assault on the ear drums.

My small box first, the one I'd known that I possessed. Tilda's birth certificate was on top. A slew of feelings, memories, impressions filled my head. My dad's sweaty curls and distressed forehead when he learned I was having a second child and had no interest in getting married to its father. Dad's dislike of Luke and Luke's of him. Luke's temper and his passion, the passion I had felt misdirected at all kinds of social injustice and at sporting fixtures instead of at me — I'd been a thirty-odd-year-old woman and thirty-odd-year-old women can be complicated creatures, and thirty-something male journalists too. But after we broke up Luke stayed more than merely 'in touch' with his much-loved daughter. He paid for Tilda's ballet lessons. When he came to watch her in last year's ballet production (she was a buttercup), he gave her a dozen pink roses covered in glitter and accompanied by a stretchy rubber cockroach. Against my will, he took her regularly to McDonald's, and that is something I confess a father and child should do, have occasional allegiances against even the mother. Also, Luke had insisted vocally and in writing that he would not, never, no way, no how, let Tilda be forever separated from him. Tilda needed a father, which was him, as well as a mother who, despite my being such a supernaturally insufferable female, was me. He bellowed that he had no doubt in the universe he was Tilda's father and I could take a ferry ride to burn in the sump of hell before he would stop seeing her.

You'd expect this difference between their fathers' attitudes to create a rift between Tilda and Jarret. Maybe it did. The rift that binds. And I acknowledge that several times Luke and I had nearly got back together. Love. It's thorny.

Underneath Tilda's birth certificate was the title to my house. Underneath that were papers about the dissolution of my marriage to Gifford, Jarret's birth certificate, slips of paper saying I gained moderate results in the few university courses I took (I will not bore you with humiliating details), a reference from my high school principal (why the heck keep this? I'd been a useful member of the crowd scenes in school productions and my grammar and spelling were impeccable), and my birth certificate. *Suzie Emmett, 15 April 1965. Mother: Mary Emmett, née Green, occupation housewife. Father: Frank Emmett, occupation scientist. Place: Christchurch New Zealand.* To be absolutely factual, my birth certificate was stamped *Certified Copy*.

That was all the box contained. Why had I been paying around twelve dollars a month to protect these hardly crucial documents? Because my mother said I should. I remembered her voice distinctly, that husky tone, that definite way she ended her sentences. I even saw the little nod she'd give as if she were dotting the punctuation with her head, the little rap with a wooden spoon on the side of the preserving pan, the dot of paint after the last letter on the *Save the rainforests* banner.

All alone in the private room, I finally let myself open up the second box.

On top was a copy of *Little Black Quasha* by Helen Bannerman. A big blue plastic paper clip marked a page. I opened it, and the words on that page were masked by a piece of paper in handwriting, not Mom's: *We're sisters. We share.* The facing page was the picture of two grinning tigers surrounded by a pool of gore, torn limbs, black and orange scraps of other tigers. The little girl was up the tree and crying.

This did not strike me as necessarily strange. My mom Mary was contrary. I put the book aside. What did strike me as peculiar

— in fact it gave me a jolt — was the birth certificate I found beneath the little book. *Suzannah Quinter-Hurren. October 15 1964. Mother: Maria Hurren, occupation elementary school teacher. Father: Laurence Quinter, occupation student. Place: Boston Massachusetts.* Quinter? Even beyond the grave, Mom could mystify me. *Laurence* Quinter? The private room in the bowels of the bank filled with my puzzled laughter. Larry Quinter was the most arrogant and least successful rock star who ever made the cover of a magazine. Quinter was such a dick of a name for a rock star. Quinter had been great at making headlines, but abominable at music. He squandered millions, funding his own records. My father would never let the air in his house be sullied with the sound of Quinter's rock. This birth certificate — which, if it was pretending to be mine, also pretended I was some months older than my true certificate — could only be another of Mom's practical jokes, an elaborate one, as good as that more simple one I remembered from the San Diego airport. I imagined how Dad would have reacted and started to laugh. Mom was a funny tricky lady, and I loved her. Now in this little private room, my laughter disintegrated. Tears began pouring down my cheeks as I wept for my mother. I'd been waiting for this moment for several months. This was the first time I had wept with all my body, shaking down to my core, for Mary, contrary Mom.

After my shuddering grew less, through the dazzle of crying I hauled more papers, mostly old letters, out from underneath this fake certificate. Under them was a bulging envelope with my name on. My nose dripped, my shoulders jerked with sobs as I glanced into the envelope and saw two wads of money. One in US hundred-dollar bills, the other local fifties. Was this another of her jokes? Were they fake dollars? There were also many documents like fancy bank notes, which I suppose they are when they bear pictures of famous Americans like presidents, scientists, and Paul Revere, with a heading UNITED STATES SAVINGS BONDS and the advice that interest ceases thirty years after issue date. The amounts ranged from 5,000 to 10,000 US dollars, the issue dates from a year to twenty-five years back. Oh my goodness. There were two thick boxes, around one of which was a rubber band with a slip of paper tucked under it. In my mom's printing, like a crooked fence, it said: *from Thonia*. When I opened the boxes I found gold coins. I picked one out. On one side was an antelope or some-such animal with hooves and horns: the other side said SUD AFRIKA SOUTH AFRICA around the head of a middle-aged bearded bloke. Krugerands? Oh help. Oh dear. Oh God. Right underneath everything there was a handwritten letter addressed to me.

All of this for my dear Suzie, said my mother's writing like swooping birds in the thick blue pen she liked to use. *There are rights, then there is what is fair. Each generation has the right to decide for itself what is both right and fair. Mom.*

The date below her signature — do you call 'Mom' a signature? — was two months after Dad had died. Three months before she died herself, before the unexpected *poof*! in her gentle brain.

This was added underneath: *I should write an explanation but it's harder than I thought. Let's hope I don't die for a while yet.*

I rested my head on my arms, over my mother's last letter to me. I missed her very much.

chapter nine

You may think I am a callous cow not to have wept so fiercely for my mother before this point. You could be right. Philippa and Lara cried cyclones starting with all the letters of the alphabet. They were the older daughters, so knew her longer — I didn't know how those things worked in families. When Dad died, I had been a puddle of tears but during those terrible months after Mom's death it felt as if a metal cap descended on me and denied me the ability, even the will, to look beyond myself and my kids. My eyes leaked water constantly though for some reason I sobbed only when I was in the shower. Jarret and Tilda treated me like glass. I could not talk about my mother, not to my sisters, not to anyone. Caine had been a rock for me, silent when I needed it, kind, a pair of strong clean arms, a chest on which to lay my head, that bed of his to float away on. When I thanked him, he would blush. Being with him made me remember I was *there*, a person, that I mattered. A few weeks ago, I had started to think I could talk to Caine about Mom. But almost at the same time I began to have this pain deep in my heart, to think it could not work out with him, that I should end the relationship before it went the way of all the other important relationships in my complicated years of adult life: down the s-bend.

Instead of crying for my mother, I had begun work on that footstool. Philippa said if I taught myself how on one of my own, she'd pay me to upholster two bigger ones she had. The activity was curiously compelling; something in it agitated a crucial element in my race history: placing padding over rough, raw wood, smoothing fabric over the padding, *bang*! with the staple gun to hold it all in place. All that pioneer/colonial Do It Yourself, the making-do, the covered-wagon mentality that was part of my growing up in California, my father's six-months-in-a-leaky-boat attitude.

Now, wrung out with crying for my mother, I sat in the private room in the bowels of the bank. I had countless thousands of dollars of two countries in my possession and no reason to imagine my mother came by it dishonestly — although *Thonia* was unusual as a name, either a wanky choice by the person's parents or an equally wanky shortening of Anthonia. But that was by the by. I had permission (I thought) from my mother to use the money as I wished. I could buy Tilda her own ballet company and make sure she danced the key roles. I could buy Jarret his own school and ensure he was head boy. I could buy myself a perfect life, new house, new car, a fancy new kitchen — I stopped those thoughts right there.

Unable to hold the book properly, still sitting in the minuscule private room with its glowing desk, I skimmed *Little Black Quasha* and gave one tiny puff of laughter on the page where all it said in big black lettering was: '**and was drowned**!!'. The facing picture was a tiger floating on its back, legs straight up and its tongue stuck out.

My tears had dried. My face itched. What to do with all this money? It had been safe in the bowels for goodness knew how long. The bank book, bonds and coin could stay, but I decided to deposit some dollars in my cheque account. I did not want to come running to the bowels each time I needed cash. I folded Mom's last letter in my wallet too. Then, lest I was missing something crucial, I skimmed the bunch of letters. Don't you hate it when a person in a mystery has crucial information and doesn't look at it straight off? These letters, typed, seemed to be to my mother from someone crazy — mad but intelligent, you know? We all need friends like that. These letters invariably said how much this person — a woman, I was sure, because of that fey intelligence — missed the person they were written to. I should say that they were not addressed Dear Mary, but always to Dear Friend. The one I liked best began, *As that little prick Nietzsche said (and because everyone misquotes him, so may I), if you want to give birth to a dancing star you must nurture chaos for a time. Yes, it would have been helpful if he'd mentioned the black hole you have to fall into again and again. We march onward, not on our stomachs as claimed by that other little prick whose name begins with N, but with solitary courage. I'm not at all ashamed or sorry for my subterfuge. Stuff your principles, dear friend, and let your daughter choose her own. Hug that dancing star for me.* It continued with mundane detail about a snippy tourist in the Russian Tea Room, a crammed shuttle to Boston, but ended with this: *Forgiveness and tolerance are still alien conceits in the neighbourhood of Filene's, as well as in Times Square.* It was signed with a huge looping T. Filene's? A big department store in Boston. It had a bargain basement, that's all I knew. I was glad Mom had made such a friend in the States — and had possessed all this money. She had often seemed strangely lonely to me, though always self-sufficient too. And I could now tell my sisters that Mom's simple way of living was her choice and ask them how we should all share this treasure.

I emerged from my private room, thanked the attendant prettily as we tidied the boxes away behind their doors (my mother taught me manners), queued up and put five thousand local dollars in my account. Little movements of my right hand such as tucking the deposit slip into my wallet hurt like the dickens. I glimpsed Caine in his plain clothes, straight-backed, his crooked nose in profile, standing outside the main doors. It gave me a strange wormy feeling between my heart and throat. I didn't think he'd spied me — he must have been on the lookout for some criminal, if not merely on a break from work (which, after all, was just round the corner).

My brain chugged with more energy. Though I still couldn't imagine my mother coming by this money illegally, I decided to conceal this matter at least for a short while, concealed myself as well in a group of American tourists leaving the bank — thank goodness for cruise ships — and visited a smaller branch of my bank north along the main street. I paid off my Visa account in full, with more of my mother's dollars.

As I headed back along the Quay I caught sight of a sorrowful woman coming towards me with scarecrow hair and one white clown-like hand: myself in a shop window. I had forgotten the new hairstyle and that I was wearing Annie's clothes. They seriously did not become me. She's petite and suits lace. I am lanky and suit very little. The haircut Annie gave me only added to the Orphan Annie impression I was giving. In the first draft of a thriller, my friend's name would have been globally changed right at this minute, lest readers grow confused. All I can say is, my own confusion rode me like a cloud. Oh boy, I looked forlorn. It would not have surprised me if a social worker on her morning break had stopped and asked in gentle tones if I needed help. There was, of course, a great deal of help I truly needed — I should go to the police. Or should I go home first, to check? My dread of going there alone reeled around me like the bogeyman.

I went into Kirkaldie and Stains to freshen up. The lighting in the ladies' room was kind, but I looked weary, scared and guilty. If I kept delaying like this, the kids might get home first and then what about the pantry? I did a weak best with the hairbrush from my bag, but still failed to turn myself into someone who might be taken seriously by the police.

More coffee might revive me, as Annie's midnight soup had helped last night. First things first. Feed the inner man, as my father would have said, and feed the inner runt, as I said now.

Everyone who works nearby comes to Kirk's at tea break or lunchtime, to buy, to look, to covet, or have lunch. Want to catch someone unawares? Just lurk in Kirk's. It has a classy coffee shop on the second floor where successful well-dressed women meet their successful well-dressed daughters. One day I hoped Tilda and I might meet on the second floor but in the meantime we both liked the lowly one at ground level. I nipped down the staircase and through the kitchen department.

As usual, this lowly coffee shop smelled of stewed tea and sausage rolls. This took me right back. When she reached menopause, Mom claimed she kept her weight down by sticking to this rule: *never eat anything bigger than your hand*. Should that include the fingers, or did she only mean the palm? The sausage rolls here were as long as from my wrist to my second finger joint. I did not fancy sausage rolls today because they reminded me too much of my mother. I picked two potato-topped pies instead.

I chose a table tucked against the wall, where I could look over to the kitchenware. I liked to sit and watch people covet utensils that I too could not afford. Today of course I could have afforded many, also designer clothing from upstairs. I was aghast at having such a thought at such a time — designer clothing was what those two dead women had been wearing. So similar to my sisters. So firmly middle-class.

I sipped my tea, took out the copy of *Little Black Quasha* to leaf through again. I remembered how I'd laughed and laughed, as Little Quasha laughs and laughs, when my mother read it to me. I remembered too when I had finally learned to read for myself. Very slowly, I had read out loud until Philippa with a sneer to end all sneers said, *You can do it silently, Suzie. You can read in your own head.* She meant to make me feel ashamed and stupid. But this idea was striking. Silently? I tried it. And, do you know, it worked!

In mingled sadness and the memory of success I glanced up. Through the crowd I caught some exchange between a tall man in a particularly well-pressed suit, his back to me, and a shorter man in a slim dark suit who had another slimly suited man beside him. It looked like someone being given a court summons. The shorter man held out a blue envelope, the well-pressed man brushed it aside, the shorter man insisted, the large man grabbed it in an angry way, turned and strode towards the delicatessen. It was Roger, my brother-in-law who used to be a dentist. I got ready to wave hello. But as he read the note, he came to a sudden stop blocking the end of the aisle where you buy expensive kitchen knives. His face said, *Oh God, this is worse than I thought.* He glanced up. I waved. His face said, *Oh hell! It's Suzie and she's spotted me!* I inhaled a crumb of pastry. He whipped around and vanished up another aisle past the Corningware. By the time I'd stopped coughing, he was long gone into the early lunchtime mix of happy shoppers. The two little guys in suits had gone as well.

That was not polite of Roger. But he had still appeared stressed out. Maybe he was just remembering he had to buy something for Philippa, if she had turned up. That man was so uxorious: when Philippa wanted, Roger ensured she got, and fast. I could have helped him choose her a present, I could have given guidance, I knew the kind of clothes and *objets* my sister liked: expensive. Helping Roger would have meant I could put off my going to the police a little longer. And I love to shop in Kirkaldie's, to look if not to buy. From where I sat, for instance, I saw someone had just bought a big fancy notebook with a picture of Edvard Munch's *The Scream*, the very upset woman in black with swirling sky behind her, an image that has become a modern icon. You can even buy blow-up dolls of *The Scream*, and I know because once I bought one for Tilda's father and told him it was exactly how he made me feel. He blew it up and popped it!

You see how I was delaying. Once again, I felt ashamed. I left the potato pies and I got going.

First, I ran to re-do the pay and display. Guess what? Too late. Another ticket. Though I could pay them all easily now, I still felt despirited, too disconsolate to go to the police. Just consider — how idiotic I would feel if I went to them with my story, and when they came to investigate the body in my kitchen they found it had been an illusion all along.

It was time I behaved like a grown-up. The only course was to check for myself then, depending on what I discovered in my pantry, call the police or a psychiatrist. And feed the cat.

I parked outside my house. It was after midday, nobody around except a woman with a dog. I hovered at my gate, jingling my keys as I summoned the nerve to go inside. The dog bounded over, strings of saliva dripping from sloppy lips. I scampered up my steps, shoved in the key and slammed the door. I tried the light switch. It worked. So far, so good, but I was sweating and I'd hurt that wound again badly.

Everything was still in chaos, the sling that I'd used for all of three minutes yesterday dangling from the handle of the closed kitchen door at the end of the corridor. Beneath a fossil rock on the hall stand was a yellow slip of paper. I didn't remember it there the day before. Maybe that dinky policewoman had left it for me. I picked the note up and unfolded it. In Jarret's writing and dated today, late morning, it said: WE'RE OKAY. YOU'RE SAFEST NOT TO LOOK FOR US. STAY CALM.

No matter what I had experienced before, I had not felt this kick of fright — I snatched the phone, nearly dropped it, heard the dial tone — thank God! — and fumbled with the phone book. It fell out of my hands and I crouched over it on the floor while I flipped to National Library. I asked to speak to someone who knew where Jarret's grandma might be, where the conference was being held — but I was put through to her at once.

'The children?' she said. 'With me? What conference? I haven't seen Jarret for weeks. Dear girl, you know what Gifford's like. He's got it wrong again.'

My moment of pure fright was lengthening.

'I've been meaning to call and ask Jarret how he likes his new school,' she went on. 'Suzie? Are you there? Are you all right?'

Heaven knows what I answered. I only remember holding the phone as if a lifeline had transformed into a snake, and putting it down very carefully. Then I walked towards the kitchen. Heart thudding, I reached out and pushed the door to let it swing open.

My jaw dropped. I blinked. I shook my head. I glanced back into the hall as well as over to the dining room to make sure this house was mine. Try it, see what you do if you are fearful of seeing a corpse and a chaos of spilled food in your old painted kitchen with its peeling and scorched bench top, chipped cabinets and a missing cupboard door, and instead you find the place has been redone. There were new doors on every cupboard as well as on the pantry. There was a beautiful jade green bench top with a small white card lying on its spotless surface. The floor had been scrubbed clean.

Blood drummed in my ears as I stepped over to the pantry and pulled it open. A new little light clicked on and showed me every shelf was regimental. My only jar of pasta sauce had gone. The cans of catfood sat there.

More important, the only dead things were in cans labelled *Sardines in Spring Water* and *Chunk Tuna*.

chapter ten

How high can confusion rise before it tips over into madness? In the manner of those Filipino faith healers who appear to dig into a patient's belly and bring out tangled eels and other unexpected items I thrust my good hand into my hair to drag out a sensible thought. Come to think of it, this gesture was very like that woman's in *The Scream*. Her thoughts must have been at least as wild as mine. Where had these new cabinets come from? Had there been a dead body here last night or not? And the kids — why leave me such a terrifying note? And why had Gifford lied to me about where the kids had gone? I didn't linger on this one. He had such a history of untruth that his lies over the years were woven like an Oriental carpet, to be amazed by, not possessed or understood. He didn't care about the kids who, after all, had scampered off before. He would merely have decided that to whisk me away under the noses of Luke and Caine was excellent entertainment.

But the kids. Had they been forced to leave a message? It seemed unlikely, though several unlikely things had happened. Would someone abduct children from the house of a detective?

Could disgruntled criminals be trying to get revenge on Caine for putting them behind bars? They might have thought the kids were his kids. Bright criminals would have done their homework better. My kids might have been abducted by dumb criminals. This was not a thought to lift my spirits.

The kids could of course simply have been bloody-minded: Jarret had been in a strange mood. No — I remembered they'd been promised pizza. I doubted my kids decided to leave Caine's place on a whim. They didn't know Caine meant to feed them Hawaiian.

But did they discover something at his house — perhaps they'd snooped around, as all kids will — something that made them decide to leave? Something connected with the unoccupied new pantry? At this third possibility my scalp crept as if with head lice. If I found whatever the kids found, would it give me a clue as to where they might have gone? Maybe I had better return to Caine's and do some snooping of my own. Was there anyone to help me? My government official sister could not snoop. Her husband could not snoop. I didn't know where Philippa might be. Roger — he'd been having that little argument in Kirks and looking ill on it. Annie and Zoe had done enough for me already.

I picked up the small card on the bench. It was poor quality, the kind you print for yourself at airport machines. One side was blank. In cheap type, the side that had been face down said: **Stay put. Know whats good for you. Shut up plese**.

Nameless appeared on the windowsill, thrust his tawny side against the glass and writhed. He nestled his head on his paws and squirmed those haunches. He squalled and showed his buck teeth. His eyes glared through the mask-like markings.

I stepped to the pantry but as I reached towards a can of Chomp, my hand rose instead to tangle in my hair again and 'Luke' is what I said: a very unexpected item. Who else was there to help me find the kids? Only the Child Youth and Family Support people, who are always overworked and I did not wish to be assigned a file number and asked all manner of intrusive questions about my lifestyle. That would not be fruitful, I knew, because I asked myself intrusive questions about my lifestyle in the dark hours when I woke and couldn't sleep: that is, most nights.

I phoned Luke and was hardly coherent. He shouted for me to make sense. I screamed bad things. He crashed the phone down.

I looked at the window. Nameless had disappeared. *Be calm*, I thought, *be coherent*. And: **Stay put.**

Okay. I phoned Tilda's school: she was not there. I phoned Jarret's and found the same, though this took longer to establish. I began dialling Gifford but became mired in distrust. Had he been trying to keep me out of my home last night? Did he have anything to do with this new kitchen? Was this a nice surprise? Was it a gift? Though Gifford had surprised me in the past, it was not often pleasantly. More likely, some home-owner elsewhere in this street was incensed their new kitchen hadn't been installed yesterday as promised. Perhaps the card — **Know whats good for you** — was an aggressive new marketing ploy.

I tried the new cupboards. The doors swung evenly, less weighty than the old ones but with scientifically advanced hinges and bevelled edges. The bench top was an invitation to roll pastry, chop onion, grate a lemon. I had certainly not ordered a new kitchen. Until I'd found the money Mom had left, I could not have paid for one. And besides — the pantry. That bare foot. Okay, about that I might be hallucinating, but where were my kids if not at school? If there was no need to panic why did Jarret leave that panic-inducing note?

Before me was yet another trial to undergo this awful week, and it was only lunchtime Tuesday. With my ace detective ex-boyfriend and erratic ex-husband off my list of people to confide in, Luke was definitely my only resource.

Under the central library I parked in a space reserved for the handicapped — to hell with social ethics on these occasions — and ran through the little arcade to Willis Street. It was years since I'd entered Press House. This building, the beating heart of the city's daily paper, is a heart made up of one extremely old side, one very swish and new. I knew that on the Boulcott Street side at the reception area where you deliver letters and so on, there used to be at least one burly security guard meant to prevent me from entering although, more usually, they didn't glance up from their newspapers which I assumed they got for free. With my bad luck at the moment the security boys would surely glance up, decide I was a terrorist and pin me to the wall with one of their staplers. I hadn't taken the time to change out of Annie's clothes, but again I tried to smooth my hair, gave up, rummaged in my bag for Caine's perfume, found Philippa's damn car key again as well as Tilda's sneaker, spritzed Anaïs Anaïs on Annie's tee, swallowed a jolt of nostalgia for that man I'd dumped, and entered Press House.

Oh — you were no longer able to go straight up in the littlest oldest elevator in the world. There was a swish new door and a security swipe device. I hung around until a journalist I recognised came whizzing out through the new door wearing jogging gear. I begged her to let me in with her security card.

'Oh hell,' she said, 'it's more than my job's worth these days. Regulations are tighter than a Christian Heritage Party sphincter. Hell again, I haven't time to go back up with you and see the sparks fly. Never mind, I'll hear all about it later.' She swiped her card for me and I said thanks.

I trusted my left brain-right brain links again. I headed down a corridor, through a double door into a tiny outdoor section, then in through another door and there was a little elderly elevator waiting for me. I pressed a button. After leaving the elevator, I clattered down a maze of corridors like something out of Kafka combined with something drawn by Escher and all the while I hummed 'One Night in Bangkok' because that's what Luke was singing loudly and badly at the party where I first met him. He and Tilda have no ear for tunes though they are both good movers. Luke dances like an eagle constructed by Disney and though Tilda may be no ballet star, she knows how to bop to the beat.

I shoved through more doors and found the bear pit they call the reporters' room.

A glossy-haired woman swivelled round on her computer chair and stared at my bandage. 'I hope you're not my shoulder massage.'

No, I told her, I was here to see Luke Fitz. She waved towards the far side of the bear pit. And there he was. The father of my younger missing child.

The only people I had come upon who handled the English language worse than journalists were the teaching staff at Tilda's school. What is a copy editor for? Going by Luke Fitz, it was to put in the punctuation for sports writers. In the past I had teased Luke about his punctuation many more times than only once too often. When we decided to call Tilda what she is called and I made what I thought an extremely clever joke about punctuation, Luke didn't understand because he had never heard of a tilde but this is probably not unusual. (In case you haven't heard of a tilde either, it is a wiggle like this ~ in fact a diacritic mark placed in Spanish above the letter n to indicate a palatalised sound, as in señor. Try it out. N-y, n-y, just like in onion. You can look up 'diacritic' for yourself. People often seem — I think maddened is the word — at how much I know regarding things about which nobody else gives a five cent stuff. This will be no surprise to you by now.)

Across this bear pit Luke stood at his desk, an oversize coffee mug in hand. He glared at me. 'Can't Help Falling in Love' by UB40 this was not. Luke's glare is more intimidating than that of any other person I have met: his eyebrows are black thickets in which small beetles might get lost.

I wove through the maze of desks. There were curious glances from his co-workers but basically they left us alone apart from 'Relationship alert!' from one who I remembered prided himself on his gift for irony and, from an even less subtle wit, 'Wa-hoo! The Happy Family!'

'Luke,' I said, 'whenever kids tell their parents not to worry, a wise parent worries harder right away.'

He glared.

'I want to be a grown-up,' I continued. 'I promise not to raise my voice if you promise not to raise yours. This is all about our daughter. I have calmed down, and I seriously need help. Where can we talk? If you tell me you've got a deadline, I will kill you.'

My voice was steely until I reached those last three words, when it became a shuddering quack. For a moment I thought Luke was going to rear back and flap his great arms as he was wont to do when I made him angry, a Disney eagle smelling of sulphur, ready for take-off. I was wrong (I never like admitting this). One long arm did reach up, true, but only to set his mug on top of his computer. He grabbed his jacket off his chair back, yelled 'Twenty minutes!' to someone in another cubicle, and we were off down the Kafka-Escher corridor to the stairs, into the oldest working elevator and out into the end of lunch-hour hustle.

In his flapping jacket, Luke sailed over the road and through the arcade towards the library. I straggled in his wake like a Raggedy Anne from the Two Dollar Shop. Up the library stairs to the mezzanine coffee bar he sailed, scanned for a table, and flapped one of his arms towards the only spare, at the very furthest end near the glass doors out to City Square. I scuttled with obedience while he fetched two coffees.

By the time he arrived, I was composed. He had bought me a cappuccino, himself a trim milk latté, and a plate of three muffins. As if cleaving enemy heads, he cut them in half, buttered them, and pushed the plate to the middle of the table just as he used to do when we were an operative partnership. In all this time, he had said nothing apart from the 'Twenty minutes!' he called to his co-worker. He took a bite of muffin, a sip of latté then regarded me, his great arms folded on the table.

There was beige froth on his nose. I indicated, he wiped it off and still said nothing. I knew why: if he said anything to me it would be a shout. In the past we had both been unforgivable. I drooped my head and glanced sideways through the glass doors at the airy ball of silver fern suspended over the square, the happy normal people wandering in happy normal directions beneath a bright blue sky. I felt sick.

'You're a good man, Luke.' I told him why I needed to talk. The woman in the morgue whom both Roger and I had been taken to identify. The apparition in my pantry and the pasta sauce beneath her. Caine and his suspicious un-cop-like behaviour (Luke smiled at this, a snarly smile), about my self-centred ex-husband Gifford (Luke snarled and smiled here as well). I said the kids had somehow returned, left a scary note on the hall table and disappeared again, that I'd been given a stunning new kitchen with another odd note (**plese**), and I did not know what to do. I had nowhere to turn because there was nobody left in whom I had much faith.

'So you trust me,' Luke said at last.

I picked at a crumb of muffin. 'If you were investigating this as a story for the paper, what would you do?'

His eyebrows thicketed more thickly. 'I'd trust you five metres less than I could throw you, and I could toss you a good two metres. I'd think you were having me on.'

My mouth opened to yell but one of his great hands came over mine and squashed the muffin.

'Suzie, this is not something I'm investigating or reporting. If you say something is the matter with the kids, no matter how bizarre it sounds, I believe you. You are the most frustrating person in my life. You turn me into a sub-human. But when it comes to your kids, you are a prince.'

'Prince?'

'I'm using non-sexist language.'

Which comment reminded me I hadn't mentioned the politically incorrect children's book my mother left me in the safe deposit box. I had not mentioned it because I did not want to mention all the money. I wrestled in my mind now whether to tell Luke, but decided no. I wanted to discover more of why my mother possessed such riches before I told anyone else. But I brought the puzzling *Story of Little Black Quasha* from my bag. Luke glared at the cover.

Inside my head there was a sudden shift in consciousness. For the first time in the nine years I had known him, I realised that because of those remarkable eyebrows, any expression on Luke's face was like a glare. The apparent glare, at this moment, was in fact his blank confusion.

'Why are you staring at me like that?' he asked.

It was not the time to say I finally understood why I'd always insisted on making love with the lights off. I turned the conversation back to Tilda. To Jarret. To where on earth my kids might be.

'We go to your house and I see this new kitchen for myself,' Luke said. 'We sit at your dining table and write on file cards everything that may have some relevance to the fact the kids are missing, though if they left a note it indicates they're more or less okay — I hope. We frown at the cards and try to make sense of this.'

I put *Little Black Quasha* away.

chapter eleven

To know I was about to be so busy went a tiny way to quiet the dread that had increased in me, the sense of having limbs out of action, those limbs that were Tilda and Jarret. And when Luke and I approached my car beneath the library, the traffic warden who had been about to write me a ticket for hogging a handicapped space, instead engaged Luke in discussion about the stadium as a venue for rugby test matches. I took this for another sign that life would soon improve for me. This was one of the world's great small cities, where traffic wardens engaged sports journalists in idle conversation, where traffic wardens looked like cute sports referees and sports journalists like giant eagles. Little sisters and big brothers could not stay missing in such a city. I was so happy and keyed-up that I didn't step away fast enough when a car backed from a parking space, revved up and roared out of the building. If Luke hadn't yanked me by the neck of Annie's jacket, I'd have been sideswiped. As it was, I was nudged by the side mirror. The traffic warden growled did I want to be handicapped for real. Luke wanted to drive, but I said I was okay. I was trying very hard to be a grown-up.

Once more I parked in the street, still doubting I would ever brave my gloomy garage again. Inside the house, Luke hulked at the door of Tilda's room and surveyed her mess of toys and books. I knew from the slump and then resetting of his shoulders that he was the best father in the world for my little girl. I hoped he wouldn't pick up the music box he gave her and open it to hear the tune because that would be so B-grade. He didn't.

In the kitchen, he shook his head about the streamlined cupboards and checked the pantry. He scrutinised the cheap and nasty card. 'Whoever wrote it doesn't know you. You would never stay put and shut up.'

I was tempted to shout, but I had promised.

He got on the phone to all the people I had called last night to see who knew anything about the kids. None did. In fact my answerphone was choked with messages from people asking if I'd recovered from the upset. Those we contacted again were troubled to learn they were still missing. Annie, for instance, was so shocked she turned absurd.

'If the police can make no headway, phone the American Embassy!'

'What good would that do?'

'Put on your American accent. Pretend you're an American citizen whose children have vanished. Don't argue with me, Suzie. It may be no help, but it can't hurt.'

'That's what little nations do when they're in trouble. Call in big brother. It can be a big mistake.' I hung up.

We sat at my dining table with a large pot of coffee. We didn't use file cards, we used big yellow stickies, several pads of which Luke had nicked from Press House when he'd returned to tell his co-workers he'd be gone much longer than only twenty minutes. I jotted many things and, at Luke's suggestion, jotted things that could have no relevance at all. Such as: to whom had I ever mentioned I would like a new kitchen? About that, in clumsy lettering because of my clown-size hand, I jotted *Everybody*.

Luke walked his fingers through the Yellow Pages and phoned a kitchen company. 'How long does it take to install a new bench, cupboards, a double pantry? Just the doors and shelves once they've been measured? As quick as that? And did you install one in Brooklyn last night? Yes, last night, after maybe eight o'clock . . . okay, we don't need a comedian.' He dropped the Yellow Pages, *bam*! on the table over a row of stickies. 'Jeez, Suzie. Five pages of kitchen designers to trawl through.'

I wrote *designer earrings* on a stickie.

'What the hell's that?' Luke asked.

'Can't you read?'

'We've promised not to shout.'

'They're what the woman in the you-know-where was wearing.'

Luke pointed to another yellow stickie: *a mum's blouse*. He pointed to a third: *hairdo*. I took the glare he gave me to be a question.

'Both dead women looked like Philippa and Lara. The jewellery, the clothes, the well-cut hair. They could be clones. That's if the second one was, you know, a real dead person . . .'

In a large and noisy movement, he sat down. I felt frightened — Luke wasn't glaring, he looked as scared as I felt. 'Two women are dead, and they looked like your sisters. Philippa's card was found near one of them. Is Philippa missing? God forbid, I hate to say it but she may be dead as well. You've been told to stay put, by this badly printed card left here in your brand-new kitchen, as well as by the kids. Suzie, you could be in danger too.'

I snatched another pad of stickies and he grabbed my left arm. I yelped.

He flung both hands up. 'I hardly touched you!'

I pushed up the sleeve of Annie's tee. Below my elbow was a high-coloured rectangular bruise. I hadn't felt much at the time, but that big dark car beneath the library had swiped me good. It was the second time in two days I had nearly been bowled by a car.

Luke bammed the table with his fist. Oh, this was glare in spades. 'Why the hell won't . . .' He clamped his own mouth and jaw in both huge hands for a moment and spoke gently through the trap. 'Suzie, we have to call the police. We can't do this on our own, I'm a sports journalist and you're a . . .' he stopped, glanced at my bandaged hand. The phrase *clumsy stand-in chef with only one opposable thumb* burned in the silence.

I made an effort too and it was hard. 'Luke, let's get back to the stickies.'

What also simmered in the air was that, very carefully, he had not said the kids might be in danger. Last night, the blood drained from Roger's already-pale face after he learned my kids were missing. When he saw me this lunchtime, after he'd been given that blue envelope, Roger ran. And Luke was right, nobody seemed to have seen Philippa for days.

Let me iterate how hard it is to cope with stuff like this when you do not trust the police. Your mind throws up all kinds of explanations for wacky behaviour. Philippa might well be in a huff, the way she used to act. How unnerved Mom would get, how red and sweaty in the face my dad, and Philippa would have been hiding in the shady cave of branches beneath the shrub that attracted bees, waiting till their panic reached full pitch. Maybe it was genetic and my kids were hiding too because they were mad at me for some terrible neglect, real or imagined . . . On the other hand, Philippa may have been kidnapped. That could be good cause for Roger to look ill and run away. I felt sick again myself.

Luke gnawed the knuckle of his thumb and studied the stickies that quilted the table like strange feathers. Can you have a quilt with feathers on the outside? Why not? It's the way that birds wear feathers. I longed to crawl beneath a quilt — how I wished I was still wrapped up in that security we call childhood, tucked under a coverlet with a kiss and a promise that it would all be fine by morning. With scraps of clothes, some well loved, others greatly loathed, Mom had made cryptic rugs of memories. Appalachian design, the Wedding Ring, and Covered Wagon. Pioneer art. My mother was not American though many turns of phrase fooled people that she was. She dodged questions about her upbringing. Neither of my parents, I recalled, ever talked about when they met or where they married. But such is the selfishness of safe childhood wrapped about with quilts made by your mom, that I did not recall we had great curiosity about those moments that had helped create our family. Sometimes my sisters and I giggled to ourselves that Dad must have been the quintessential nerd, and who would want to remember their young nerdish years? Anyway Lara had been more interested in school politics, Philippa in social who-was-who. As for me, beneath the quilt of safe childhood I'd been tangled in that runt of the litter syndrome, catastrophising, telling myself I was disinherited and disregarded like a footnote left unread . . . how was that for a muddle of metaphors? And I wished I hadn't thought of footnote. Again I tried to forget that elegant flat-soled purple shoe and five bare toes of last night. I thrust my hands behind my back to stop them wringing.

'Roger,' murmured Luke, still chewing his knuckle.

'What about him?'

'You say he's been behaving oddly. Would he engineer this crazy situation? Philippa missing, and you get a new kitchen. A dead body as an extra. I can't see why. However, I could never trust a man who used to be a dentist. Call me unreasonable.' He slid me a tiny grin. Luke and I had called each other unreasonable and far worse, myriad times.

I gave my jumbled brain a shake and came up with this: Lara had been annoyed with Roger because of something to do with Customs. He imported Asian foods. Philippa and her campaigns for the animals of Asia . . . We all like to be nice about orphans and shocked about poverty, but is it a misuse of energy to campaign about some issues? Of course animals have rights. I happen to think more work should be done first about the rights of human beings. Sometimes, being unkind, I referred to my sister's charity as Hug a Gorilla (do the acronym yourself) or the Offices of DEAD, for Don't Eat Asian Dogs. Dogs scare me, alive or on a plate. But I was being younger-sisterly again — Philippa and the women with whom she ran Suite Three were creative, they raised money for some things I admired, some things I thought were crazy, and none of it was any of my business.

I put my mind back to the job of finding the kids, of digging up — whatever: Philippa and Roger's interest in antique brass, in Asian artefacts. Their recent purchase of that smudgy Frances Hodgkins. Philippa not badgering me to give her back those car keys — surely if everything is normal, a woman needs her car. Scraps in the ragbag of my brain.

I unstuck from the table all the yellow stickies that were to do with Roger, and stuck them down again in a column. Luke next to me, we read: *ex-dentist*; *whisky*; *Kirk's kitchen utensil department* . . . I'd forgotten the men in suits and hadn't taken much notice of them at the time. After some concentration I pictured them more clearly and wrote *MIS (Asian?)*. Then on three new ones I printed: *Philippa missing? Philippa kidnapped? Dogs on the menu?* (I scrunched that last one up and felt ashamed.)

I scrawled *import* on a stickie, and *Asian foods*.

'From anywhere in particular?' Luke asked.

I gave him a look and wrote *Asia*.

'Beetle!' shouted Luke. 'There's a beetle!'

'Where?' I thought he meant a cockroach in my kitchen.

'Jarret obsessed about it for a while. Regulations and fines. To do with imports.'

'You're right,' I said. 'The Asian long-horned beetle.' I puzzled about how a beetle Jarret obsessed over might fit with what was happening.

Luke grabbed the phone and called a colleague, harassed him for some detail and repeated it to me, shouting over the receiver: 'It's as long as a joint of your finger . . . It has antennae ringed with white . . . It's struck mega-terror into the heart of this planet's strongest nation, a — how much? Wow. A multi-billion dollar disaster! Trees especially tasty to the Asian long-horned beetle are . . . what? Maples, horse chestnuts! Poplars, willows, elms, mulberries — My God, America is a smorgasbord for that thing! Thanks,' he said to his colleague at last, and slammed down the phone. 'Suzie, there is no way to rescue infected trees. They must be felled and burned when the beetle is dormant in midwinter.'

Well, of course. Otherwise the adult beetles might fly away. Wouldn't you, if were you a bug? Then they'd infest another area.

'Luke, this is no use . . .'

Shouting over me, Luke sketched out a scenario: Roger, used to drilling holes, deliberately injecting wooden packing cases around china from China with the larvae of the Asian long-horned beetle, routing them to Queensland or New Zealand . . .

'But Luke . . .'

He kept on shouting: thence to Fiji (where there are so many tiny islands that it must be very hard to know who comes, who goes), from thence to Hawaii (ditto) . . .

I had to shout back to be heard. 'But what could Roger gain by . . .'

'Then to the coast of California . . .'

'He'd have to pester Lara for documentation. He'd be a very desperate man to pester her.'

'He pestered the hell out of Lara!' cried Luke and flapped his arms.

You see how crazy this journalist would be to live with? 'Oh please,' I said. 'Give me a break. How many months would it take to set up? How long before the beetle caused enough destruction in the United States for anyone like Roger to benefit? Could he hold the United States to ransom, over a beetle?' From my knowledge of Roger, I considered him a man who liked an easier road, immediate gratification. I doubted that he belonged in a real-life eco-thriller. Unless, perhaps, there was exotic whisky in it.

I was a grown up. I had stopped shouting. I pressed my lips together and looked at Luke. His eyebrows quieted. I asked him to rinse out the coffee pot because I couldn't use both hands to tug the plunger, and I made us some fresh. I think Luke was sulking. He doodled beetles on all Roger's yellow stickies. One reason I used to shout at him was this, his doodling. He said it was to help Jarret learn to draw, but I knew better.

A movement at the kitchen window made me jump. It was Nameless again. Not bothering any more to writhe and be appealing, he sent messages with narrowed thuggish eyes to let him in and give him food.

I stood up to fetch the Chomp from the pantry. 'We're off on a false trail. This is not finding Tilda.'

'God, Suzie, if she's in trouble . . .' His voice choked off. He covered his eyes with his hand.

It was strange to see such a large man in sudden distress. I was close to breaking down myself and dropped the can of catfood on the bench to pour the coffee. I set a cup in front of Luke and said sorry that I didn't have trim milk. He blew his nose. We both heaved sighs.

'Jarret's probably just wagging school and dragged Tilda along for company,' I said to make a joke of it, and stood up again for that catfood.

Luke blinked and glanced at me obliquely, like an eagle. 'Jarret loves the new school.'

He does? How did Luke know?

Luke flushed. 'We — share hamburgers. Often.'

I banged the Chomp down a second time. My God, I yelled. Not only Tilda but Jarret, seduced by unhealthy fast food! Jarret telling me how against commercial exploitation he was, but being seduced by it anyway, and Luke seeing Jarret when I didn't know about it, and my boy confiding in Luke!

'Boys like hamburgers!' Luke shouted. 'Life is one series of contradictions!'

'Get out of my house!'

Oh God — I hoped he wouldn't.

He scowled at me. I shuffled. He shuffled. From the sideboard, I picked up that staple gun I'd rescued from Zoe. It was small and cost only a few dollars, which was good. When you used it, it gave a deafening *click*! which invariably made me scream and that was bad. You try reupholstering a footstool with a scream following each *click*! I put the staple gun back and said the word I must.

'Sorry. I am sorry. If only we could trust the police.'

'We can't trust your ex-boyfriend,' Luke reminded me. 'But you say he's planning to retire. Once he has, we'll trust the police again.'

I remembered Caine sneaking into my house — then remembered Beth, the skateboarding student. She was doing Asian studies. And she kept an eye on my house, my kids, my doings. I wrote a stickie for her: *suspicious neighbour?*

'I have to talk to Caine. It was his place that spooked the kids.' I went for the phone but Luke grabbed me. I yelped again.

'Sorry!' he said in his turn, for hurting my bruise a second time, and yanked his cellphone from his pocket. 'Tilda's my kid as well as yours. Nobody should be surprised that I want to know where she is.'

Good sense. I told him the number of Caine's mobile. Jittering around, trying not to get too close to Luke, I fiddled with the staple gun again.

'I'm trying to find Suzie,' Luke said to Caine. 'What? God's sake, that is ridiculous, they don't have passports. Who's in charge of the invest . . .' I saw the warning signs, the spreading shoulders, the leaning forward, and then *bam*! the man exploded. 'This is my daughter! This is Suzie and the kids you're messing with!'

My hand squeezed tight. The staple gun went *click*! I screamed.

'Suzie!' Luke shook his wrist. 'Oh fuck,' he said more quietly, turned off his cellphone, and sucked the speck of blood where the staple had hit him. 'Now Caine knows for sure you're not in Fiji.'

'What?'

'According to him, Jarret called and said you were all going out of town. He knew Jarret was lying, and told me that if I should see you, I was to ensure you didn't do anything foolish. He said to make you lie low so you won't screw up any further.'

Stay put! Lie low! What did this mean? One thing it meant was Caine didn't seem to know the kids were genuinely missing. What kind of detective was he!

'Don't point that thing at me again.' Luke tried to take the staple gun but I held onto it. A knock on the front door saved me from more yelling. I marched down and jerked it open. A fair-haired man in a suit stood there.

'Ms Emmett?' he asked. 'Ms Suzanne Emmett?'

A sedan was in the street, a woman in a city-black suit standing by it.

'Who are you?' I demanded.

The guy slipped a hand inside his breast pocket. I'd seen this in movies.

'Hold it!' I aimed the staple gun.

The guy froze. Luke emerged from the dining room. He froze as well. I didn't know what should come next. Across the street, a couple of the students came out on skateboards. The man backed down my steps. As he reached the gate, he took his hand from his pocket, slipped something in my letter box, and both suits smiled uncertainly before they took off in the sedan. Luke sidled up, eased the staple gun out of my grip and stuffed it into his pocket.

I didn't remind him about the safety catch. I ran to the letter box and found a business card inside for a realtor. Oh. I hoped my father had never been faced someone like me when he tried to do his job. I remembered the New York dream again, where he had a shiny bald head. That would be so typical of Dad if he wanted to disguise himself, to shave his head but not his red moustache, then wear a ginger fur hat. I remembered awful music and banners in Times Square and started to cry. You go through what I experienced, see how rational you are. I wanted my kids home. In thrillers, in the final pages the many strands tie up in a neat package and explanations fall *pat-pat* like the cards in Happy Families. But this was a world of many packs of cards and too many jokers, many of whom were clad in suits.

chapter twelve

We locked the house. Luke spotted another half-eaten mouse near Jarret's bike and shoved it off the veranda while I scrabbled for my car keys. Though the students' house was quiet, something made me glance over. A shadow moved in a second-storey window. It could have been the reflection of a cloud or the movement of a frond of tree fern in the breeze. But I sensed the movement was behind the window. The idea of being watched made me uneasy. I wanted the comfort of Luke with me, my sidekick in all this. But amid the terrible feelings I had right now, my anxiety for the kids, my frustration at this tangle of events, was one that had become like my familiar. Mistrust.

'Luke, tell me something with an honest heart.'

He blinked. This was the form of words we used back before Tilda was born, to ask how much we loved each other. To be fair, it was also the form of words we used for a couple of years after she was born. It was the form of words we used when we needed reassurance.

'How important is Tilda to you, Luke?'

In the pause, I unlocked the car and climbed in. He opened his door, packed his big hulk in the too-small passenger seat and turned towards me frowning.

'You well know Tilda is the first equal most important person in my life.'

I did not ask who was the other. The pause grew longer. The corners of his mouth tucked straight.

We are supposed to learn in life through having role models. There are other ways, of course, like making mistakes. I wrestled in my mind as I was driving. Until the term *teenage* was invented — sometime after World War Two — were human beings between the ages of thirteen and nineteen not complicated troubled creatures? Before then, did boys aged fifteen, the age of Jarret, move smoothly from childhood to maturity, or was the word invented to acknowledge this troubled period of a young male's (and yes, young female's) life? This is a rephrase of that old question: which came first, the egg or chicken? Let me tell you, Jarret had experienced egg on his face before and that was a great worry. That boy. He was sweet and kind to his small sister now and then. He was protective of his mother on occasion. He was as obedient as you could wish a boy to be, which is to say he had a good mind of his own. I would not wish a boy to be forever and always obedient: to me that would indicate he had no strongly held opinions, no capacity for being individual. I yelled at him if he skipped chores. He had been known to yell back, to sulk, and so had I. But more often, he was quiet, even reclusive, also normal in males that age. Other mothers of boys had reassured me on this matter, that they have periods of dynamic and enthusiastic energy then lie in their fuggy rooms for days, emerging only to the dining table or to open the refrigerator (certainly not to have a shower or clean their teeth). Other mothers had expressed with wistfulness how lucky I was to have a teenage son who was still sometimes pleasantly articulate, who did not communicate solely in infrequent sub-verbal expulsions.

However, from the time he was able to talk Jarret had asked unusual questions. When he had just turned eleven he asked if I lay awake at night as he did and worried about black holes. I may have been curt with him at that particular moment because I was more anxious about the minus figures in my bank account. But that night I lay awake and worried about Jarret worrying about black holes.

Did this make me a bad mother for my son? Did it mean I was incompetent? I loved that boy. I loved him with such fervour that I trembled for his vulnerability. To me, there was nothing more heart-wrenching than my fifteen-year-old obsessing about beetles and black holes. Perhaps rushing to his school, as Luke and I were doing now, would help us find him, help us figure out where he had gone.

So why had he been dismissed from his first secondary school ten months back? He totalled the deputy principal's car. He did not deliberately drive it into the pine tree. He had been sent to fetch something from the vehicle. Other boys were involved. Somehow there were shenanigans as you should expect if you deal with young males and mix them with cars. The handbrake was let off — on a downhill slope. But the deputy principal was already nudging the highest possible stress levels because of his domestic problems (it would not be right or kind to gossip about those) as well as issues such as recurrent high jinks at the school, and we all — the principal, the deputy, Jarret, myself, with input from Tilda who was firmly on Jarret's side, but none from Gifford who, true to his nature, didn't turn up at the family conference — agreed that Jarret had talents, such as maths and athletics, and a deep interest in quirky subjects and issues to do with humankind (such as the Asian long-horned beetle and America its smorgasbord), that his only real lack was in artistic skill, and who gave a toss for that? Nevertheless in the interests of universal peace of mind and because I did not intend to fuss about Jarret needing physiotherapy after that accident, which happened on school property, we agreed he would quietly and with grace be removed from that school and attend another. And I ask myself and you, what the dickens was that deputy doing to have had so many accidents with his vehicle that the insurance company refused to pay out for any more? (I suspect this involved the domestic troubles the hapless man was having, but as I said, I will not gossip.)

All these thoughts were in my web of worry about role models. Did Jarret not have a good male role model? Certainly not in that deputy principal and not in his own father. Except now I knew Jarret had hamburgers, often, with Luke. Was Luke enough of a role model? Was Caine? But of course, I must remember that Jarret disliked that top detective. Besides, I'd dumped him.

Also in that web of anxiety, I fretted about my mother. If I was possibly not a good mother, why was that? Did I not have a good role model?

How dare you.

(I did not promise I would be coherent. Still less did I promise to be reasonable.)

But had my mother screwed me up somehow? And as a consequence had I screwed up my son?

At that moment, mid-afternoon, the sun hot when it beamed through scudding clouds, as I drove with Luke to Jarret's school I was disregarding both the cryptic message from the kids and the cheap aggressive card telling me to stay put. How I hoped I could stay calm, not shout at Luke again. I needed him for the kids' sake. But I also thought how independent my mother had been, how, though she was often floaty like Indian cotton, she also often yelled at Dad and had that steely core of self-reliance. As she stirred pans of feijoa chutney, as she sat in the sunshine hand-sewing quilts and painting banners, as she tended her herbs and hummed to a tape of the Creedence Clearwater Revival she used to warn me not to be impulsive, to think things through, then stick with them no matter what.

I promised myself to be like any good protagonist in any mystery and any good mother as well, to seek until I found.

In the visitors' area, knowing what I do about boys and vehicles, I locked my car. Luke wanted to hunt out the school secretary but a horde of boys scrambled around a corner towards the sportsfield, *wolf on the fold* like the Assyrians, all noise and wrinkled socks. They spilled around Luke and me, and I stood there sniffing hard. This was not because of tears. I was trying to be resolute as my mother said I should. No, I sniffed hard because that mix of grime and sweat and energy reminded me of Jarret and I wanted to inhale as much of it as possible. Then I dashed towards the West Block, Luke flapping in the rear.

It is invariably a mistake to try and see a secondary school teacher if you have not made an appointment. Ms Baxter came running out with a pile of books and folders. We scurried beside her as she sped back up towards Main Block.

'I'm late for my last class!' she said. 'How's Jarret?'

'Still missing,' I puffed.

Ms Baxter stopped so suddenly I had to return to stand beside her. Luke too. As I explained Ms Baxter looked more and more confused. 'And so,' I said at last, 'we have to figure out what's going on. Why is he in trouble here?'

Her mouth opened and shut. And I was talking to an English teacher. You would expect a more articulate response from such as her, especially a teacher with the surname of a very fine poet, though I sometimes think poetry sucks. *Sucks* was one of Jarret's favourite expressions and I had not asked if he knew exactly what it meant: in this instance I did not want to hear my son say *yes*.

'Ms Emmett,' Ms Baxter said eventually. 'He's not in trouble. Your son is a contender for the Moynahan Cup.'

The what?

'A social studies initiative. It's personal research. He's written a very solid essay on cultural misappropriation. UNESCO. Artefacts. Sharing. Ownership. It's deeply philosophical.'

My son was a contender? I pressed a hand to my forehead where I'm sure the lines were deepening by the moment.

Ms Baxter tucked her chin over the armload of books. 'Did Jarret go on the school trip, maybe? He probably thought you knew without his uttering a word. Boys can be vague, especially clever ones like Jarret. If you're truly worried you must go to the police.'

'We'll do it on our own,' growled Luke.

Ms Baxter glanced at me, smiled a troubled goodbye and ran on, up through the swing doors of Main Block.

Luke raised a large arm and pointed after her, towards the office. At this time I must say I have heavily disguised this school as I do not want to be sued for defamation.

A moment by moment account of our conversation with Janine Truby, school administrator, would try the patience of us all and anyway, an editor would slash it. All you need know, as I did before we fronted at the sliding window in the foyer, is that she was no help. Janine Truby scanned the list of boys on the trip, not showing us in case that was a breach of privacy (for dickens sake!) — but Jarret's name did not appear. When she informed us what the trip was for, Luke and I were not surprised. Jarret detested tents and tramping. He had no interest in songs around a campfire. This was a boy who drank sports gunk, did press ups in his room, worried about cultural misappropriation and black holes.

Luke and I walked back to my car. My nerves thrummed.

'Maybe Gifford was right,' I said, 'Jarret simply doesn't like Caine and refuses to stay at his house.'

'Who'd blame him?'

'Caine's not so bad!' Although, maybe he was. 'I dumped him, anyway.'

Luke let out a caw of approval. Anger prickled up my neck, but I couldn't afford to bicker with my sidekick.

By now it was too late to catch anyone at Tilda's school but just the right time for ballet. Madame Avril was in dialogue with a lanky boy and his father. Waiting in line was Tilda's teacher with her older girl. We joined her.

'Suzie. Luke.' Glenda Nelson spoke softly so it would not disturb Madame. Even parents were intimidated by her. She was so ethereal-looking while so eminently sensible and those high kicks at her age made her seem a superior life-form. 'Tilda was not at school today — is she okay?'

I explained the situation. Glenda went kind of taller with the shock.

Luke scowled at her. 'Was Tilda all right yesterday at school, and when you brought her here?'

I started to protest. 'She was fine when I collected her . . .' My lungs juddered at how mistaken I could have been, so engrossed in my own problems that I hadn't noticed any anxiety in Tilda. Then I recalled what I had been through. No mother who'd been asked to identify a woman in an 'm' room should be ashamed of not taking enough notice of her kid during the next hour or so. And we had talked, on the way home. Tilda had told me with great smugness how she'd kicked someone during ballet.

Glenda beckoned Luke and me closer to hear. 'She seemed bouncier than usual during ballet. Nursing a good secret, I'd have said.'

Madame Avril had finished with the man and lanky son. They looked chastened. Glenda nudged me and stood back. 'Your need is more urgent than mine.'

Usually, though I'm taller than this beautiful creature we knew as Madame Avril, when I was next to her I felt like a bargain basement reject. To put it in a way more suited to her occupation, my spirit flopped as if I were a rabbit hiding its broken zipper behind a fake mushroom. Today, despite still wearing Annie's orphan costume, inner steel supported me. I asked Madame Avril if she could tell us anything about Tilda's behaviour yesterday that might help.

A flicker of something crossed Madame's eyes (you know what I mean). 'Nothing.' Madame tilted her head with its tidy grey French pleat.

'She said you scolded her,' I said.

'That would not have bothered Tilda. She and I have an understanding.'

'Didn't Tilda kick one of the boys?'

Madame smiled. 'We both dislike Cormac. He's a very dislikeable child.'

'But what actually happened?'

Madame's skin took on a pearly flush. 'My methods are unorthodox. Whatever gets results, that is what I want. Your daughter may not be the most agile of my students but she has a speaking gaze. I see much of myself in that child.'

She did?

'We'll keep this to ourselves?' Madame included Luke in her nod. 'Cormac has talent, but he is too much the show-off. I pay Tilda two dollars a time to kick him when I indicate. I scold her for kicking, then tell Cormac to observe your daughter's stage presence. It keeps him confused. Your Tilda has remarkable stage presence.' She glanced to make sure nobody but we could hear. 'She will be my fairy godmother.'

She would?

'I like to invert expectations,' Madame Avril informed us. 'There is very little dancing in the role. She'll use her fine sense of comic timing to charm the socks off everyone. It's to be a surprise. She's planning to tell you she has to be the pumpkin.' Madame took my hands. Her grip was steel butterfly. 'She earned four dollars yesterday.'

As we left though the maze of sun from the overhead windows, my eyes blurred. Outside, instead of using the pedestrian crossing

I tried to walk over the GIVE part of the GIVE WAY sign painted before it on the road. At a screech of brakes, I leapt back to the sidewalk.

Luke gave a big finger to the male driver. 'For God's sake, Suzie, be more careful!'

'Shut up!'

I stood with my arms on the roof of my rusty heap to rest my aching hand, trying not to yell again. What had I discovered in the last hour? Jarret and Tilda both keeping such big ones from me. So bad a mother, I had not understood either of my kids. Jarret, not at risk of being expelled, but a contender for the Moynahan Cup. Tilda to be the Fairy Godmother, when I at her age was a static rabbit. I ferreted (please excuse the unintentional linked pun) in my bursting brain to find out if I was jealous. I was not. I was so proud. I hoped to the heavens that Tilda would be on stage, Luke and I applauding fit to break our arms to bits. I remembered how proud Mom had been of me even though I was a useless rabbit, proud even though I would never be as good as my older sisters . . . a thought came like a lightning bolt: had my sisters been jealous of that? Not Lara, but Philippa — on some level I'd always been aware of it but now with these ideas about jealousy spilling in my mind, I wondered if there was something about the way my mother had protected me. Sometimes, I'd felt it was me and Mom on one side, Dad and The Girls on the other . . . but surely that was only the usual psychological tangle that exists in any family. My mind kept sliding away from the unexplained riches Mom had left me . . . but why had Gifford brought round that safe custody key on Monday, that particular day when other things went so awry, that day I saw Caine snooping?

'Luke, there's no other way. I have to talk to Caine,' I said. 'I have to go and see him.'

He slapped the roof of my car. 'You've dumped him. You can't trust him. Stay away!'

'That is so typically overbearing of you! Stop being so impossible! What's the alternative?'

'You would drive a saint to murder!' shouted Luke.

chapter thirteen

I left Luke glaring on the sidewalk and drove off, so furious that I could hardly see. It's not good to drive like that. After-school traffic clogged the roads. I figured I should pull over, calm down, do some thinking now I was on the loose without a sidekick.

When I reached Oriental Parade, I swung my rusty heap into a shady space beneath a Norfolk pine and rummaged in my bag for a peppermint. I found Tilda's sneaker, the usual female accoutrements for all seasons, Blu-tack, a pack of throat lozenges so ancient they'd gone furry, those business cards and pens that spawn while no one watches, then the new pack of peppermints I'd bought yesterday. I also found a card of painkillers and popped the last two. And *Little Black Quasha*. How I'd loved that book, how my sisters had curled up with me and Mom to hear her read . . . how Philippa would try to shoulder me aside, but despite the biting incident, despite the scorn, I had wanted so much for her to love me. I remembered the toast. Oh goodness, how pathetic that had been . . . One morning in San Diego, in her room that had a wall of mirror tiles, Philippa asked me to go and make her toast. *I won't*, I said, as little sisters do. She fixed me with her rich brown eyes. *Make me toast and peanut butter and I will love you forever*, she promised. My obstinacy melted on the instant! I sped to the kitchen! I slid bread into the toaster and waited with bated breath for it to pop! I slathered it with peanut butter, ran with it back to Philippa and watched her while she ate. She licked her fingers and put the plate aside. She picked up her book. *Do you love me forever now?* I asked. She turned a page and shook her head. *It wasn't hot enough*, she said.

With *Little Black Quasha* in my hands now, I didn't know whether to feel sorry for the child I'd been, or simply laugh. I opened the book. My mother, who was fond of cryptic crosswords, may have had some odd belief it would contain a crucial message to me in an hour of need. Why else would the eccentric soul have left it for me? I studied it now, my mother's peculiar legacy. The pictures were not very well drawn but had raw charm and energy. I remembered the envy I used to feel about Quasha's curly hair and big dark eyes. She looked much more like Philippa and Lara than me. I used to imagine I could be that little girl, given a few more years I'd grow such curly hair, my eyes turn dark instead of being this indeterminate mud shade. Now at least I had big hair, though it had nearly got me shot by the man I'd later dumped in public.

I started reading. Quasha sees a ball of orange wool on the road, winds it up, comes finally to the old woman who had dropped it. As a reward, the old woman says Quasha can have an apple, but there's no apple in her bag. Instead she gives Quasha a penny.

Quasha wants to buy a toy with her reward, but as is the experience of every child who wants to buy a toy with her own money, those she can afford are no fun and those she likes are too expensive. And this story was written in — I checked the front — 1908. How things don't change in a century.

Next, a man resembling a thin Santa Claus is selling books. Quasha buys a book about a little girl like her, and off she runs to read her book beneath a jungle tree. She still reads aloud! Now and then she bursts out laughing. Tigers hear. They gather round and decide not to eat her until the story's done.

I used to be perplexed at this next scene. At an especially funny bit the tigers laugh aloud too and frighten Quasha. But instead of insisting she finish the tale (as I wanted them to do), they say they'll eat her up at once. This is inconsistent: I didn't know the word when I was small, I just knew it made me puzzled.

Next! Out pops a frog! He promises to save her if she gives him the funny book. The frog tells the tigers they can't all eat Quasha so, to decide which one will have the feast, the tigers fight. The ground is puddled with gore, ears, tails and paws strewn around, and — I turned the page to the one my mother had marked — all the tigers have been torn to bits but two.

I moved the slip of paper in Mom's handwriting, looked at what came next and read it twice. I looked at the cover in case it was the wrong book. I looked back to the page about sharing. It did not say what my mother used to read: *'We're sisters.' The tigers smiled. 'We share.'* What happens is, the two tigers smile with open mouths and say: *'We are brothers, we are not going to fight, we are going to divide Little Black Quasha between us.'*

I felt so annoyed and cheated I nearly tossed the book out the car window. But I flicked on through. The frog tricks one tiger into drowning, then hops into the final tiger's mouth. Frogs are poisonous. The effect of biting them is that you froth and froth. The tiger froths until he disappears. (I used to wish Philippa would go and eat frogs.) Quasha's funny book is too heavy for the frog to carry so he gets a dish of milk instead, which he likes much better. The End.

More bewildered than ever, I closed the book. I guessed that everyone's mother is inexplicable to them in many ways. It occurred to me the tigers and frog never hear the end of the story Quasha reads. Also, though everyone keeps their bargains in this book, they keep them in an unexpected way.

As I sat puzzling beneath that Norfolk pine a notion flew at me from left field. Did my mother mean to tell me that my sisters are really brothers? Was I in the midst of a real-life saga of sexual identity, transvestism, gender crisis? The idea of Lara in her opal earrings, tailored jackets, of Philippa in her elegant knitwear from designer stores, being transvestites . . .

To leash my mind back where it belonged I found a pencil to write a list of questions to ask Caine (to hell with Luke, to hell!), and flipped to the end pages. I'd call Caine on his mobile, arrange to meet him . . . I stared at the end page of *Little Black Quasha*. It was already covered in Mom's printing. She had drawn a family tree. It took me some time to make sense of it, but it gave answers to several questions and posed many new ones.

If what I saw was true, I was not even me.

Rather than a family tree this was two little saplings that might or might not make it a thicket. Frank Emmett, scientist, of Christchurch had married Mary Green in 1960. The names of two children dangled under this on the first tree: Lara, 1961 and Philippa, 1963. On the other half of the page was the name of Robert Quinter, who had married Christina Rose — no date. Dangling under this information was Anthonia (no issue) and Laurence (*aka* Larry). Next to Laurence was a dot-dot-dot, then the name Maria Hurren. My ragbag brain knew dot-dot-dot means Laurence and Maria didn't marry. Dangling under the dots was Suzanne, Boston, 1964. Was I this child? Frank and Mary had adopted me? That fake birth certificate wasn't fake? Quinter was an unusual name. For all my childhood dreams of being a stolen royal child, was I in truth the bastard offspring of a truly bad rock star, Larry Quinter, famous only for his poor musicianship and financial prodigality? I checked the wad of money and, from my wallet, my mother's cryptic letter saying *too hard to explain,* and *each generation must decide for itself what is both right and fair.* As a revelation, all of this only increased the mystery. It also meant I might be an American citizen — at least, born in America, and months earlier than I'd always been led to believe. Annie's absurd suggestion about contacting the embassy might have merit.

But in all the sisterly things Lara and Philippa had hurled when I was small, they'd never thrown that spiky one, *nyah-nyah, you are adopted*. And why would my crazy mother and father, already with two kids under five, and in a foreign land, adopt a third?

The shade of the tree had edged backwards from my car. Sitting there, the blue of the harbour crinkling up and down before me, I sighed. My tricky hippy mom. I guessed if you mixed the barefoot domestic dream of the sixties with my mom's strong maternal urge and steely principles, you might adopt a dozen kids. This explained her particular attitude to me, the cracked egg in her basket, runt of the litter. I felt complicated in my stomach where you keep your deepest sense of self. They try to tell you it's your heart. Forget it. It's the belly, every time.

I saw clearly why I'd never be a detective. There were so many loose ends to tie up, too many mean streets to walk down.

I walked down the particular street of the tiny key that had unlocked this box of secrets. Gifford had left the key on the day of the ransacking. The ransacking happened just before the deposit of the body in the pantry, and that had happened just before the installing of the new kitchen. According to Lara, Gifford was importing used earthmoving equipment from Japan and had asked her to squeeze rules apart. As had Roger. And Philippa — not in touch with Lara, nor with me, for days. She hadn't told anyone she was going on holiday, it was too early for skiing, I'd seen Roger still in town. Too many coincidences — they must connect somehow. Luke had said my sisters might be in danger — he had said I might be, too. The note from my kids, and the misspelled card, each told me to stay put. But my sisters — the word flipped inside out and spun around beside my heart — they were still my sisters. There was emotional connective tissue. I did not want to see Lara or Philippa in the same state as those other two unknown, well-dressed, deceased women.

And, in a nasty mental hologram, I saw Roger again last night with those poached-egg eyes, Roger asking Gifford if my kids had gone to Gifford's mother.

Lara would still be at work, but I turned the ignition and zoomed in the lull before the five o'clock traffic, up to Khandallah. This time to my sister Philippa's house. My younger older sister by adoption, if the family thicket held water (so to speak).

As once again I passed the paint shop, the liquor store, Archie's Security, reached the enormous pet store with the plaster dog grinning over the main road, I hoped I could do this on my own. I was miserable and scared that Luke and I had yelled again and I had lost my only helper. I still loved the man, of course. You cannot spend a length of time with a guy, have a child with him, then dismiss him from your emotions for all time. My face heated dreadfully at what I had said when we split up, that Tilda was not his kid at all. Deplorable. And stupid, because Luke demanded blood tests. Roger, with his ex-dentist's knowledge of things medical, helped us interpret them. How the family carried on around that time. In sweaty silent fury Dad organised my move to the house he bought, sprained an ankle but continued to hobble round like an angry martyr, Mom was making relish out of whatever she could find (pumpkin, cauliflower, tomato, cabbage, those endless watery zucchini), Lara was in psychological bruises from that terrible media onslaught, and Philippa — *euph*! — the word bitchy does not come close to the state that woman was in, the fervour with which she was promoting the Don't Eat Asian Dogs fight for Suite Three.

The yellow stickies were on my dining table back home but I jotted more clues in my mind. If a blood test can establish the paternity of a child, can it also establish whether siblings are truly siblings? My unforgivable behaviour towards Luke could have led to Roger — and therefore Philippa — discovering strange fruit on the family tree.

I did not see how that tied up with the body in my pantry, let alone the woman in the 'm' room. Though I was scooting round the twist in the hill road now, I was getting nowhere fast inside my mind. Two dead women — two tragedies — murdered or not? The first woman — something untoward had happened to her head — maybe an accident. But the second woman could not have died in my pantry because a jar of pasta sauce fell on her. I was not being flippant, I wanted to sort this out in my own thoughts. Some other person must have put her there, or killed her there. Though the puddle underneath her may have been pasta sauce. There had been a scent of basil and my only jar of pasta sauce was missing. Her waxy look — oh God, had she been frozen before she was stashed in my pantry?

I was glad I'd reached a straight bit of the road.

I would have thought that I knew only normal people. A few eccentrics, like my mother, like Bernard at Thee Ultimate Café, like my son who let me think he'd been expelled when in fact he'd been made a contender. People like my sisters who frustrated me and racked me off. But people who would kill? Even by accident? What could turn an ordinary person into a murderer — or manslaughterer, as you don't have to have violent motives here, merely the performing of some misadventure that left another person not-alive.

In my state of fright and my awareness that I'd racked off Luke, my only sidekick, I felt it best to leave my car a distance from Philippa's. As I walked up the front path between green fragrant growing things, it seemed that I was living in a dream. Maybe I'd banged my head on a cupboard door at Thee Ultimate Café and had been comatose since then. I hoped when I woke I would forget all this. I hoped when I awoke, Tilda and Jarret would be arguing about whose turn it was to clean up the catfood Nameless had scattered on the floor in our old kitchen.

I hoped I'd still have all the money Mom had left me.

I knocked on Philippa's front door. I peered through the window and saw the Frances Hodgkins, a little smudgy one of old farm machinery. How could Roger and Philippa have afforded it? Suite Three was not a profit-making organisation. Can you buy expensive art on time payment? For the first time in my life, even sharing with my sisters, I could afford to buy a Frances Hodgkins in one lump sum, but what use was that to me without my kids? A quake ran through the odd emotional plateau I seemed to be on. I recognised one tremor of it: jealousy. Philippa had her daughter safe in Philadelphia as an AFS scholar while my two . . . but I did not wish the situation to be reversed. You could not truly wish your sister's child missing instead of your own . . . I sank onto Philippa's front steps, my bag beside me, and hugged my arms around my chest in sorrow, fear and grim self-knowledge. I'd do anything, wish anything, to have my children safe with me again. Right that minute I hated Philippa for throwing light on my dark side.

Inside, the phone rang, stopped, and I heard a click as the answerphone switched off. Sitting where I was on the top step, there was a sticker for *Strait Security* at eye level on the front door. Brick's company. Though I'd never been able to afford his security system I'd heard Jarret weaselling curious details from his uncle on evenings when, whisky flowing like a darkly golden stream across the heather and encouraging indiscretion, I had cooked Brick omelettes (this is not to imply my son's a weasel or my omelettes brick-like).

Around the back of Philippa's I found the green recycling bin with wine bottles and an empty single malt lined up inside it, and a large cardboard box folded flat and stashed neatly behind the wheelie bin for the household rubbish. On the box was the picture of a filing cabinet, a cabinet made of wood, with brass corners, ready assembled. There was a label on the box in Chinese letters but I brushed the long-horned beetle from my mind. I knocked on the back door. As expected, there was no answer.

But Roger, I was sure, knew something about where my kids might be.

Further up the back path was nothing more exciting than the garden shed and native bush. I thought of rats, my skin crept, so I did not explore. Nor was I foolish enough in this set of circumstances to enter any unlit outdoor building; I just peeped through the cobwebbed window: a bench with tools, a bigger staple gun than mine (why hadn't Philippa let me borrow it instead of paying for my own!), containers of garden chemicals. On the floor were large crates and cardboard boxes, a box or two also bearing Chinese lettering (Roger being in Asian imports). Bolts of fabric protruded from the top of one. There was a roll of netting, a ladder and a lawn mower. I did not think Roger or Philippa would have used the mower themselves for many years. Philippa and Brick were nicely served by Green Lawn Buddy in his overalls of tasteful tan, and by Jarret doing odd jobs now and then. Jarret and I had argued many times over who would mow our lawn. I wished I'd never argued with my son, wished I'd shown more interest in his problems yesterday and discovered they were not problems but a triumph . . .

I forced the handle of the shed and wrestled out the ladder. It was awkward and painful to do this, but so what? I carted the clattering set of steps to the back door with far more noise than a regular burglar would make. This late in the afternoon was an odd time for a thief to be working — if what I'd learnt from Brick didn't work, if I triggered the alarm and the cops arrived in consequence, I could show them Philippa and Roger's family album. There would be a shot or two of me to prove I had some right to be inside.

Immaculate: that's what it was, inside. Even as I clambered in the laundry window I smelled how clean it was. At home, the messy space along the back porch I called my laundry was full of fluff-balls, discarded socks. Life, for me, was a sock without a mate — at least a series of mismatched ones. But here, the shelves were tidily arranged, the detergent sitting in precise advance of two waiting refill packs, pale blue hand soap and blue hand-towel as fresh as if nobody had touched them since the day they came home from Kirkaldie's. Neatly folded washing on top of the drier. Not a speck of fluff in sight. If Philippa was missing, our well-groomed Roger was doing a fine job on his own. I knew they didn't have home help. I can still hear Philippa, eleven she must have been, commenting to a friend that pine needles had surfaced in their aubergine shag pile carpet four months after Christmas. *But my mom has a Mexican maid*, said the girl. The mother was a social tennis player, with alarming long finger nails — no housework for that one. *I hope your mother doesn't pay her much*, Philippa replied, *because then she'll pay for what she gets. Not much.* Though I was but nine, I knew the whole point of having a Mexican maid was that you didn't pay her much. I'd asked Philippa if she was so big on tidiness in other people's homes, why was she so haphazard about her own stuff? The result of that? A bash with Philippa's own racquet.

I closed the laundry window behind me, slung my scruffy bag over my shoulder and moved to Philippa's kitchen. I will not describe the chrome, the streamlined surfaces. To me, this kitchen was for photographs, for spreads in magazines. It was not meant for cooking.

Now out into the hall. The security alarm beeped with surprise to see me. I flicked up the little flap and performed the crafty thing Brick had been indiscreet about while I cooked omelettes. This is an indication of the way a younger sibling learns. Try teaching them formally and there's disaster. They are bossed about so much at home that a stubborn wall arises in their minds. Let them learn in their own way — especially if they think it will annoy their older siblings

— and all manner of information is implanted. The number of times I heard Philippa say, *Don't do it like that, you'll make a mess, too young,* the times from Lara, *Don't dart off on your own, why can't you ask for help* . . . then grudging silence as they saw I got it right.

Right now I was doing precisely what a woman on her own should never do, venture into the house of a person who may possibly be a bad guy. This was when the spooky music ought to start.

I didn't think uxorious Roger could be a bad guy. Nevertheless it was eerie, tiptoeing to the squeaky clean downstairs bathroom, the dining room, the living room, front hallway, the TV snug that adjoined the kitchen, Roger's study with a photograph of Philippa on the desk. A closet in his study was where they kept the sports gear. It took nerve to open it but I found it stacked only with what was proper, such as skis, ski poles, tennis racquets and two red Frisbees.

I made a full circuit of the lower storey and saw neither sister nor a clue to her whereabouts. The flashing answerphone said twenty messages were stored up. I was tempted to play them, but snuck up the stairway first.

My niece's bedroom was neat and clean of course, because of her being in America. Only seventeen — how could they encourage her to go away? We don't have our children long enough in any case . . . my quaking returned. I did not wish to consider how little time I may have had with my own two, if they never came home. In tears again, I sank on Stacy's bed, arms braced around myself. I tried not to sob aloud in case I missed the sound of a car crunching up the drive. The shuddering stopped and I continued my search. I checked out another immaculate place of ablutions where I stole two Panadol from the medicine cabinet to still the continuing burr of pain in my right hand, then came to the main bedroom. The door was closed. Wondering if I'd find Philippa prostrate with 'flu, I pushed it open.

My nerves bristled. For goodness' sake, it was like a film set, as if nobody lived here at all. That Roger! Such a well-trained husband! The only thing even slightly out of place was a folded piece of paper on the dresser.

Philippa wasn't in the en suite. I didn't want to check the wardrobes. I didn't want to check the large carved Oriental chest at the foot of the bed.

Damn it, I had to.

I cracked the top of the chest, peeked quickly and saw blankets. I cracked a wardrobe door, saw large-sized well-pressed suits and shirts with size 42 collars, a row of gleaming shoes. Cracked the other one — a row of empty garments including a yellow ski jacket and blinding tennis whites, shelves of knitwear, and no dead bodies.

I did not snoop inside the bedside cabinets. That's where people keep intimate paraphernalia. Although you might want to know a lot about your sister, only the kinky want to know precisely how normal or not their siblings might be in their bedrooms.

There was only Philippa's study still to check. This was where her true nature would show, her turbulence, the ferment of her soul. When I was six Lara had ordered Philippa to confiscate my Barbie dolls because she did not approve of how untidily I kept their teeny accessories. Philippa's toys had been in far worse array but Lara had been forced to project her disapproval onto me, the prickly doormat. Nobody, not even Lara, liked to prod Philippa's bad side if they could help it.

I pushed the door gently and gasped at the state of the room. Usually, if you looked into her study, any number of murdered matrons could have been stashed behind file boxes and under rafts of paper. But today it was so neat it made my teeth hurt. At that moment a car slowed on the street. I didn't breathe again till it moved past.

A Chinese robe was pinned on one otherwise clear wall: it was tacked onto a backing, and map pins held the backing in a frame. It must have been antique. It was scarlet, with gold and crimson embroidery of fish and birds. The method of display seemed unusual in a way I couldn't define. But the best way to figure something out is to treat it like a cat, pretend interest in something else, then it comes trotting to annoy you. So I rolled open the upper drawer of the wood and brass filing cabinet.

This was an even bigger shock. It too was tidy, and I knew my sister's method of filing from way back. Her system was to cram everything into a cardboard box as it came in, and at the end of the financial year scrawl on the side: *dead letters*. But now! Neat typed labels, folders with their corners so aligned they could have been done with a set square. It smelled clean and new — like the rest of Philippa's house — but the point was this must have been done by someone else. For the first time, I was genuinely frightened my sister was dead.

A metallic click came from the front door lock downstairs. A male voice called out a soft *Hello?*

Footsteps came up the stairs. I moved the study door to almost closed. I was embarrassed. I hoped Roger would not enter. I expected him to go immediately into the bedroom to change, or use the bathroom, then I'd sneak out and knock on the front door in a normal cool manner . . . but the steps, definitely male, seemed lighter than his. Or else he knew I was here, and he was creeping. Yes, a creeping male was coming nearer, briefly entering each room in turn as I'd done. My throat dried up with fright. A man does not walk in such a slow and creeping manner, stopping at each door, unless he's after an intruder. Or unless he himself is an intruder.

I crammed myself as well as my bag beside a bookshelf. The study door swung open, wedging me in. I hoped the bookshelf was tall enough and me skinny enough not be noticed, though my head must have stuck up like a lollipop.

The man entered but I couldn't see him. I quickly discovered it was stupid trying not to breathe. The harder you try, the more desperate you become to gulp in air. Suddenly I thought, if this male is lighter on his feet than Roger, it might not necessarily be a smaller man, it might be a teenage boy — it might be Jarret.

I could not resist the yank of motherhood. I peeked.

It was Caine. His plain clothes had been changed for a burglar's outfit, trousers and sweater all black, even to the beanie on his head. He rubbed the side of his nose as he stared at the Chinese robe. I drew back and the door gave a bump. His feet moved on the carpet.

I closed my eyes just like a two-year-old — if I could not see him, surely he couldn't see me. Silence. Then I heard sniffing.

'Suzie?'

I felt my jaw go stubborn.

'Come out,' Caine whispered. 'Come on.'

How long could this continue?

He pulled the door at last. I opened my eyes. He didn't look dangerous so much as that he considered me a thorough pest.

'How did you know?' I asked.

He waved a hand. 'You told me your sister loathed Anaïs Anaïs.'

That broken nose of his worked fine.

'Where've you been hiding?' he continued.

I gave him a kind of a look. 'Behind the damn door, Caine!'

'Hush.'

I lowered my voice. 'I've got a right to be here. What about you?'

'I'd rather explain later.'

'They always say that in . . .!'

'Be quiet! We haven't time to argue.' He indicated the Chinese gown and leaned across the desk, touching the fabric lightly with both hands. 'How long has she had this? What's it doing up here?'

'She's not my favourite sister. How would I know?'

Outside was another roll of tyres and a car crunched up the drive.

'Shit,' Caine muttered. As he turned and put forefinger over his mouth, his other cuff brushed one of the lower map pins. It dropped to the carpet. He didn't notice. He took my arm, firm and gentle — this felt strange, considering I had dumped him. Caught between my detective erstwhile boyfriend and my possibly dangerous brother-in-law, I didn't see I should trust either. But it was obvious we could not both hide behind that door. As we left the study a soft movement caught my eye. The corner of the backing where the pin had gone was beginning to curl up revealing a photograph of something tacked behind it.

Caine tugged me towards the stairs. We saw the heads of two people entering below. One was Roger, the other a woman concealed in a big black hat and an Indian silk scarf I recognised — Philippa!

Involuntarily, I moved forward but Caine drew me back, warned me with a finger to his mouth again to stay silent. Roger was talking in a low voice. In his own house?

We crept back along the hallway. Given Caine thought we should hide, I thought we should hole up in Stacy's room but Caine hauled me by the sleeve of Annie's jacket and we entered the main bedroom. I did not like this. The more we tried to conceal ourselves, the worse it was going to be if we were discovered. He tugged me into Philippa's wardrobe and slid the door shut.

'This is absurd!' I hissed. 'Is this police work? What's going on!'

He squeezed my arm. I elbowed him and he let go. But I shut up. With luck, Roger and Philippa would settle in the kitchen and we could slink away.

Had my luck run hot so far this week? Roger's voice was coming up the stairs, my sister following. There seemed a certain amount of low-voiced energy, unusual in a long-married couple but if Philippa had been away for a few days the embers of passion could flare again, I guess. Oh, jeepers, I did not want to listen to my brother-in-law and sister . . . Caine rolled the closet door open a sliver, I jabbed him again and tried to ease it shut. Too late. In the dimness of the racks of Philippa's outdoor gear, I saw Caine's very cross eyes (don't be picky, I know I've done this twice) at my interference.

You know how it is when you really don't want to watch something? The devil makes you sneak a little look.

Roger sat heavily on the bed and put his face in his hands. 'It's on the dresser,' he said. 'Oh God. We can't let Suzie know, but I have to stay with this for now — oh God.' He gave a muffled sob. 'Just read the note.'

Philippa gave his shoulders a hug, unwound her scarf, removed the disguising hat . . .

Oh no! This was just another middle-class, middle-aged affair with a family tree twist! As fast as possible I slipped a ski beanie off Philippa's shelf, dragged it on, eased the yellow parka off its hanger and wriggled into it, teeth gritting as pain shot through my hand, jabbed Caine again and tugged his beanie down to cover his eyebrows. I banged the closet door open and backed out.

'Zat should do the rats for here!' I shouted in a gruff and guttural accent. 'Ah, 'ello, Mister! Welcome 'ome! You 'ad a busy day? Me too! We're off!'

There was a glimpse of Roger's horror, of my sister's startled mortification as she looked up from the blue notepaper. I headed down the corridor talking loudly about pest control, the need to check any other wardrobes against the eaves at a later date, and stacking several rat traps in the van. 'Zis suburb! Too mucha da trees, in da winter! Don' worry, sir, no overtime, cost all in original quote, no da extra!'

It didn't matter how ludicrous this was, all I wanted was to get down the stairs and out. Caine dogging me, I strode along the driveway, waving my arms and speaking in a guttural and European manner that switched between mock Italian and fake Russian. Caine kept hissing to shut the hell up but his gestures tied in well with Russian fervour. We reached the street. I stuffed my hands into my pockets, shambled on and stopped around the corner.

'That was ridiculous,' Caine said.

'That was my sister!'

'I realise that, Suzie, she's identical to . . .'

I gesticulated wordlessly.

'You mean — it wasn't Philippa? It was your other sister? Lara?'

I squeezed my eyes shut for a second. I had not wished to be a voyeur in a wardrobe while my sister had it off with my large ex-dentist brother-in-law who was her brother-in-law as well. I felt peculiarly disappointed. I felt wounded on poor Philippa's behalf. I stalked towards my car, which I was pleased I had discreetly left a half a block away.

'Suzie.' Caine tried to hold me back. But I did not want to talk to a guy who had left the police force — or was about to — only to become a private detective sniffing about in people's closets. This was as well as the fact that I did not want to be involved with the guy anyway. I'd learnt, and was still learning, to distrust him. I told him so, hissing in my turn so the neighbours didn't catch an earful. We must have looked absurd in our beanies, Caine dressed in black and me in yellow, hissing, on a lovely sunny evening.

Caine stared at me. I couldn't cope with what was happening in his eyes. I stepped back. After a moment, so did he.

'Say hi to the kids, then, Suzie. Goodbye.'

He still didn't know the kids were missing? What kind of detective was he, public or private? What kind of man was he, good or bad? I didn't trust myself to speak and gave a smile like the one you see in Charles Schultz cartoons, the wiggly mouth that indicates rueful torment. I raised my hand, goodbye. He walked in normal fashion down the road to his car, climbed in. I waved again, moved up the road to my car, fiddled with my keys until he was off and out of sight.

I tried to be logical, to see if I could come to a conclusion.

a) Caine was very interested in the Chinese robe.

b) He hadn't noticed what was under it, which was a picture of — I don't know — a green Lego man?

c) He didn't seem to know my kids were genuinely missing.

d) Maybe my kids weren't missing, but hiding.

e) Why would they be hiding?

f) From something they saw in Caine's house?

g) Why would Jarret tell Caine we were going to Fiji?

h) Well — so Luke told me, after his phone call to the ace detective. Was Luke lying? I didn't think so.

i) Why was Lara with Roger, in the main bedroom? And in disguise? A disguise that was Philippa's black hat?

j) If they were having an affair, why would she wear Philippa's hat?

k) Did it in fact mean that Lara and Roger knew where Philippa was and were trying to fool someone? Like Caine?

l) What was written on the blue paper to make Lara look so much her actual age? To make Roger look like desperation?

m) There were more bits and bobs from China stored in the outdoor shed.

n) Why was the term 'outdoor' shed? Who has a shed indoors?

Okay — I had to get a grip. I would check the shed more thoroughly even though I'd vowed before I was not foolish enough to do such things and nervousness tracked up and down my spine.

It was too complicated to decide whether to remove my yellow gear or not (that is, my missing sister's gear) in case it was too easy to identify where it came from should I stuff it under a hedge, or if Roger recognised it if he spotted me in it again, or whatever, you see how tricky even little decisions can be when you're embroiled in a mystery? So I removed the jacket and stuffed it down in the back seat of my car. Even though the fingers of my good hand were weak with fright at what I meant to do, I turned the beanie inside out so the purple inner showed, yanked it back on and slunk up into the back of the property belonging to Roger and Philippa's neighbours. I thought of bush rats — and wriggled quickly through the hedge.

There was an autumn smell of layers of wet leaves, the smell that means it was time somebody cleared up after the vigorous growth of summer. I trod carefully because the concrete path was mossy. Philippa hadn't had Green Lawn Buddy or Jarret up here lately. So messy outside, but so meticulous within. Even in her study! So odd. So very unlike her.

Oh dear God, this was scary.

Approaching the shed from this side, I saw more wooden cases stacked against the back. I entered the shed, and started to root around as quietly as possible in the boxes. I was thankful for the beanie. There were spider webs as thick as muslin. No doubt there were larger insects too. Why are some insects so terrifying, but some so cute? It must be the scary ones seem as if their minds work in a thoroughly different way to human beings, while the fuzz on a bee (just for example) makes it seem a little cuddly. I thought my older sisters sometimes had the souls of scary insects. I didn't remember getting cuddles from my sisters — oh all right, some-times from Lara.

The rolls of Chinese fabric turned out to be cheap brocade, probably one of Roger's import disasters. I tried to protect my bandage, but both hands turned grey with dirt. Ignoring the mess of paraphernalia on the makeshift bench, I'd worked through four or five boxes when I heard a rustle outside. Once again I expected to hear ominous music or at least the *squeak* of rat. What I heard instead was Caine hoarsely saying my name, and here he came, for goodness' sake, ready to spring. And spring he did! He pulled me to the ground in the dirt and spider webs, and this was not for romance. Pain shocked my hand. I screamed. Caine clamped a hand over my mouth, but the fear of Caine and the fear of scary insects still possessed me. I kicked. I jerked away and bumped the bench. Tools toppled down. The staple gun struck my shoulder, a can of paint remover hit Caine on the beanie. He sighed. He rolled off me onto a broken-down wooden pallet. He lay still.

I had rendered a top detective unconscious. Well — he was either still a top detective on a case, or at least a minor villain of this piece. He was breathing. A pulse beat in his neck. I checked the weight of the can — part-empty. He'd be okay — maybe.

The devil or his analogue made me do it. I grabbed the industrial strength staple gun and stapled Caine to the pallet along the sleeves of his burglar's sweater, down his sides. I let out those little screams with every *click*! but I did a darn fine job. He would not be able to wriggle free in any hurry. I began to gulp hysterically at the image of Caine trying to run after me with his arms pinned wide as if he were a biological specimen. Spread out like that Chinese robe.

It wasn't till I had squeezed back through the hedge, shielding my aching hand under my armpit, that I thought, *If Caine is still a top detective, I will be in big trouble with the law for the hindering and stapling of an officer.*

You'll realise as fast as I did, this made it even trickier to talk to the police. Brushing twigs and spider webs from my shoulders, I rushed down the neighbours' side path, reached my car, grabbed off Philippa's beanie and whanged it against the car roof to rid it of any insect life. I may have got carried away. I whanged and whanged, and why should I care if my sister's beanie had spider's legs on it, but I'd just had another tangle with that ex-boyfriend and, oh God, by now I was so afraid that Philippa might be dead — Lara, in the bedroom with Roger? Was this the reason for those other deaths — you know, in books how people murder other people to throw them off the scent of the real person they mean to kill? It is false serial killing, I suppose. But it seemed a strong likelihood that Roger had done away with Woman One and Woman Two in order to hide the reasons for his wife's demise — and somehow he'd had to hide one of the women in my pantry? Jeepers, and Lara was involved. This would not be the best career move ever, especially if she wanted a top job. No wonder he had said, 'We can't let Suzie know.'

. The beanie had unravelled at the seams. I drove around the corner to the village, empty by now apart from one or two parked cars, and pulled in by the phone box. I felt a little safer once I'd slipped inside and pulled the door behind me, thankful it was not one of those mean-spirited doorless ones where stray dogs sidle up and sniff when you're not looking. As succinctly as I could, I told Caine's second in command at Metro Central that his possibly erstwhile superior officer was spread-eagled in an outdoor shed in this well-to-do though rat-infested suburb. 'Call it a lovers' quarrel,' I said to the hush on the other end, and finished the call.

I sensed something outside the booth. I whipped around to say *good dog, please go for walkies* . . .

'Hello, Suzie,' Roger mouthed through the glass. He seemed distressed, not quite like you'd expect in a combined adulterer-murderer but then, as far as I knew, I'd never met such a person before.

I pushed open the door. 'It doesn't make sense,' I told him. 'None of it makes any . . .'

'I'm sorry. I have to do this.' He took my left arm. He slid his hand down to my wrist and slid it up again beneath my sleeve so quickly I just felt puzzled till I also felt a brief sting on my forearm. I don't think I even said *ouch*. My puzzled state deepened.

'This is only to protect you, Suzie, I promise,' Roger said.

My bewilderment had gone pillowy and soft around the edges.

'Sit in the car?' he suggested. 'Give me your keys?'

That seemed a nice idea. I folded into my passenger seat like a cloth doll. The world outside folded too. It grew darker with each tick of time. *Tick. Tick.* Roger closed the car door. *Tick.* My thoughts slid over each other and away like folds of cheap brocade. One nearly final thought was this: *Oi! — such fading into oblivion is exactly what happens to a heroine just when she thinks things can't get any worse, and then they do. How much badder can they get for me?* My very final thought was: *badder is not right — it's not good grammar.*

part three

MEN IN SUITS

chapter fourteen

I didn't know if I was awake or not. It was dark, soft and warm, like being tucked up in a basket. Perhaps I was dreaming I was a furry creature, hibernating. Hibernation seemed a good idea. Hibernation would be a long time out, an elongated sleep, dreams scrolling through my mind, then when I was up and about at last that first breakfast would be the very peak of tastiness — the savour of bacon after long starvation, the crunch of toast, the bitter-sweet of marmalade. And coffee! Oh, the coffee. Nothing ever does as much for me as that first coffee of the day. I always want a second, though I've learnt long since it never does as much for me as that satisfying first. All of a sudden in the dark it came to me: the way around this was to buy a bigger cup.

My wish for coffee reminded me not only that I was human, but an adult. This was not a pleasant realisation. My dad was not going to knock on my door and call out *Rise and shine, li'l Suzie-pie*. I would not hear Lara and Philippa bicker in the bathroom. Mom would not bustle in tying her yellow dressing gown as if she were a parcel preparing to send herself somewhere. She would not swish my curtain open and place her palm on my forehead if I looked feverish because I wanted a day off school so had been breathing hard beneath the blankets to get that flushed appearance (some kids have one trick, some another).

The good thing about this — about no Dad, no Mom — is that I would not have to eat Dad's oatmeal. He made the porridge because Mom invariably forgot the pinch of salt. I think she decided to forget the salt on purpose. She had very little time for making porridge, busy as she was chivvying me out of bed and refereeing the *who's-hogging-the-mirror* spats between my sisters. Dad used to buy the porridge mixture too, the *down home* kind that had shucks in it, and hurt my gums. Shucks made me snivel. I wanted pancakes, French toast, waffles. *Shucks will make a cowboy of you, Suzie*, my dad would say, *shucks will put hair on your chest.* He was a man of principle and not a few bad jokes. If he decided something simply had to be, that is the way it was. Here, possibly, was why he was a better realtor than a botanist.

The bad thing about this — no Dad, no Mom — was that they were both deceased. Dad must have died while on some hefty medication, imagining as he did that I was getting back with Gifford. Mom died working on her herb garden — a simple *poof* inside her brain and she was gone.

I felt the old familiar smarting in my nose that means you are about to cry, sat up in this dark nest and bumped my head. I realised, not only was I awake and grown up, but I was in complete darkness and not in a familiar place.

The bed smelled musty, unused, like beds in a holiday house. I stretched cautiously to my right, and with my finger tips felt plump things that might be rolled up bedding. I stretched to the left and touched an upright piece of wood against a wall. I stretched out with my feet — no wall. I put my hand above me where I'd bumped my head, and felt a row of slats. This was possibly a bunk. Was I on board a ship — a ship to Fiji? I listened with my body to feel a rocking. I sniffed to search for salt but only found that musty smell. I reached to the right again. This was like a box, a pitch-black box stored with musty lumps of sleeping bags, and me.

I was too scared to call out. I might not like whatever answered. I might not like who came to lift the lid of this strange box.

Maybe I was still dreaming. I closed my eyes and expected my mind to do that slipping and sliding that indicates you are asleep. I was interested to see what would wander along for me in this dark box of sleep.

What came along was this:

a) I remembered Lara's gong reverberating as if it had been the signal for the end of round one in a wrestling match;

b) I recalled Roger next to my car by the phone box, his sliding a hand up my sleeve before my thoughts slid away like silk — the end of round two;

c) I also recalled Roger used to be a dentist though I did not wish at this point to speculate what that had to do with anything;

d) I remembered Lara's tartness at the idea of my seeing Gifford, and the silver and sparkle cat brooch I had pinned to my capacious bag;

e) I saw, also in my mind, two keys for safe custody boxes and that large amount of riches from my mother, as well as those unexpected little family saplings in the back of *Little Black Quasha*;

f) I flinched to remember how furiously Luke had shouted over my wanting to see Caine;

g) I flinched again to think how angry Caine himself would be when he regained consciousness and discovered himself stapled like a scientific specimen.

h) Hunger came along. Real hunger. This may seem

selfish. But that coffee, bacon and toast would be delicious and I did not care what I had to eat as long as it was something, even oatmeal. My stomach wriggled inside me like a famished cat, as famished as poor Nameless had to be; but —

i) I remembered that Tilda and Jarret went missing in early evening and they didn't have coats with them. I did not wish to feel anxious and afraid; but —

j) I saw in my mind again that hallucinatory woman lying jammed up in my old vegetable rack;

k) I also saw the new cupboards and clean pantry;

l) I saw that photograph or printout, concealed behind the Chinese robe in Philippa's study, the supine man made up of blocks;

m) I realised I had to use the toilet urgently before breakfast. Here is something rarely touched upon in books and movies concerning people who get into difficulties such as this — kidnapped, or abducted, drugged, and not able to find a bathroom.

As I sorted out my thoughts, I discovered a bottom-of-the-fridge taste in my mouth from whatever drug I'd been injected with, far worse than that unaccustomed Loch Ness whisky of the night the kids went missing. What I would have liked to do now was weep till I was rescued. I would have liked to be a fairytale heroine who merely cried *oh help* and a stalwart champion appeared. But if I should wail I suspected nothing would happen or nobody would come or, as I said, that somebody I did not like would come and, what's worse, in whatever case, I might embarrass myself socially because of having so badly to go to the bathroom.

My kids are safe, my kids are safe, they have to be okay, I told myself.

Then, *mind over matter*, I said and rolled off the bunk. After feeling about for my bag in case whoever put me in this place was thoughtful enough to leave it beside me (no such luck — you will already have assumed that whoever put me here was not a nice person, and I was guessing it was Roger — for my own good, he said? *Ha!* is what I said to that), I decided to crawl in the darkness. Next I had to decide in which direction to crawl, away from the wall, or along it. I chose against the wall. Then I had to choose which wall to crawl along, the one I crouched beside, or the one at the other end of the bunk. I chose the wall right next to me. That was three difficult decisions before breakfast.

Doing my best to protect that damn big bandage and ignore the way my whole hand felt too hot, the way it had begun to pound, I struggled over and through the lumpy sleeping bags. I knocked against rough shelving, cardboard boxes, piles of dusty magazines that made me sneeze, suitcases. I crawled because I might trip over all the junk if I tried walking. There had to be an exit. After all, somehow I got in. You may be wondering why I was not panicking. The answer's simple. I did not wish to wet my pants. A more complicated answer is, if I panicked I might lose my mind, let alone my physical dignity. The time for panic was not yet. *My kids are safe, they have to be safe.* The only thing to do was keep crawling through this dark box crammed with junk.

Into my mind came a time when I was maybe seven years old and still in Santa Barbara. A new boy joined our class. His name was Trevor. He had blue eyes and curly brown hair. He had smooth skin with a bloom like peach. I fell in love with Trevor. One day, the teacher sent us both out of class to the big box-like school hall to check through some list or other. My heart burned with the thrill. Trevor and me, together in the hall. We just did what we were told, we checked the list. Me and Trevor. Thrill. I never breathed a word to my sisters because I feared the way they'd sneer. I never breathed a word to any friends in case they loved him too. I used to daydream, a serial imagining each night before I went to sleep: Trevor and me captured by a giant, kept in the giant's shoe box. We couldn't get out. We tried and tried, but had to stay in there together.

My kids are safe, my kids are safe.

Now, crawling in this blackness that for all I knew might be the interior of a giant's shoe box, I kept going, powered by the embarrassment of remembering I used to love a boy called Trevor. I fell out of love when my sisters discovered it, as older sisters always do. They teased me so much I hurled my *Life on Our Planet* at the dining room window. Luckily for me, the window was open. Unluckily for me, Dad was dealing with loop caterpillar on the bougainvillea that twined up to our terracotta roof, and *Life on Our Planet* struck him on the head. Luckily, Dad had heard how badly my sisters teased me. Unluckily, he still figured I should be punished. Luckily, Mom declared that if he'd heard teasing and not intervened, he deserved to be hit by more than *Life on Our Damn Planet*. This caused an unusually prolonged argument, my father and sisters all involved, recriminations of *favouritism*, *principles*, and *pig-headedness* batted round on every side. It was one of the more spectacular of our family arguments, caused by a soft-skinned kid called Trevor. Such arguments were often healed as in other hippy-ish families of the sixties and seventies by a ragged little cigarette, though only smoked by Mom. She and Dad had fixed ideas of right and wrong and didn't always share them as a couple. I found it hard myself to reconcile how they reconciled the theme of love and peace with the arguments they had, the long hard silences that followed or else the chuckles of Mom as she murmured *families, strangest organism on the planet, who needs families?* But what I say now is, who understands their parents?

By now I had counted three corners in the darkness. I wondered if it was time to panic yet, but no. There were many mysteries to be cleared up, like what had been in my pantry (with a bare foot) and why my kids had gone missing, not to mention where.

You may have thought I should have realised something else by now — and at this stage it did occur to me.

I was missing too.

This made no sense. I started with my normal close-to-meltdown life on Monday morning. Something unusual happened — I was asked to identify my sister's body (though it wasn't). Second, my house was turned upside down (the inside of it, that is), and I was given the key to that second safe custody box. I discovered a second body (or hallucination) in my kitchen, my kids vanished, and when I tried to enlist family help the whole damn lot of them arrived except the missing sister. *All odds and sods of it*, as my mother might have said, *the whole damn passel*. Among the motley lot was not only my second brother-in-law who used to be a dentist before he moved into wheeling and dealing and who could therefore have had access to some anaesthetic (out-of-date anaesthetic?), but also my ex-husband (proven yet again to be untrustworthy), my ex-partner Luke (I could trust him), and the boyfriend I'd dumped publicly and who may or maybe not be still a detective, and who I had stapled in my sister's garden shed tonight . . .

If it was still tonight. I doubted it. It had to be tomorrow at very least.

I'll think of it all tomorrow, says Scarlett O'Hara at the end of her story, but for me, tomorrow was now. If I was truly in a thriller, one thing was for sure. This would not be one of those where you have to read (or skip — I do) long descriptions of forensic pathologists establishing the time of death in unusual circumstances like those of the corpse found hanging near the sixteenth hole of a golf course, discovered by a golfer who played on through, not informing the police of his find till he'd finished his round. (The deceased, in life, was just over five foot tall. In death, over the more than two weeks he'd been there he had stretched to about six foot. This is gross and disgusting information which is why it's in brackets so you can ignore it. Please.) Nor would it involve stories of maggots and how long it takes to complete their life cycle, and what other entomological assistants, bugs and beetles, might be involved. I did not do that modern, high-tech, state of the art stuff, thanks. (To tell the truth, it's not that modern. Forensic entomology, according to a review I read of some book on the topic, might date back at least to thirteenth-century China. In a crowd of peasants brought before a magistrate, the murderer was picked out because his was the only sickle surrounded by a swarm of flies. Smart, guy, that magistrate. But I wonder why those peasants all brought their sickles with them?) No, no. I was a stand-in cook. I designed and sewed, sometimes. My highest educational achievement was English 202 where I received moderate marks laced with a little praise for my spelling and handling of grammar. That's when I met Gifford. He had dropped out of university to get rich quick and I guiltily suspected he still owed Bernard, the kindly owner of Thee Ultimate Café, several thousand dollars which by now would have accrued a stack of interest.

I hoped this would turn out one of the thrillers when the main character — who I assumed was me — stayed alive to tell the tale. I hoped I was not an expendable secondary figure. Mind you, you did not have a thriller unless there were several gory deaths and the main character too was under serious threat especially towards the final chapter . . . I stopped this line of thought at once.

There remained one corner to find and count in this dark unknown place, then if I came upon a fifth corner I'd know I had gone around the square and was in fact back at the first corner. Would I? I could be going in any direction, around any shape, a tetrahedron or polygon — don't ask me, I don't know maths. But here was a fourth corner. So where was the door?

As I'd been crawling, I had also been feeling the wall to check for some hint of an opening. A hatch. A sliding panel would be nice. I snagged Annie's trousers on something. My knees hurt. So did my back. If I'd known I was to be in a thriller, I'd have exercised more often.

I gave up. I banged the wall.

'Get me out of here!' I shouted. 'Get me out or you'll be sorry.'

There was movement on the other side of the wall, the scrape of hurry.

'You'll be very sorry!' I yelled. 'Open up!'

'*Mmph?*' something said.

'These are your sleeping bags and suitcases, I presume. So let's not be polite, I need to pee!' I banged the wall and kept on banging.

Further along a rod of light appeared. I stopped banging and heard scratching, like claws. Large claws. In jerky movements, the light widened to a tall rectangle. After so long in the dark I squinted and had to shade my eyes. A roundish shape shoved through the gap and pushed it wider. It was a fuzzy head with pointed ears. Hoping to God that strange visions were an effect of the anaesthetic, I struggled to the gap and tumbled out at the foot of a flight of steps. I tried to stand. My legs shook. I crumpled to the floor again. I was still blinking, my eyes watered.

'*Grmph,*' said the head, next to mine.

I was right, it wasn't human. It was the head of a Samoyed. I tried hard not to think 'dog' — if I thought 'dog' I would freak out. So, *Samoyed, Samoyed, Samoyed.* I knew about Samoyeds, they're not the smartest animals though people who like them might claim they are fine-looking creatures. This Samoyed looked confused. I guessed it was supposed to keep intruders out, not release them from somewhere inside. At least it hadn't sunk its teeth into me yet.

'Good — animal,' I choked out. 'Nice boy . . . nice girl.' (I was not about to check that fluff for certainty. But next time I saw Roger, I would take no responsibility at all for my reactions.)

The Samoyed sniffed me — I managed not to scream! —

turned and trotted up the stairs. I glanced back into the basement, finding it hard to believe how exceedingly crammed and neat it was now that I saw it with some faint illumination, and followed those powder-puff haunches into a corridor. There — my one piece of luck for a while that was good instead of bad — was a door with a porcelain tile screwed to it bearing in gold italics the blessed word *bathroom*. I shut the animal out and used this room, so immaculate it must be kept for guests. I washed my good hand and the fingers of my bad where they poked out from the bandage, rinsed my mouth (thank God) at last, splashed my face, ran fingers through my hair. I did not care to look into the mirror. A dark red-purple swelling spread out beneath the bandage. For a second or so I considered unwrapping and cleaning the wound, finding a new dressing, but I couldn't face the sight of those spiky black stitches. A sour parsnip taste still lingered from that drugged sleep and I drank water from one cupped hand, which takes a lot more skill than drinking from a pair, but I still swallowed what must be pints and pints. Beside the basin was a tiny bottle of Opium that looked like a free sample — not my kind of thing, too musky. There was lavender soap shaped like a shell. There was a cream hand towel with lavender embroidered roses.

Whose house was this? Why would Roger put me here?

When I emerged from the bathroom, cautiously, the animal was sitting with its tongue out. I was not sure what this meant. The Samoyed beside me, I walked slowly down the corridor — *keep calm, keep calm, if this animal was going to bite, it would have bitten you by now. Maybe*. We passed a room that appeared to be a home study with curtains drawn, a hall bookcase with titles like *What Colour is Your Parachute* and *The Beauty Myth* (how did that go with the dainty bathroom sign?) and came to a very country kitchen, striped blinds pulled down to the windowsill, copper saucepans on a rack, a display of willow pattern plates. The bench top was clear of signs of recent use. On a small side bench was my bag, beside a phone.

There was an empty aluminium dog bowl on the floor and a matching one half-full of water. I glanced at the animal, now standing in front of the fridge. My own poor Nameless fled across my mind. The Samoyed eyed me and nudged the fridge door, but I didn't want to hunt out pet food in case someone accused me of stealing. I tiptoed to fetch my bag. The Samoyed growled and showed its pointed canines.

Awash with fright, careful to move slowly, I rummaged in my bag. My wallet was still there, and the wad of dollars. I didn't think the animal would appreciate furry cough lozenges. But there was half a roll of peppermints.

'Yummies,' I whispered. Hoping the animal had a tooth as sweet as mine, I dropped a mint. It disappeared into the animal's mouth with a *goll-op*! like something up a vacuum cleaner pipe. I took up the phone, tried Luke with no success, then dialled home. No answer. It was becoming harder not to panic.

'Which way to the door?' I whispered to the Samoyed.

There was intelligence in the creature's eyes, which now gleamed at my capacious bag.

'Out,' I tried. 'Out. Walkies?'

The Samoyed backed from the kitchen and trotted along the corridor, glancing to make sure I tagged along. I kept a hand in the bag. Each time the Samoyed stopped, I dropped a mint and whispered, 'Out?' We passed a living room with one lamp on, the curtains there drawn too, and came to a closed double glass door through to a reception area. I had seen no clues, no photos in brass frames, no letters lying round. This home was so plush and orderly it was painful.

One peppermint was left. As I began to offer it, I realised my blood sugar had nearly bottomed out. I shoved through the doors, made sure they closed again with the Samoyed on the far side and popped the peppermint in my own mouth. The creature snarled and flung against the glass with flecks of spittle. A warning buzz began. I saw the red blink of a sensor and hurtled for the front door. Pain lanced through my hand as I unsnibbed the catch. I dashed into the night past a double garage. I thought I saw movement next to it, and that, as well as the *yah-wah-yah* of the alarm and furious barking, meant I'd better not stop dashing. I crossed a lawn, tripped over a low stone wall, nipped under a camellia onto a road — I saw darker shapes of hills, and turned about. Below me, jewels spread around a black silk sea — the motorway rim to the harbour. I was in the suburb where my sisters lived. I walked smartly to a side street and ducked on down. In the distance a siren ululated, perhaps a police car heading for the well-appointed residence with a large basement and a disappointed fluffy guardian mammal.

My watch said it was eleven o'clock. It also said it was *Lun* 19 but as *Lun* is compressed French for Monday, you will realise I'd never figured how to reset the date, which therefore could have been anything.

Ahead of me was a cross street, which I walked to with (I trusted) a leisurely air, and just around the corner was a bus shelter. I sheltered there. I should ask someone for help but there was not a soul around. I would not knock on strange doors. The police? You must be joking.

My sisters and brothers-in-law? Give me a break.

The main thing was to find my kids. A timetable on the wall of the shelter said a bus would be along in a few minutes — if it was a weekday — and take me into town.

But did I dare go home? Besides, where was my car?

I tried to straighten my clothes — that's Annie's clothes. The rip in the pants was three-cornered. I smelled very stale indeed.

This suburb could have been something else designed by Escher: go up one road and find you're in an opposite direction. But I murmured tunes and eventually my subconscious sent me trudging past the little supermarket. My car was no longer near the phone box. I hadn't been stupid enough to expect it would be, but I had to start checking somewhere. I was shaking more and more, a dragging sensation deep inside me that I might never see my kids again. As I shivered from the chill night wind and with the shock of all I'd gone through, there was no tad of consolation in the thought that, just like me, main characters in thrillers never have much notion as to what might happen next.

At nearly midnight, then, I crept closer to Philippa's house. Philippa and Roger, as I may have said already, had an automatic double garage, but Philippa's car was parked outside. It hadn't been there when I last visited — the afternoon of Roger and the needle. Was my sister home? I doubted it, given my grave fears for her. Through the garage window, in the gloom, was the shape of Roger's BMW and next to it my rusty heap. In other circumstances I might have said, nice guy to keep my rusty heap locked in securely while his wife's new Mazda sat in the driveway begging to be stolen by teenage hoons who had not yet learned social responsibility.

At last I knew why Philippa had never asked me to return her keys. Whether she was locked up herself somewhere or she'd genuinely forgotten it, this was one of those fortuitous little tricks a plot can play. I used her key. I stole her car.

Though I still didn't know for sure what day it was and although it was so late, I drove to Luke's and rang the bell.

Guess what? His girlfriend answered. She opened the door as narrow a gap as possible and claimed he wasn't there.

So why was she dressed in a dinky little bathrobe, her hair all cute and mussy, and why were candles burning with the smell of incense?

Do you really need an answer?

I hid my throbbing hand under the front of Annie's denim jacket. 'This is about Tilda,' I said.

177

She smiled in a way I labelled evil, and closed the door on me.

My stomach hurt from holding in my tears but I refused to sob out loud and let the pain escape for Luke's girlfriend to hear. The loneliness of fear for your children is something I wish never to describe.

chapter fifteen

This is not world news but a statement you are welcome to dismiss or not, just as you choose: if you are over twenty years old it is not possible to sleep in a car and be comfortable. Perhaps as a teenager you slept in a car and with exhilaration discovered what your hormones could lead you to perform, but in that case the term *slept* is euphemistic. In my opinion human beings over twenty are unlikely to be victims of their hormones to a degree where they can ignore intense discomfort. This may be in order to prolong the physical mobility of the human body into middle age and onwards, or merely to enrich relationships. For genuine romantic involve-ment as well as for true sleep a little comfort is essential. A floor with a blanket is okay. Double sleeping bags are fine. Single beds in cheap motels might pass the test. Cars? No. Definitely not Philippa's new Mazda, not even on my sad and lonely own-some and for true sleep. I didn't even bother to try sleeping in the driver's seat. I tried the passenger seat at full recline, then tried the back, curled up like a troubled caterpillar. The passenger seat had been minimally better but I was too wrung out to move again.

I entered that unpleasant state when you don't realise you're asleep because you are dreaming you're exactly where you are. I kept waking up and finding it was true: I was kinked up in the back seat of my missing sister's car, a hole in the knee of my best friend's pants, in the parking area at the northern end of Wilton Bush, fairly close to the main road. I do not recommend this as a sleeping spot. It was reasonably quiet between 1 a.m. and 4 a.m. except for the insistent calling of a native owl. I wanted to shoot it. I've heard it said their *mooor-poork* cries mean someone's going to die. The birds call *moor-poork* every night and each night someone dies, and so the legend is spot on. The owl did not scare me, but it was the only thing that didn't during this long uncomfortable night. This northern end of Wilton Bush is not the place for a grown woman (and I am over average height) to catch z's in a car because she's too scared to go home. I was so unused to having money that it was not till morning I realised I could have gone to a hotel. I also didn't realise I could have gone to the twenty-four-hour emergency medical centre to sort out my purple hand.

I was not an ace detective. I did not have the organising ability of either of my sisters (for want of another kinship term right now) or brothers-in-law (big ditto). What I had were my instincts as a mother. Intuition. During that night, in my half-dreaming, half-alert state, I knew the moreporks called out clues. They clutched pieces of the jigsaw in their talons and, should they be persuaded drop them, the fragments would float, stir and buffet till I snatched them from the currents of the wind and sorted them into a pattern. Some clues were tiny men in suits, others were neon signs for a popular carbonated drink, green plastic rectangles, angry voices behind closed doors, the muddy machinery in a Frances Hodgkins painting. All the clues were almost in my reach if only the moreporks would stop teasing and let the pieces drop and settle.

Families. The strangest organism on the planet. We don't ask to be put together with those people, we simply occur that way, like lichen, like — oh well, a tree, the family tree, or thorny family thicket. We're born into it, or gathered into the family by ways like marriage or adoption. If you were bitter, you could say you're hung on it, and I don't mean like the fairy doll at Christmas. Good luck or bad, we're stuck with the other members on the tree. Unless we run away.

I wished that Tilda and Jarret still had grandparents, not just Gifford's charming (though scary) librarian mother. My own dear mom, my dad (for want of more knowledge and correct kinship terms) — you know about them: both gone. Now, with *moor-poork* sounding in that ghostly manner from the trees around the parking area, I knew why my own grandparents were never mentioned in my family. The revelations inside the back cover of *Little Black Quasha* said it may have been because I wasn't a blood-child of my parents. Even so, I'd have thought there might be photographs of Lara and Philippa's grandparents in a dusty box or a tattered album. Were there mementoes — an heirloom Doulton teapot, a silver-backed mirror, a battered oak barometer? Not a sausage. As children, any questions we had about our grandparents were dismissed. Mom was too busy organising a march for Greenpeace just at the second, Dad had a phone call he must make. I guess that if you're pioneers, you must cut ties, and my parents had implied we were pioneers twice. The first time was when we went to the States, the second time was coming back. It was harder coming back, my father said. Your own country lay before you like a strange land. You saw it with new eyes. It was difficult to recall where you fitted in. My mother never said what it meant to her although her face went still, she chopped vegetables for chutney with more vigour, sliced up fabric for her quilts with more attention or puffed longer on her untidy cigarette.

As I uncramped my left leg to rest my ankle on the back of the passenger seat, I thought: no, Mom's face didn't exactly go still, it was more as if she adopted a mask, a pleasant, cool expression like Caine's detective mask when he didn't want a soul to know what he was thinking. So I assumed Mom's memories of what happened before I had my first memories (which were all of Boston, then of Santa Barbara and then of San Diego) were not ones she cared to dwell on. All I remembered was that her father used to be an electrician — that's what she and Dad always said and laughed about a little. Dad had been so conservative that I'd even wondered sometimes if nobody talked about my grandparents on Mom's side because they were circus people. Or entertainers, at the very least. I'd thought this because of how Mom seemed so good at adapting: all those American expressions she used, how she could put on any accent. She used to do a comic Australian as well — *geddin, yerright* — that had annoyed Dad and made us laugh. And her aristocratic Oxford was a treat. Jarret had that same ability and sometimes it was very annoying.

My mother was something of a chameleon, I thought, as I drifted again into the last shreds of dreaming before the owls called it a night. In my dream-state chameleons turned into patchwork toy lizards full of pinto beans, then into small prehistoric creatures. I woke hazy with tears because I remembered Tilda sobbing once when she saw a picture of a baby tuatara on its keeper's hand, the soft crumple of its newborn lizard silver against the weather-beaten hand of the man who held it, how Tilda wept because it would grow up to be a gnarled ugly creature as big as a cat and become so old that its back turned green with lichen. *Someone should scrub the old ones,* Tilda sobbed, *they don't like to have mould on their shoulders.*

As I wept, I chuckled too because I dreamt how frantic my father became, the summer we came from the States to live in this quaint Wild West country and rented a holiday house. Where was it? Some beach. I can't recall where. I loved that beach — the sand was white and squeaked beneath my feet with cleanliness, not like the sand in California that seemed to have been covered, every grain, with grease comprised of sweat and suntan oil. This new beach seemed more like the Californian desert with harsh sun, clear sky without the softening haze caused by pollution — oh, we had all loved that desert. Each spring we took a picnic up to the Anza Borrego to see the wildflowers — I remember bright yellow poppies, clover, blue lupine, the sprawling purple sand verbena. Were they all blooming at the same time, or is it just a jigsaw of my memory? Driving further into the heart of that place we would come upon the astonishment of blossoms on the cacti: a barrel cactus as big as me, saucers of pale yellow petal among its long sharp spines; great spidery ocotillo that seemed about to paint the sky with their flaming red tips; a scatter of tiny unnamed splashes of colour, delicate and magical, that sprang directly from the sand. How I had adored those family picnic days, each one of us exploring. *You must see this! And this! Look, there goes a jackrabbit! Brer Rabbit!* One afternoon we even went from sweltering Palm Springs up in a cable car to the mountains and threw snowballs in our satin shorts and sandals!

That first summer on the beach, back from the States, the sun burned everything clean. Sand hoppers sprang like crazy-bugs, fat beach plant crawled along the dunes, the air was spicy with hot fennel. I spent most of the time alone — in sight of Mom — on the long white squeaking shore. The Girls spent their time together in a kind of emotional twinship. Mom was nearly ill with nerves one morning when they went out in a dinghy without Dad. Before now, the only boats they'd been in on their own had been rides at places like Disneyland and Knott's Berry Farm. They returned carrying a lizard in a bucket. *Look at this cool animal*, they exclaimed in their American accents. *We're going to take it to the store. We'll charge money for people to see!*

Dad sat up in the lounger beneath the sun umbrella, pushed back his towelling hat and glanced into the bucket. His face went a funny colour beneath his tan.

It's such a big gecko. We found it on the island. Wow, this place is better than Disneyland!

You'd have thought a scientist would be intrigued. My mother was. *Will it bite? Can you keep a lizard as a pet? Can we train it? It doesn't seem to move much. Is it sick?*

For crying out loud, it's a protected species, Dad said in a desperate whisper.

Though I was fascinated by the lizard, something more than ecological purity was driving his distress. *Don't say a single word about this, girls. Not one, not to anyone, you hear?*

Philippa protested, *We could get our names in the paper!*

But by then Mom too was ensnarled in Dad's anxiety. As I dropped off to sleep that night, a burl of low voices from my parents unlike their bigger arguments, rode me to sleep. By morning the giant gecko had disappeared. *Scotty beamed him up*, Dad growled, a fresh band aid on one thumb. But the dinghy wasn't where The Girls had left it: it was pulled up further along the beach. My parents hadn't wanted to draw attention to themselves. Modesty? Or something more?

Dear Lord, my sister's Mazda was uncomfortable. Traffic began to build on Churchill Drive and blackbirds had begun the morning howdy-do. A yellow blur passed the car window and I caught a man's old-fashioned look as a black Labrador tugged its rain-jacketed owner through the barrier gate onto the grass for the start of its morning walk.

Morning walk . . . and morning talk. Oh goodness, that's right — my parents had been aghast when we were back in town, had started at our new schools and I said I'd given a morning talk about the lizard in the bucket. *I should whip you!* said my dad. He'd never said such a thing before and was appalled at his own words. I'd just toasted the heel-slice of a loaf for myself, but gave to him because he looked so red and upset.

Why? I asked. *Are you ashamed because you killed it?*

I put it back, said Dad, *it's not important but I told you not to say one single word.*

You told that to The Girls, I said, *not me.* A little smart-ass. But he thanked me for his favourite part of the loaf.

Back at school I told my teacher I'd made up my morning talk, and asked her what would happen if someone had a protected lizard. *They'd get fined*, she told me, that look in her eye I've learnt to recognise in teachers and in parents, now that I'm a mother myself. At that age, I figured *fined* was like the notice in buses: if you gave information about someone damaging the vehicle and they were convicted, you received a hundred dollars. I used to sit in the bus and wonder how easy it would be to lie about seeing someone damaging a bus, but work out you wouldn't get the money if it wasn't true. When I thought some more, that seemed okay: it wouldn't do to get money for being a liar. For a whole year, I went through the same process each time I was on a bus. Dumb kid. Dumb youngest kid.

A Rottweiler doing heavy breathing tugged its owner past the car I had stolen from my sister.

Now that it was light, I had courage enough to go home. I needed the bathroom. I needed a long hot shower, a poached egg on toast. I needed to add a few more yellow stickies. I needed to change out of Annie's long-sleeved tee and ruined stretch pants into something of my own. Then I needed the doctor. With luck, and a guardian angel watching over me, I'd find my kids had returned. I was ashamed I hadn't had the courage to check last night.

When I pulled up outside my house it was as if I'd arrived in a Mexican stand-off. Two cars were there, Caine's personal old white Laser and Luke's red sports car, both men sitting in their vehicles. From the set of their shoulders, they'd been waiting there a while. On her porch across the road sat Beth, in what might be her pyjamas or might be trendy street-gear for the student set these days.

Neither man would have recognised Philippa's car, which I

hoped gave me a moment's leeway. I gathered my bag to my chest and tried slipping up my steps, a shadow of a shadow, as Caine had done on Monday night.

It didn't work in daylight. Caine and Luke tumbled from their vehicles and barrelled towards me, both shouting. I did not like their collegial air one bit.

I nipped inside alone and shut the door. Swiftly I looked at the hall table. There was no new message from the kids. There was no nasty surprise in the bathroom when I used it for a quick pee. Stickies covered the dining table, and there was no body lying under it. There was no nasty surprise in the kitchen, just clean new-smelling wood, smooth modern surfaces instead of the inimitable DIY carpentry that had caused such dark and quiet arguments between my parents. The mouldering cupboard along the back porch that I laughingly called my laundry was as makeshift as it had been since Dad helped me move in. By now, there was a lot of knocking on the door, two deep and angry voices calling me.

Oh, I hadn't expect my kids to be home but their absence hit me afresh. I felt as if my heart had been removed, as if I had no limbs to use. I felt nauseous. I wanted to lie on my side and weep with the ache of *my kids missing*. But into the pain a small idea slipped like a knife edge. Each breath crushed and tore me. It was a struggle to reach the front door again and open it. Caine stood aside to let Luke enter, but Caine was the one who dived and caught me as my knees gave out.

'I'm all right,' I whispered. 'I'll be fine in just a second.'

Caine tried to lie me on the sofa but I wriggled up and shoved Luke aside as well so I could get through the dining room and see the kitchen. I clung on to the dividing ledge, staring over at the nice new woodwork.

'Suzie, sit,' Caine ordered.

No Rottweiler was I, nor Labrador, nor Samoyed, but even though I was pulverised by my children's absence, my sniffing-out instincts were still working. Why had it not occurred to me before? I might have got a new kitchen not because someone had made a mistake, but because someone seriously wanted the old one.

Someone scared me out of my own home so they could get their hands on my old joinery. This was a kitchen sink drama.

My ability to breathe returned and I was fighting mad. I stormed to the front steps and shouted for Beth to come over. I stormed back to the kitchen, shoved a plastic bag over the swollen hand and began to poach eggs.

'Where the hell have you been!' Luke asked. A scabbed-over line ran down the side of his face. He was extremely rumpled as if he'd slept in a car himself.

With a spatula, I pointed at his scratch. 'A gorse bush?'

He flushed. 'She should have let you in last night. She knows you and Tilda come first, I've made it clear.'

There's not much you can say to that, but your eyebrows can speak volumes if you let them. I tried to keep mine quiet. 'What day is it?' I asked.

'Thursday.' Caine was unshaven. I had never seen this man with growth. I liked it as much as I liked him clean-shaven but I should not be thinking that way now. I handed him my watch, which now said Tuesday in shortened French.

'Please fix it.'

His fingers did the job as if he didn't even have to think about it. 'Where have you been since . . .' His jaw worked and I wondered how he was going to say it, especially in front of Luke. 'Since you — and I assume it was you, Suzie — used the staple gun on Tuesday?'

I apologised for ruining his clothes.

He shrugged. 'Police issue. But you must have known I was trying to protect you.'

'How could I know that?' I yelled. 'Is it protecting me to

throw me down in an outdoor shed? Is it protecting me to sneak around inside my sister's house? Roger drugged me! I was locked in someone's basement for a night and a day and a whole evening!'

Caine's look said *told you so*. To give him due, it also said he was serious and upset. 'You should have let me know about the kids. God in heaven, I had to hear it from Luke. Suzie, why didn't you tell me!'

This made my insides feel extremely complex. So — he hadn't heard about the children missing from his colleagues. Did he know about the body in the pantry or not? I wanted to be quick, before Beth arrived. I filled the men in with what had happened to me — Roger the ex-dentist, the lonely Samoyed. I told Caine to check with Central to find if there was news of Jarret and Tilda. By the time he had (and there was none) I had spread tea towels across the yellow stickies.

Beth sidled in and I asked her to sit down. 'Beth, you're going to be interviewed by this small nation's finest. Detective and journalist, both. I cook, you talk.'

'I've been wanting to get my feet under your table for weeks,' Beth said.

Each man showed, by trying not to, that he picked up the flirtatious note. I told Luke he was responsible for the toast.

'Do you guys want to alternate your questions, or go one at a time?' I asked. Caine indicated Luke could have first shot. I figured this was cunning detective work because most people are pleased and excited to be interviewed by a journo, but we all know what they do on TV shows when they're being interviewed by a detective, even when they're innocent. They peg out laundry, shelve books, go about their daily business and avoid direct answers. This must be because of the visual side of things, you know, keep the audience watching some action because talking heads are tedious. And even in books, I figure, it must be difficult for the author to show on the page exactly how an interviewed person in a criminal investigation reacts in a way that gives the reader exact clues about what's really going on. Therefore as Beth replied to Luke's questions about the last few days, and then replied to Caine's, I was impressed. Mind you, Caine put pretty much the same questions as Luke had. Beth was straightforward. She didn't try to help me with the cooking. She didn't behave badly and snap off witty one-liners to show her cute personality, didn't talk to the detective over her shoulder while she tried to fold my laundry. She'd be no good as a character on stage or on TV. Beth simply sat, looked Luke and then Caine right in the eye, screwed up her freckled forehead while she pondered once or twice, but in the main was so straightforward (which I have said earlier in the paragraph but you need to be reminded for it was indeed remarkable) that she was the answer to some of my prayers.

Here's what she told us.

Mid-Monday evening, maybe nine o'clock, an unmarked van arrived. Three builders in white overalls and caps leapt from it and disappeared into my house. Beth was not there when the van actually drove up but she believed it arrived when the flatmate who was into mountaineering and had been waiting for the weather on TV said it did, and it was definitely there when she arrived back from rehearsal.

'Didn't you think this was weird?' Luke yelled — at least, said loudly with asperity.

Beth wrinkled her nose. 'I reckoned it was something to do with the lights being out, earlier. I reckoned that's why Suzie went to sleep at her boyfriend's place, that's all.'

'Ex,' Luke said.

'Shut up, Luke. But what about when Caine came in on us holding his Glock . . . ?' I asked Beth.

With the hand furthest from the guys and hidden by the table Beth motioned to me as if she held a cigarette. Ah. Right. My boyfriend, who was in the police, would not like me to have a friend who used pot, and that's why she had fled with such alacrity.

When Beth had woken around seven next morning the van was still there, or there again. She had thought this showed particular zealousness on the part of the builders. Most builders arrive noisily at 8 a.m. before you wish them to, and vanish like clouds in your coffee at 4.30 p.m. on the dot, leaving festoons of wood shavings and sawdust in small Saharas. But she figured three such cute guys as those builders might well want to show extra zealousness to a cute older woman like myself.

Luke burnt the toast.

Beth thought the van departed a little after eight-thirty in the morning. At least, she heard an engine start up but she had her lines to assimilate over her toast and jam, and was not a voyeur, thank you.

'You'd noticed they were cute guys,' I pointed out.

Beth shrugged. By now I had prepared four breakfasts of poached eggs, fried tomatoes and onion, and a pot of coffee as well as taking over responsibility for the toast. I figured if you intended to interview what might be a key witness, you ought to keep her happy. McDonald's burgers, which you see being fed to witnesses in TV police dramas, were not what I cared to put before someone who had served as guardian angel to me earlier that week.

Caine and Luke fell upon their breakfasts. As sometimes happens when you cook, though I had been ravenous before and, except for that one peppermint last night, hadn't eaten since a muffin with Luke at lunchtime on Tuesday, I only picked at food myself. About to get up instead and call for Nameless, I suddenly realised that in all this questioning and exchange of information, two things still had not been mentioned. The note from the kids. And the body in the pantry. If Caine knew about the body, he wasn't letting on.

'May I ask a question?' I asked. Both Caine and Luke were adorable with their mouths full and expressions of embarrassment on their faces (at being so hungry, at my asking if I could ask questions in my own house, at realising they had been doing a guy thing — you name it, it's only right they were embarrassed). 'Builders usually have skips. You know, bins. Trucks for the rubbish. What did these guys have?'

Beth tucked a wedge of toast into her cheeks like a hamster with a nut. 'They had the truck, that's all.'

Cleverly, because he did not use words just a grunt and a flourish of his fork, Caine asked if Beth was sure. She was.

'Did you see them carrying the new joinery into the house?' I asked. 'Did you see them carrying anything out of the house?'

Beth frowned as if she did not want to say.

'Beth, I really need to know anything at all that you or your flatmates might have seen.'

Her chin became defiant. 'If I tell you everything, you'll know how much of a voyeur I really am when it comes to you and your house.'

I gave her The Look.

She blushed. 'A girl can dream, okay?'

I poured her coffee. A good author would be telling you by now how Caine and Luke reacted to this by-play: I can't take the time.

'So all right, I was curious.' Beth tucked more toast and flipped a rosy, freckled half-smile towards Caine. 'They were definitely cute guys, the three of them. I'm not prejudiced.'

'So you'd recognise them again,' said Luke at the same time that Caine, rubbing his slightly broken nose, asked her to describe them. I had intended to get to that myself.

Beth's freckles turned darker rose. She shook her head.

'What is it?' I asked.

'I lied. I am prejudiced. They were Asian. That's all I know.'

'And you're doing Asian studies?' I remarked.

She grinned, a little repentant. 'Plus, they were wearing those white caps all the time.'

It had been a very smooth operation, planned long in advance, to steal my old kitchen. But why set the whole thing up — the ransacking to get me and the kids out of the house that night? Why couldn't they simply have told me I'd won new cupboards in some lottery? Believe me, I would have asked no questions.

Beth slipped into the kitchen and started washing up. Caine followed and began examining the insides of the drawers, cupboards, pantry, for maker's marks or other clues. He seemed just a little desultory. Perhaps Beth was in his way. Anyway, I didn't want her feeling too much at home so I thanked her and packed her off.

'Why do you trust Caine now?' I asked Luke on the quiet.

'When we couldn't find you, we got drunk together last night. He is on the side of truth and justice. He thinks Tilda's a tough little number.'

I'd trust Luke's paternal instinct to the end of time and then some. If he said Caine could be trusted, I'd consider it.

'Besides, you were right the other day, Suzie. We have no option.' Luke leaned on the divider to watch Caine. 'Shouldn't you get a forensic team to do that?'

Caine gave his mask-like stare. 'I am not on the case.'

'You're a liar,' Luke said.

There followed a slight pause. 'I am on leave.'

I made a disbelieving sound, because what I guessed was that he'd been suspended.

He turned the stare to me. 'I had planned some leave. I hoped to spend it in Fiji, chilling out in sun and sea.'

'Now you're spending it looking for your ex-girlfriend's kids,' said Luke. 'I hope to God there's someone serious on this case, not just an out-of-work guy on so-called leave.'

What the heck was going on here? What happened to that trust Luke talked about? As I tried to interpret what Luke's eyebrows meant, I noticed the scratch on his cheek looked inflamed. Not a surprise. I fetched antiseptic. He seemed appreciative, though Caine did not. Why should I not have a little sympathetic moment for Luke? I would not want the father of my daughter to be the victim of blood poisoning, although a scar would suit him well.

As I applied the cream to Luke's face I took the chance to whisper in his ear. 'Why didn't Caine tell you about the pantry? And I don't think you have told him about the kids' note?' Luke closed his eyes in a squinch that indicated no. 'Why not?' Luke squinched his mouth.

Okay. The missing link was trust, that crucial word.

I picked at a little more toast. 'Guys, I'm exhausted. I must have a shower.'

'You've got to find that house with the Samoyed again,' said Caine. 'I'll take you out there. We'll get to the medical centre first: you need that wound checked and you probably need more treatment. Don't think I haven't noticed. We should hurry.'

Luke's eyebrows moved together in suspicion. 'You should get someone to arrest Roger. I want to see who's in charge of this investigation. I'll take Suzie down to Central when she's ready.'

'I'm going to do that,' said Caine.

So close was I to yelling, my eardrums popped.

Choices, choices. In a usual mystery there is one person officially in charge, or at least there is one who sorts things out. A police detective, say. In this case, Caine had a personal (though dumping had occurred) romantic interest in the case, he may not even have been an official police detective any longer or he may have been simply suspended, judgement pending.

The person in charge in some stories is a journalist, possibly drink-sodden, over-womanised, or in other ways a trial to his colleagues in the newsroom. Luke was hot-tempered. He was lazy with punctuation. He was entangled with an evil-smiling woman who had scratched him. I didn't think these provided enough bad qualities for him to be in charge. However he was also the father of one of the missing children and that gave him the right to be very involved.

Another person suitable to be in charge would be a forensic pathologist, a woman in solid middle age with romantic problems and, as like as not for added personal interest, a young relative with gender problems. I had the romantic problems. I admitted to being in early middle age. But my teenage relative was off being an AFS scholar and, though intelligent, was still in the stage where she turned giggly about clothing and hair gel. Also, I hope I made it clear already that I am not into gory dissection.

Then there is the feisty female private eye into serious aerobic working-out who sustains a hit on the head or is otherwise in great peril, but who rescues herself, ties up loose ends and all the bad guys, then heads off to dinner (maybe more) with one of the hunkier good guys who has sprung up in the narrative.

I do not get excited at the idea of physical danger: crawling in that basement had been more than enough fright for me. I wanted a tall, cool, father figure who was into finer things like art and poetry, an elegant male police inspector of the cerebral British kind who would calmly take control and find my kids.

It just wasn't going to happen.

I thanked my breakfast guests for their time and company, saying 'Shower, shower, shower!' and pulling at Annie's ill-suiting clothes. Caine left only when I agreed to keep all doors locked and bolted till he returned, and that Luke would stay as long as he could. Caine also came out with a string of assurances that the boys in blue would be doing everything and more because of this personal connection even though it was one of the reasons he himself was, at least officially, off the case. When I made a comment about him being noted for his straight talk he avoided my eye. He said — this piece was not assuring in the least — that Philippa had not been reported missing, but he feared she and I were in danger, and he would definitely be giving his colleagues this data about Roger and the basement. He would be back in less than one hour, and I was not to go anywhere till then.

I smiled as if it were a promise and closed the door on him at last.

Luke's face was heavy. And because Luke is Tilda's father we sat, tentative and awkward, in the living room. He and I looked at each other with faces that didn't smile but said silently we were in enormous trouble.

'What does your paternal instinct tell you?' I asked.

He bunched his rustly jacket to his chest as if it were protection from something large and cruel. 'All it says is that I am, and will be, a mess until the kids are found again.'

The kids, he said. He didn't even think about it, he put my son and our daughter together in one word. Once more I came over shaky — I leaned back in my chair to hide it. He was still the only person I could trust. He must have seen this in my face because he left the sofa and knelt beside my chair. I lurched towards him. The arm of the chair hard between us, we held each other and allowed ourselves to weep.

The shower was bliss, the shampoo was heaven, even though I had one hand shoved in another plastic bag. My own clean knickers were joyful to me. I was bamboozled by the bra strap once again, thought of calling Luke to help, but rejected that idea the instant it reared its tricky head. I worked out that if I slung the damn thing backwards around my waist, hooked it up then turned it round and wriggled hard, everything should end up in the right place. Bingo. Clean jeans, a denim jacket with no lace — such small important pleasures.

Luke left to check in at work because Caine was due back to take up protection duty any time. My ratty side began to bare its yellow teeth. Nobody thought I could handle this, they assumed I was incompetent — even the kids — and *stay put, plese*! To quiet my snarling rat of anger, I decided to clear the table. The tea towels were spotted with tomato. I lifted them off cautiously so I didn't disturb the yellow stickies.

You might expect at this moment to learn my caution was not needed because all the yellow stickies had disappeared. Not so. However, there were fewer than I remembered. When had they gone missing? Had I not taken proper notice when I hurried to spread the tea towels over them? Had Luke and or Caine removed some?

Keys to the house: of the three official sets, I had one, Jarret another, and that third set had been missing for a while. I suspected Gifford — but those Asian guys in boiler suits had got in without trouble. I should change the locks today.

It seemed to me the stickies that had disappeared were ones to do with Gifford. This meant Gifford could be the one who'd done the stickie-thieving or it could mean whoever had done it wanted me to think that Gifford was the thief — or wanted me to forget about Gifford's possible involvement. To throw me off the track — or put me on it? Another of my mother's favourite stories came to mind: Brer Rabbit who managed to escape from Brer Fox and Brer Bear each time. In one story Brer Fox kotched him, but wily Brer Rabbit begged and pleaded. Roast him, hang him, drown him, skin him, but *don't fling me in dat brier-patch,* begged he. I always thought Brer Fox should have just eaten up the bratty little critter but he was tricked just like Brer Rabbit wanted. Into the brier-patch that rabbit was tossed. And underneath the thorny bushes, safe and sound, that rabbit snuck on home.

False direction. Double crosses. Ploys and tricks.

If anyone could pick a lock, or carry a set of master keys with not one question asked, it would be an ace detective. And I had seen Caine snooping, Monday night. It may well be he knew about the body without being told. He may have seen it — he may even have helped put it there. He was also snooping at Philippa's, just before Roger kotched me in the village.

Caine and Gifford came together in my mind.

My snarling rat side flexed. I slipped another note to the kids on to the hall table.

chapter sixteen

Had I left a thread behind me as a spider does, a silvery network would have woven over the city. Now the thread tracked into the centre. Why? I knew I should get back to the GP. And shouldn't I have tried to contact Lara again by now?

Have you forgotten she was with Roger in the main bedroom? I don't think anyone realises what a suspicious nature they have till they're in suspicious circumstances. One scenario I had at this point was that Roger and Lara were having a relationship and had got rid of my younger older sister. I couldn't see how it might tie up with all the other stuff, but I didn't want to get hold of Brick — how can you talk to a nice untidy guy who is happiest in his tartan slippers if you think his wife is cheating on him with an ex-dentist? I was trying to protect Brick. Lara too. I mean, would my sister really do away with my other sister unless there was strong reason? Oh, and those squitty family trees . . . the whole caboodle made me feel very weird.

I was still driving Philippa's Mazda. I was temped not to give a toss where I parked when I reached the city. Her car could get towed away, be ticketed, wheel-clamped, why should I worry at a time like this?

But it was not Philippa's fault the kids had gone, and not her fault I had such a self-pitying, self-dramatising time being youngest sibling. However it did occur to me it may well have been her fault Roger was driven to have an affair — it must be hard work being as doting as that man. But then I would imagine having an affair with Duchess Lara hard work too. Affairs are often cries for help, so I have heard, and my job was not to reason who was yelling for help this time.

When I tried parking under the library again it was full. That self-pity rose up like a fountain, but a woman ran out from the elevator, saw me stymied and waved urgently. I had no idea who she could be. She grabbed something from a car and dashed right over.

'I over-paid,' she cried. 'It's a shame to waste it.'

Astonished, I thanked her. Self-pity receded like the tide, I put her parking slip on my dashboard and took the space she left.

If you didn't already know the name of Philippa's charity it would be damned hard to find. It had always seemed to me if Philippa's little team wanted their non-profit work better noticed they would have had a more prominent frontage. The office was tucked in a boring grey building tucked between other boring buildings, and the entry to her stairway was not even the main entrance of her building. I'd only visited here once and never met the women Philippa worked with. With their interest in things Asian you might have expected good luck symbols, maybe no more than a solitary jade plant, but there was nothing except a sign that said Suite Three (fifth floor).

A notice in front of the elevator warned it was out of order. Looking at the steep narrow stairs, I felt my legs would never cope. But the longest journey begins with just one step, so one step is what I took and I'd begun. Though a mother may find it near impossible to enter her own house when she has discovered one stranger's body thawing out on pasta sauce, she would climb a million stairs to find her kids.

On the first floor was the office of a money lender, on the second the office of an adjustable shelving system. Third floor was an employment specialist, poorly lit, and I wouldn't try there for a job if I were you. The fourth floor had an office for something biological. Through the dirty glass of the window on the security door it appeared so seedy I figured it must be some crackpot scientist who'd been tossed out of the university.

By the time I got to floor five I was gasping. I tried the stairwell door. It did not open. I knocked. If I was lucky, the women Philippa worked with would hear and let me through.

They didn't.

Not for nothing had I lugged my trusty bag with me. I sat on the stairs and checked through my wallet. I had cards for the library (of course), the Automobile Association (no single woman should be without a membership), various stores (customer reward points). I chose one for a pharmacy chain. Health and beauty. I was not feeling so great myself, but the Zen of this one ought to have effect. I emptied my mind of impure thoughts, floated up a little prayer to whatever angel might be listening out for mothers and slipped the card into the crack of the door beside the lock. There was a click. I turned the handle. The door swung open. I thanked Caine for being a good teacher, and Beth for reminding me of this trick.

No lights were on in the vestibule, an imposing word for the dreary space between the elevator and the office door. Suite Three was dark as well. This could be awkward if someone turned up but the Blu-tack in my bag was handy now: I pressed a wad over the lock before I slipped into the vestibule. And here I was, in front of the out-of-order elevator, and outside my sister's non-profit organisation.

Also outside the door to Suite Three was a courier package

about the size of a paperback. Couriers are not supposed to leave packages where any passer-by can snaffle them but nearly all couriers do. Surely this courier could have pushed the small package through the letter slot in the Suite Three door. I noticed the address — for the building next door. Bernard once asked for some premiere blue vein cheese to be couriered for a particular festive lunch. The courier left it at the wrong door, on the lowest floor of that jumbled hillside complex that held Thee Ultimate Café and, not only that, in a metal letter box. In full sunshine, midsummer. By the time Bernard found it, the cheese had turned to water and trickled away. Do not trust couriers.

I knocked and turned the handle though I didn't expect an answer, nor that the handle would turn, then used my card again. It broke — so much for health and beauty — but the door snicked.

It pushed against something as I opened it. I told myself not to scream if it was another body, just run downstairs and fetch the police. However, it rustled and slid — a pile of unopened mail. More packages, manilla envelopes, one or two old-fashioned aerogrammes with the address done on old manual typewriters with the letters out of alignment. Even at a glance I saw many of the stamps were from India, Korea, the usual suspects for the territories Suite Three dealt with.

I used another wad of Blu-tack on this second door too. This was the dark side of the building and the only window in the office was through in Philippa's cubicle. No wonder she used to meet potential sponsors at Thee Ultimate Café with its fine view of the harbour. Once she'd come in when I was working in the kitchen and ignored me, her own sister! It was beneath her to have a sister who worked as a chef in a café! She had treated me as if I were a servant! Even Bernard, kindly Bernard, raised his eyebrows, whiffled his beard although of course he was friendly and polite to her, as always. I'd always suspected Suite Three was in truth just Roger's tax break but don't ask me how that worked.

I flicked the lights on. The air seemed porridgey, cold and thick. I tried to open that only window. It had no view except of an even smaller window in the neighbouring building across a narrow alley. At first the window stuck, but when I bashed the frame it suddenly slammed wide. The air began to stir.

The answerphone in the main office space was blinking. I listened to many messages, some dating back to last week. Several were from me and Lara, a few others, repeated, both personal and work-related, for the other women, Maisie Forrest and Katherine Tiller. If I'd ever heard these women's names before, I had taken little notice. They were a different breed from me: good houses, conventional dress code or so I supposed, so why would I care? By the end of the tape, some callers sounded very cross indeed. Listening between the lines, so to speak, I gathered Suite Three was on the brink of folding up for lack of money and those Asian animals could go begging.

Hmmm.

I returned to the pile of mail and opened some. One was from an Indian gentleman extolling the excellence of his brother-in-law's dance academy in Sambalpur and wanting a reference to the American embassy here. A second came from a Singaporean entrepreneur saying he had interests in dog meat and did Suite Three need a line of supply? A third was from a New Zealander living in Fiji: he had written a thriller with international settings and wanted a list of literary agents who might kindly peruse his manuscript. To me, the word peruse does not carry a ring of credibility as to a person's skill with words and story. I held out no hope for him.

Given I'd snooped into the mail, I figured to compound my crime and snoop into the desks as well. My sister's first. It was not as scary as the desk in her home study. Her desk drawers contained the usual in a mess: pens, pencils, paper clips, a hand-sized hand-knitted rugby player clutching a ball, a glossy newsletter from an aid organisation still in its cellophane mailer, the kind of thing you set aside to read but never do. I glanced at the front and back items, did a kindness to my sister and slid it in her rubbish bin. A book on Imperial Chinese antiques. A bottle of nail polish, plum coloured. I doubted Philippa did much work here. It was more a thing to talk about at cocktail parties . . . the shame of that notion. Though I did not want her dead, my feelings towards this sister were complex. Were she dead, I'd feel a load of guilt at the convolutions of my feelings.

I moved out to the second desk where a label said Maisie Forrest. A calendar showed last Thursday's date. The drawers contained more or less the same kind of stuff as Philippa's, minus the knitted toy and plus a pair of hand weights. In a bulldog clip was a sheaf of recipes (chicken, pork, beef, lamb — oh yes, and fish), another couple of newsletters, under them a business card folder and beneath that was the bottom of the drawer. A faint perfume, some rubber bands and a pill bottle, labelled garlic and echinacea. It had a childproof cap so I bashed it with a hole punch. I swallowed two tablets and dropped the rest in my bag. I was a tidy visitor and brushed the shattered plastic into the waste basket.

It's hard to snoop when you don't know what you hope to find. I moved to the third desk. No name on it, but it had to be Katherine Tiller's. One of those big desk pads was on top: its edges were pristine, when usually they curl and look ill-kempt. I opened the top drawer of the three, and felt a little strange. I opened the second. My skin prickled. These drawers were unnaturally tidy. There was even a pink plastic truck, a cleaner cart to sweep up pencil shavings and dust from when you file your nails — I played with it briefly, moved to the filing cabinet and opened that. The labels, hand-written, were identical to the labels in Philippa's home study. This woman must have been in my sister's house and done that intimidating job on all her papers. I turned back to the desk, slid open the bottom drawer and found it packed with neatly rolled pieces of string, precise regiments of little boxes.

I returned to the window in Philippa's cubicle for a breath of air to clear my mind. Through the opaque window opposite there was a flash of pink. My heart pitched in my chest. I knew it was Tilda.

I shrieked her name but all that came out was the sound of strangulation. My heart hammered so that it was difficult to move, but I rummaged through the cubicle to find something I could throw — the Yellow Pages! With my good hand, I lobbed them through. They thumped the opposite sill and dropped into the alley. Using both hands this time, I followed it with the rest of the phone book. This didn't even hit the sill, just dropped. Still the pink shape didn't turn. I hurled the knitted football player — I missed! — I was a girl. I hurled a bulldog clip and this time hit the glass. The pink shape moved and disappeared. I leaned out the window, calling 'Tilda!' My cries faded. If she'd been wearing her pink cardigan since Monday, it would be pink no longer. It would be grey. I also heard the sound of plumbing. I had a very bad moment, and yelled *Fuck it*!

I stumbled back into the main office and went through Maisie's drawers again. The top recipe on the sheaf was for chicken simmered in Thai sauce. Red herring! I slammed the drawer shut — it was like the sound I'd made, banging in that Khandallah basement. My skin prickled again. I returned to that third desk, slowly opened the third drawer, stared into its tidiness, and was certain whoever had so neatly crammed it full was the person who owned that basement — that bunk I'd lain in, drugged — the owner of that Samoyed. Katherine Tiller.

I phoned Luke's mobile and simmered while he yelled at me for leaving home after he and Caine had agreed I should stay put till Caine returned. When he'd finished I told him where I was and sat at Philippa's desk to wait. Where was my sister, Philippa? Was everybody in this little non-profit (and how!) organisation missing? Had they simply gone on holiday? They couldn't all have been murdered. Their husbands and families would make a fuss — but did the other two have husbands, families? And why, why do away with an entire, very small and failing charity such as this? All I could think of was a news item I'd seen some years ago about a rest-home worker particularly fond of animals who persuaded elderly patients to write new wills benefiting the SPCA, then engineered their deaths. You see how poorly my mind was working. That's why, when I heard the elevator, without any fear I opened the Suite Three door for Luke.

It wasn't till the elevator door slid open and a man in a suit emerged that I remembered the 'out of order' notice at street level.

This was not the man who'd put a real estate card in my letter box. It was a small suit, and the man was Oriental. He was silent and polite. With a flourish he placed a hand over his heart, which made me notice on some level how fresh his shirt was, how beauti-fully ironed. He looked at me meaningfully (though I could not work out what his meaning was) and handed me a brown envelope. He stood there, smiling, a meaningful nice smile.

'I'm not . . . I don't . . .' I tried to indicate I wasn't part of Suite Three but he put a finger to his lips, indicated the envelope again, bowed, pressed both hands to his heart and stepped back into the lift. It went up.

I closed the Suite Three door and dropped the envelope on Maisie's desk. I had opened enough of their mail.

For something to do, I slid out Maisie's drawers again. I read her recipes and saw too much reliance on salt for flavour. I picked up another newsletter and flicked through. Inside was a photo of my sister and two women, smiling, holding a parchment for some animal welfare award. They wore designer earrings, designer knitwear. Maisie. And Katherine. The women my sister worked with.

My whole body felt chilled, even my swollen hand. I had seen these women before, one in the 'm' room and the other — yes, you've guessed it.

chapter seventeen

There was a thumping and the stairwell door burst open. Someone lumbered into the vestibule, banged on the Suite Three door, and entered. It was Caine. He was frowning worse than Luke. This I can swear to for Luke too came thumping up the stairwell and into the office. These two stood before the desk and frowned. Collegial frowns.

'Suzie!' Luke began. He smelled of sulphur.

I held the newsletter out to Caine. 'Where is my sister?'

Still frowning, Luke pointed to the photo on page three.

'No — Caine, look at the women she is with. Where is my sister now?'

Caine still didn't comprehend. I had to lean on the desk — my knees had come unstrung — and point to the middle woman in the group. 'That's Katherine Tiller. Her desk is . . .' I gestured. 'She's the woman you made me go and visit in the . . . I'm certain she's the one who owns the Samoyed!' It looked as if he finally understood. I pointed again. 'And that one's Maisie Forrest, and this is her desk. She was the . . .' I made a shut-the-door motion.

'The woman in the pantry!' Luke had got it.

'What pantry?' Caine asked.

I beat my chest with my bandaged fist and Caine looked mystified. Was he a good actor? 'Dead. In my pantry,' I said. 'We told you about the new kitchen but we didn't tell you what I found there, first. On Monday night. I went back home. It wasn't nice.'

'Monday night!' Caine grabbed the newsletter, put his nose close to the photo.

'So where is Philippa?' I cried.

From the look on Luke's face, a jigsaw was sorting into shape behind that frown. Caine straightened up. His expression had become the mask of the detective.

'We can look up Tiller in the phone book — where's the phone book?' asked Luke.

I confessed I had thrown it out the window. They didn't ask why.

'Have any of these three been reported missing?' Luke was wasted as a sports journalist.

'Tell me again why we are suddenly trusting Caine?' I asked him. 'That is, if we are?'

The guys frowned at each other. Caine's shoulders did some interesting things.

'Suzie,' he growled, as full of warning as the Samoyed, 'I don't want to say you should leave it to experts because you'd be annoyed. But you have been nothing but obstructionist since your kids disappeared.'

'Because they went missing from your house!'

'You should have told me at once about the woman, about Maisie in the pantry . . .'

'I didn't know her name.'

'Who'll believe you, now she's gone?'

'But you snooped around my house! Why should I trust you? I saw you, dammit. Just after I found the . . . found Maisie.'

Caine's mask shifted for a moment. 'I went to feed your damned cat. The lights were off so I gave up. He's a good mouser. I didn't even go into the kitchen.'

Luke looked at me. I looked at Luke. We looked at Caine.

'I still don't know if I can trust you. I would like to trust someone — oh, besides Luke. Sorry, Luke.'

'Why can't you be nice?' Luke asked.

'Why didn't you stay home today? We told you to stay home,' Caine said.

Then Luke came out with something that surprised me. 'Your problem, Suzie, is you never let yourself trust anyone. You couldn't trust Gifford and you were right about that. But you didn't trust me, you don't trust Caine . . .' Here, Luke slid another look at Caine as if that was okay because I'd dumped him. Caine's mask was set like concrete now. Luke continued. 'But Suzie, we have to trust Caine. We cannot do this on our own.'

I was gawping. 'You attack me like this, just after you've said I should be nice?'

'You're the prickliest woman I've ever met! Believe me,' he told Caine, whose mask turned rueful. 'The only thing you have going for you, Suzie, is that your kids are great kids, and they must be that way because of how you are as a mother.'

A terrible wave of fear rose in me that I was a dreadful person, not worthy of my kids — I choked it down. I was the only mother they had. If I was confusing and prickly, that was because at least one of these men was not telling me all he knew, and they both wanted me to go home, sit down and wait.

I stood up and faced them. 'I'm right not to trust Gifford. I think Gifford is the one who ransacked my house, to get me out of it that night.' Luke scowled as if he believed me right away. Caine's face was that damn mask. I found it hard to put my suspicions into sensible sentences but told the men what insignificant little bits and pieces set my intuition going — that

Gifford would have had opportunity to steal Jarret's keys and measure up my kitchen. Why, I had no idea. That the safe custody key must have been sent to Gifford in error by that foolish new assistant to my mother's lawyer. That he had delivered my mother's key to me on Monday afternoon. He'd implied he had handed it to Jarret, but Jarret had not mentioned it and, now I thought about it, Gifford had seemed uneasy when I was in that Italian restaurant with him — nervous — even deeply scared, perhaps. Unlike him.

What I did not say was that I remembered how swiftly Caine had suggested the kids and I go to stay at his house.

Caine, broad-shouldered, studied me through the eyes in his detective mask. I lost my temper. 'Caine, if I'm going to trust you, you have to trust me too and tell me what's going on. Are you on this case or not?'

There was a small boy in those eyes. Luke watched him, hands thrust into the big pockets of his jacket and seemed about to speak, but Caine sat down on Katherine Tiller's chair, clasped his hands on the table and sighed.

'There is the personal factor in this current situation — that's you and me.'

'Past tense,' Luke said in a flash.

Caine ignored this. 'I doubt anyone knows all the facts at this point.'

Luke hunched his shoulders, scowling. 'Then you're not much use to us, mate.'

Caine ignored him again. 'Suzie, the police haven't been looking for your sister. She is an adult and has every right to disappear if she wishes. Many adults get fed up with their lives and just take off, to new lovers, new careers, they go overseas, go live in caves, whatever. I can see the attraction.' He held up the newsletter. 'But I'll check this out, see if either Maisie or Katherine has been reported missing. Hmmm — your sister's card was found near where the woman in the morgue was found. Near Katherine Tiller, now you say. As far as I know, that woman still hasn't been officially identified.' He rubbed his crooked nose (I noted that he'd found the time to shave). 'The main task, as I see it right now, is twofold.'

Damn. Why couldn't it be onefold?

Caine shook his head as if he heard my thought but chose not to rebuke me, wise man. 'One: work out who would benefit from kidnapping or concealing your children. Two: work out where they would be hidden.'

My hands twisted into a knot (it hurt, so I carefully untangled them). 'They might be concealing themselves.'

'True. The children are on my list of suspects. Why would they benefit from hiding?'

I looked at him as he said this, at the man and little boy behind the mask. Something stuck inside my throat. If only I could trust this man who'd said he wanted to marry me, have kids with me.

'There is no reason I can think of, why Tilda and Jarret would hide from me,' I whispered.

'There is,' Caine said. 'I know your kids.' He included Luke in this, something I found generous. 'Your kids would hide if they thought it would help you, Suzie.'

We're okay. You're safest not to look for us. Stay calm. It was difficult to speak — what lodged in my throat was companion to anger.

'Okay. Luke, Suzie,' continued Caine, 'where would they go to hide?'

'Kids sometimes run away from home for silly reasons . . .' Luke began.

Maternal instinct threw me to my feet. 'Excuse me! A burglary that wasn't a burglary, a dead person in the pantry, an unexplained new kitchen. The kids must have picked up on something and got scared.'

Luke knew about Jarret's note — and if he hadn't told Caine, he still lugged around a passel of mistrust, despite his lecture to me. Lack of trust may have been my most besetting character flaw. Too much trust had also been a flaw. I yo-yoed between these extremes, and each became stupid.

'I'll check out Maisie and Katherine, and their addresses,' Caine repeated. 'If one of them does indeed own a Samoyed, it'll be a very good clue. Brave girl, Suzie. Go home.'

Did I give the man a glare. He looked a tad ashamed.

'Luke, go with her.'

'Me?' Luke thickened up his eyebrows. 'Okay. What then?'

So very collegial. The guys stepped around the office and took a look at this and that, doing some guy-stuff planning. I did not want to go home. I knew I had to see the doctor and get my hand attended to, or I'd be even less use to the kids. I also wanted to find out what was what. As I lowered my head to think, I saw the envelope, still on the desk where I'd dropped it . . . Why had the Oriental man-in-suit delivered it so hand-on-heartfelt? And he went upstairs in the elevator — but the sign said 'out of order'.

Luke and Caine were peering through the window, at the phone books down in the alley. Should I open the envelope? Awkwardly but quietly, I did. It was a photograph in bubble wrap. My guess was it would be publicity for a group of Elvis imperson-ators from somewhere like Sarawak. But I folded back the wrap and found a photo of Tilda and Jarret. They were at the park near home, Tilda leaning on her brother's shoulder. She wore a sweater I'd stuffed in a charity bin a few weeks back. Jarret glowered as if he'd like to punch the camera. My fingers trembled so hard I could hardly turn the picture to see if there was a note written on the back. There wasn't.

I checked the envelope again and found a blue square of paper tucked inside. In neat capitals was written PLESE TAKE NO ACTION IF YOU WANT TO SEE YOUR DEAR CHILDREN. TELL NOBODY ABOUT THIS PLESE.

A dire warning with yet another *PLESE*?

'Ahem,' I said to get Caine and Luke's attention. 'I am going to find the bathroom.' Not waiting to hear objections I ran out of Suite Three and tiptoed quickly up the stairwell.

That photograph, delivered today to my own hands, right in my sister's office, was proof at last that the mystery about Philippa was linked to the one about Tilda and Jarret. Caine's still unexplained snooping at my sister's house (before I kotched him) was proof that he knew more than he had told me. Luke's partial trust of Caine meant Luke was just a good guy. Anger with Caine rode on my fear and sent me to the topmost floor of this narrow, dingy building. Guess what? I didn't find anything. No men-in-suits. Plenty of locked doors, but no clues about which one to try and jemmy. I sat on the top landing to catch my breath and trawl for any remaining logic in my brain.

Caine was right about the kids. I should figure out where they might have gone. I tried to put myself inside my children's heads. Parents don't do this enough because it's scary. Besides, kids hate it. They can't bear to be second-guessed. They forget that you were once a kid yourself.

What I found inside Jarret's head was: his father was a louse when it came to keeping contact with his son, Jarret had built up a secret relationship with Luke, and Jarret had also been made a contender for the Moynahan Cup whereas I'd thought he was in dire trouble. This made me inadequate as a mother. I wondered if he'd ever told Luke about the way I underestimated him. I didn't think so. Jarret was a loyal boy. I found inside my son's head that loyalty hurts badly and makes a boy confused.

I found inside his head that he would protect his little sister at any cost.

What did I find in Tilda's head? She was game for anything. She was practical and loving, and looked out for number one. She adored her big brother, and liked her comfort too. She would not like to be anywhere without a TV set. She would still be in her ballet clothes, and I had one of her sneakers in my bag.

Yes, Caine was right, and in any case my children had left that note: they were hiding to protect me. The little toads. So — this meant the Oriental man-in-suit was on my side, on the kids' side. Or was this a new development, and the kids might not be hiding any more, but truly kidnapped?

I was swimming in red herrings. There must be one key piece that would unlock this puzzle. That piece could be Roger having an affair with Lara. However, Lara's disguise might mean they were trying to fool someone that Philippa was safely home. Why would Lara and Roger do that? Was dear lumbersome beslippered Brick in with them on this subterfuge, whatever its purpose might be?

What drives people into crime, I wondered? I came up with: money, status, power. Surely Lara and Brick had all three already. Roger and Philippa might not.

I switched from this lane of thought to another of those mean streets. Who would think they would get money by stealing my kids — if they were stolen? Only someone who knew I was about to find big wads of money and US bonds along with cartons of gold coin in my safe deposit box. This made no sense, because if that person — i.e. Gifford — slipped me the second key to help me find the money, he could have simply used the key himself . . . But no. The mystery key-giver could not have forged my signature to get hold of the money. Well — maybe *she* could have, were it a she, but what *he* could get away with signing Suzie? And if the kids had been kidnapped, nobody had blackmailed me yet. I'd merely been warned three times, twice with a *plese*, to do nothing. But that might be because I'd been playing hard to get, running around town instead of staying home as most mothers would if they had missing kids.

Maybe I hadn't been playing fair. Although Roger had stowed me in that basement — a dead woman's basement. He must have been feeding the dog! If so, he may have known Katherine was dead, but he was nice to animals. For crying out loud.

Now: who would know my mother had left me all that money?

On the evidence I'd seen, the only answer I came up with was: my mother and Gifford.

Who would have thought my kitchen joinery worth stealing? Dad. Maybe Mom. Gifford? What the heck could have been worth stealing about that joinery!

My parents had stuffed me up. Even after they were dead.

Was this chaos a result of my sisters finding out the joinery was worth stealing, because you can't keep secrets in families? *Strangest organisms on the planet, who needs families!*

Caine and Luke were now shouting for me in the stairwell. I should be going home as they instructed.

I unfolded that square of blue paper again to read its firm request: PLESE TAKE NO ACTION — TELL NOBODY ABOUT THIS PLESE.

I've always hated doing what I'm told, but there are times when it's best to pay attention.

chapter eighteen

The shouts faded as the men ran down the stairs instead of up. No doubt the Gang of Two would be off to my place hoping to corral me. I'd get myself home later. First, I'd go somewhere they wouldn't expect, somewhere quiet for a good coffee, lunch and a serious think.

You see, the other thing I'd realised — I'm slow, but I get there in the end — was that I was being watched, even anticipated. Why say an elevator is out of order if it isn't? To keep people away. You see a notice like that, know the office you want is more than two flights up, and you decide to come back when the elevator's fixed. The only people who trudge up will be those who are desperate. That Oriental man-in-suit had worked out precisely where and how to find me.

In the circumstances, Roger would hardly have reported his wife's car stolen so I tried not to imagine what would happen if a police car stopped me, and simply drove, letting the left brain-right brain fight it out. The conscious layer of my mind compiled a list of those

I should not trust. It proved to be extremely long and so I took another tack: was there anybody left whom I could trust?

Annie and Zoe.

Luke, possibly, though *possibly* implies not — I wasn't too sure about his trusting Caine.

Jarret and Tilda, to watch out for each other, wherever they might be.

My erratic flight across the city ended at the medical centre. They unwrapped my inflamed wound and tutted over it (those hairy black stitches made it look like something to be scraped off the road). It was cleaned and rebandaged. I was scolded for not coming in yesterday as advised (I did not tell them I had been detained in someone's basement in one of the plum suburbs), given a prescription for erythromycin for the infection and told to have it filled immediately at a pharmacy, which I did because indeed I was feeling feverish and odd. I took a tablet with a bite of muesli bar the chemist (nice lady) gave me, then drove and parked outside the store next to Thee Ultimate Café: a quiet coffee in the protection of a friend.

As usual, corner store customers were popping in and out of their cars. Bernard's van was right outside the restaurant. I looked at my hands and clothes, filthy from the stairwell though now at least I had a spotless bandage. Were I arriving at the café to work and the cockroach police arrived as well, Bernard would be given a big black mark or even have his hygiene certificate withdrawn. But I was just here for a coffee. Luckily, there were no other customers or they might have withdrawn too. There were no other staff in sight, either.

Bernard put down that wicked boning knife he'd been sharpening, covered it with one of those pretty pink checked tea towels and came to my table, several questions in his eyes and on his lips.

'Please can I use your phone?' I asked. 'And for lunch I'd like whatever will be the quickest boost of energy and brain power —

oh.' He had just picked up the notice *closed for private function*. 'My timing's off. I'd better disappear.'

'No problem, Suzie.' He put the sign on the door, smiled an apology to a passer-by who wanted to come in, and brought the phone to my table. He said he'd also bring latté and soup, and discreetly limped behind the counter.

The window I'd broken on Monday had a sheet of plywood nailed over it. Not mended yet? Bernard might be short of ready money. I broke the window, I should pay. I would offer.

I phoned Lara at Customs but she was in a meeting. Who was surprised? Not me. I called home, and left a message for the kids. I called Luke's mobile, told him where I was and not to worry, I'd be home within an hour.

A bowl of vegetable soup was put in front of me, with a side plate of Bernard's herb bread.

'Your leg is aching, I can tell. And you've given me extra Parmesan!' I started to weep.

Bernard handed me a second paper napkin. 'Stop or you'll dilute my soup. Tell me all about it, Suzie.'

This was such a nice person. He was always a little sweaty from the kitchen, but it was honest sweat and fuzz. Dressed up in a cream apron, he resembled a Santa skittle but his tubbiness was honest tub. His kindness tipped me further into tears before I was able to sip my soup. Bernard sat with a coffee while I recounted my bizarre week and my problems (of course not mentioning the money, because it was just a puzzle now). I told him how I hoped the kids were safe, hiding for some reasons of their own, I told him about the men in suits who plagued me and how one was merely a realtor. When I finished — I managed only seven sips of soup, one piece of herb bread — Bernard was quiet. I'd never seen him so still before. I'd never had him to myself like this before. There'd always been tables of customers, waiter-persons, deliveries.

After a moment, he leaned forward. 'You've been given a lot of ingredients, but no recipe. It seems to me you have three issues here. Three dishes, if you care to think of it that way. There's the mystery of your kids, and that's the most important. But I have a good feeling, they'll come home. You've done all you can, and now the hardest part is to wait.' He folded his hands into a ball. 'Then there is the mystery of your sister, and that comes second. But third, and maybe at the bottom of all this, is the secret of your mother — your parents.' He shook a finger under my nose. 'At the bottom of nearly every story is a deep dark family secret. Tell me I'm right.'

I had to laugh. 'My parents were as normal as anyone's. Mom and Dad, with deep dark secrets? That's ridiculous, apart from my being adopted, which is a shock, but not terrible because I know they loved me and that's what matters.' I still did not mention the money, nor the friend of Mom's I had discovered, the letter writer who talked about tolerance and black holes: how sad if it were a deep dark secret to possess an intelligent friend.

He raised his hands as if weighing packs of butter. 'Everybody has got something in their closet.' He let out a puff, a rueful sound and I thought he must be remembering his wife whom he had mourned these many years. His pouchy eyes were a sad kind blue. I'd not noticed the gentle niceness in them lately. I must have been too busy making muffins and arguing about Parmesan.

'So, Suzie — why do you think Philippa has displayed that Chinese coat? Did Caine break into Philippa's house especially to find it?' Bernard's gentle niceness had a clever edge. This man was on the ball.

'Mmm — he did seem to come straight up to her study.'

Bernard gave a friendly wave to a man who'd just come out from the corner store with a newspaper and a loaf of bread. 'Describe the coat. Anything unusual about it?'

It was Chinese. But that wouldn't be unusual in China. 'Coats are usually in wardrobes, or on people.'

'Not stapled into frames on study walls.'

'Probably Philippa simply likes it. She delights in expensive possessions.'

'But in her study? Not in the living room, or decorating the stairwell?'

Bernard was asking good questions. *Good questions* is what people say when they can't figure out the answers right away.

'What do you think?' I asked.

He shrugged. 'Good question.'

I nibbled more bread. Thee Ultimate Café was an oasis in the chaos of this week. How I'd have loved to sink down on a pile of cushions with a dish of dates, a jug of wine, and my kids watching television under an indoor palm.

'That coat . . .' I said.

'Go on.' Those blue eyes, the comforting pouches beneath them full of kindness.

'It was above her desk. Like — when you're studying something, you pin notes and documents where you can see them. It was pinned up, but not like an ornament. Pinned up like something to read.' I thought about the picture underneath it of the green block man while Bernard excused himself and went into the kitchen briefly to make a phone call. I heard him asking for Faludi. I hoped Faludi was over his asthma attack. I hoped I was not messing up Bernard's working hours. I may have had Krugerands in the bank and a big wad in my bag, but this man was working for a crust, and time was money.

'I'd better go. You have your private function any minute.' I pushed my chair back.

'Suzie, stay. Was there any note pinned up as well?'

I shook my head and picked up my bag.

'Nothing on the gown itself?'

'Embroidery. Little red fish. Maybe grasshoppers. Um — an embroidered fence? Could that be Chinese writing?'

Bernard's eyes pouched further. 'Embroidery. Symbols and signs. Sit down, there is plenty of time. These people might not even show, the way my luck has run lately. Let's buoy ourselves with a small brandy.'

I didn't want to hurt his feelings but a moment ago he had said I should go home and wait, now he was fetching glasses and a bottle.

'A marvellous people, wonderful country,' he said in that snow-plough growl. 'Did you know the earliest form of printing was in China? Four great inventions were instrumental in creating the modern world, Suzie. Paper, printing, gunpowder, and the compass. I would add soy sauce to that.' He poured two glasses and laughed as he relaxed. 'The earliest printed book is a collection of Buddhist texts called the *Diamond Sutra*, dated to 860-something, did you know?'

At once my brain wanted to throw up an argument: what about that clay disc they found in — Crete? — covered in little pictures. It may have been a calendar, a laundry list, or battle plan, whatever, but that was printing, about a thousand years before . . .

'Bernard, don't tempt me to stay. I have to go.'

His chin was in his hands. 'If Philippa is mixed up in something nefarious it must be to do with art. Your sister has a very competitive nature — listen to me, telling you about your own sister. I know she's fond of you, her little sister.'

Forgive me, but I let out an unlovely snort.

Bernard laughed again. 'She calls you headstrong. So you are, as well as being my favourite stand-in chef.' He sniffed the cognac but replaced it on the table. 'Do you suppose that robe might be worth a fortune? How I could use a fortune. I don't suppose you and I could sneak back there and fetch it?'

I laughed too as I stood up. The Chinese gown probably had the world's first written-down recipe for dim sum embroidered on its back. It would certainly fit how dim I was if this mystery were concerned with Eastern cooking. I kissed his fuzzy cheek. 'Bernard, does Gifford still owe you any money?'

'No, no. That's not a problem.'

'The boarded-up window doesn't look good, Bernard. I broke it, I will pay for it. Get it done and let me know how much.'

'Suzie. I will either renovate this place or burn it down for the insurance.' He laughed again but his eyes didn't crinkle. 'So, please forget the broken window.'

As I ran out he took up one of the two full glasses still in front of him and toasted me to wish me luck.

chapter nineteen

One small mystery was solved at any rate. I knew why Bernard had a high staff turnover — his dissertations on the *this and that* of history. I also knew why he had a cash flow problem — too much time talking, not enough attracting customers.

But he was right. There seemed three mysteries to solve, when one would be more than plenty. I headed for my suburb. Bernard was right about waiting, too. How hard it was, not knowing anything for sure, just filling in each second with hopes and perhaps-es, with remembering little things about my children. How Jarret looked like a pug dog when he was born, how for his first six months he snuffled through a nose that had been seriously flattened during his arduous journey into this world. He had stopped and started, stopped again, at one point even seemed to decide to back up again into the safety of the dark rather than keep coming towards the bright light at the end of the tunnel. I didn't mind his birth taking so long. My child was on his way and I was doing all I could. When he finally emerged with a hustle and slither, and the doctor picked him up and put this tiny stubborn creature on my stomach, I drew a breath of purest joy. On its out-rush I exclaimed how wonderful, when could I do it all again? 'That's not the usual reaction,' said a nurse who sounded close to disapproval. *He's not a usual child, because he is mine, mine, mine*, I thought but kept it to myself. And Tilda — I remembered what she was like at two years old if she spotted a bulldozer or digger, how she'd leap in circles with excitement, her fingers clutching at the air like small explosions. If I went home now, there was nothing to stop me remembering all that and more, and if the kids weren't there I did not think I could bear it.

I opened the door and dived at the answerphone as fast as the quick brown fox: messages from Lara, Annie, Luke, Gifford's mother, and a man who growled *dammit, wrong number*. My note to the kids was still on the hall table . . . but now it was under Tilda's music box. Someone had moved Tilda's second most precious thing from her bedroom.

My chest hurt as if steel butterflies spun round in me. My good hand refused to work, it took an age to unfold the note. There were no extra words written there, but something had been added, a drawing of — what was it? A baby in swaddling clothes? A squashed cockroach? The Asian long-horned beetle? Whatever it was, it was from Jarret. I forgave him for not being an artist, though swore at him in my head for being cryptic. I picked up the music box and opened it. The ballerina inside let out her ting! and started to revolve. I slammed the lid down on her fast.

I did not cry.

The house was stuffy so I left the front door open. The cordless phone is such a treasure — thanking the name of progress that we no longer rely on smoke signals to communicate, I carried it into the kitchen, began to make another coffee, then was brave enough to return Gifford's mother's call and ask if she'd heard anything about or from the kids. She hadn't. Though she was still charming, the melody of her voice was somewhat plangent. She offered to come and give me support, to get hold of Gifford. I said I had no wish to see her son. She replied, she could not blame me. I found this sympathy and understanding very scary.

I called Annie to give her an update as I'd promised and also let her know I'd buy her a new pair of trousers. She said I should talk to Lara, remind her she was a government employee and therefore had to be squeakier clean than anyone else, as Lara should know, having had that trouble with Brick and his security systems. An affair between someone in Lara's position and an ex-dentist might not make the front pages of the paper. Nonetheless, a threat to expose an affair with an ex-dentist brother-in-law could make my older sister more obliging.

'You mean blackmail her?' I asked Annie.

'A little blackmail is common in most families,' Annie said. 'Make her pull strings.'

What strings? Any, I guessed. Besides the person in charge of mysteries usually has some expert to get in touch with, someone who can track important information. By default, I was in charge. Lara was the obvious person for this other crucial role.

The breeze came right through the front door, down the hall and round the corner to the kitchen. I opened the window to let it out again and dialled Lara's work number. 'She's always in a meeting!' I cried to her secretary. 'This is her sister!'

Know what? I was put through at once.

When Lara is bossy, she snarls like a cat. 'Where have you been! I've been trying to get hold of you since Tuesday.'

'Roger drugged . . .'

'What were you doing in Philippa's wardrobe? With that policeman! No, don't say anything right now. Tell me where you are at once.'

'Shut up and listen,' I said. 'Oh sorry. Lara, please listen. Now this is what you do for me. You get onto your sidekicks in the

States, and find out all you can about the Quinters and the Hurrens.'

'The *who*? Suzie, I can't use official . . .'

'Philippa may have known I'm not your sister, and . . .'

'What!'

As swiftly and succinctly as I could, I explained. Our peculiarly opaque family background. The birth certificates. The fact that Roger helped interpret those blood tests for Luke and me. Dead bodies here and there. And how sure I was that Roger knew — or feared — something about my missing children and that he had put me in that basement just after I'd seen him with Lara herself, so she'd better watch it as she was on my list of very suspicious relatives. 'Lara, I don't know how or even if it all ties up. But please get on to this at once. Or else. Maybe murder. Again.'

Her silence ended with that sort of swallow that means someone's stumped for what to say. 'Oh God. This whole thing's gone so far. I've missed out on the damned job largely because of family interference, I may as well go the whole hog. Fuck protocol.' The duchess had said the 'f' word! 'But Suzie, this will take time, and . . .'

'Are you having an affair with Roger?'

'Must I dignify that with an answer?'

'Then what were you doing in Philippa's hat, with Roger, in their bedroom?'

'He . . .' She lowered her voice. 'That's what I have to talk to you about. A ransom note. Take a moment to think about it, Suzie. Just think. Don't say a word.'

When did a little sister ever do what she's told at once? 'You mean that Philippa's been . . .'

'Shut up!' she cried in her turn.

This felt just like old times.

So I was right. That blue ransom note had told Roger not to have the police involved. He was trying to pretend his wife was still around . . . but why did he drug me? 'Lara, he must know Katherine is dead. He stashed me in her junk room. He fed the Samoyed!'

Big sister frustration seethed along the phone line. 'Suzie, we can't talk about this while I'm at work. Are you at home? Stay there. I'll come right now.'

'The kids,' I said. 'Is this to do with them?'

Down the phone came a noise I'd rather not have heard. A possible confirmation kind of noise. Lara being who she is, she said it aloud as well. 'I don't see how. But it doesn't look good. I'll get in touch with a State-side contact, then I'm on my way. And Suzie! Don't talk to anyone about anything till I get there!'

I banged the phone back in its holder on the hall table. I had every intention of waiting for my sister. Cross my heart.

A man in a suit — tall, bronzed, sleek (that's the man — the suit was pinstripe) — was coming in the front gate. I should have kept my door shut.

'Five minutes of your time?' His teeth were American white and spoke of expensive orthodontics.

'Let me guess. You're FBI.'

His eyes turned guarded.

'The mafia?'

Now he took a nervous sidestep. Some women do that to a man.

'Whatever,' I said. 'My house is not for sale. I have enough insurance, thank you. I don't have time to participate in a survey about cellphones. I gave to Greenpeace last month.'

He recovered somewhat. 'Ms Emmett, I'm here in person . . .'

'You know my name?' This made my skin creep. I would pretend I had to go out, and just drive around and around the block till he had gone. I stepped back inside to heft my bag, hopped out onto the veranda and began to lock my door. 'Please, excuse me.'

'It would be no problem to give you a lift,' he said.

A tremor happened in my stomach. This guy knew who I was, and knew my rusty heap wasn't parked outside. But he didn't know I'd nicked my sister's Mazda.

'A lift would be so kind!' I preceded him down my steps, past yet another chewed back-end of mouse (I apologised yet again to ill-fed Nameless). I waved and smiled at the students' house, not that I saw anyone at their windows but there was no harm in misdirection. Pretending to fumble in my bag, I had Philippa's key ready while the man-in-suit went to open the passenger door of his big car. I scooted sideways, tried to open Philippa's door but dropped the key. The guy darted round and took my arm, right on the bruise. I shrieked, he dropped back and apologised, saying again all he wanted was some minutes of my time. I told him to back off. Just then, in this quiet suburban street in the early afternoon, Gifford's four-wheel drive came roaring up. The man cursed. Under his jacket, I saw a holster and a gun. It wasn't a Glock, that's all I can say about that.

Never had I been so happy to see my ex-husband, to know his mother must have phoned him up and scolded . . . on top of that joy was a flash of fear that this white-toothed guy and Gifford were in cahoots. I prepared to shriek again. But Gifford stepped out of the Pajero at his leisure. The guy pulled his jacket straight, raised one hand in a pacifying wave, slipped into his sedan, and drove away. He was a good actor, so natural, so much at ease.

I scooped up Philippa's car key and watched Gifford mosey towards me.

That charming look, those piercing eyes — that undertone of fear that made his hairline seem to creep backwards. 'Girl, let me apologise. I can't forgive myself. My mother says the children are still missing. I had no idea it was so serious.'

For a splinter of a second I felt the tug I'd felt on Monday evening, the sorrowful chemistry of first love from long ago. In the next splinter, rage punched through me. He'd said the kids were safe when they were not! He'd lied about what mattered to me most.

In the third splinter I warned myself, be cautious. Inside my head was like a little train set: ideas shot off in one direction, made a connection, shot back along another track. The guy with the white teeth and the gun was proof that I'd been foolish not to accept protection from the broad shoulders of Caine and from Luke's scary eyebrows. But at the sight of Gifford, that man-in-suit had fled in his dark sedan. Okay, my big sister had warned me not to speak to anyone, but Gifford was my son's father. Family had to count for something.

But till I heard the kids' stories, I wouldn't know for sure who was on my side. Besides, though it had been helpful to keep myself afloat with fanciful parallels to a thriller, real life did not pan out so neatly. In thrillers there was serial murder, and serial murder in a thriller is most usually of young women with blonde hair and cute figures. I'm not saying the middle-aged women I had seen dead would not be cute to some, but you see what I mean. Ordinary middle class middle-aged women had been killed. Somehow — in consequence? — my kids had gone into hiding. There were men with guns around. There was sneaking, snooping, drugging, and I was scared to the pit of my stomach. As far as I could judge, family counted for a big fat zero.

But there is always a place for good manners. Good manners are disarming, I'd learnt that at least from this charming and disarming ex-husband. 'Of course you may apologise, Gifford.'

He was disarmingly polite also. 'So, girl, I'd like to treat you. Let's drive out somewhere special.' His cellphone was in his hands.

'I'm supposed to stay and wait for Lara.'

A shift in his eyes told me caution was an excellent neon sign to be aware of. 'A quick coffee here, then?'

I smiled as if he'd won me at a fun fair. He smiled too. People's smiles go the extra distance when they're relieved.

'Where's your car?' he asked as I turned back towards the house.

I made gestures that meant *mechanical breakdown, don't ask me, I'm female*, then I unlocked the door again and signalled for him to enter first. As I saw Tilda's music box on the hall-stand again, I realised what the squashed baby drawing meant.

The wind turned chill as I hesitated. Beth emerged from her house and started curb-walking with her skateboard. She waved. I waved too and offered thanks to the angel who looks over mothers. Taking care to wear a smile that went the extra distance, I pointed for Gifford to go through into the kitchen and faked a need to say a word to my young neighbour. Gifford offered to relieve me of my bag, even began to take it from me but I said it was no problem. He lingered in the hallway, watching me.

When I reached the street, I dived towards Philippa's car. This time I handled the key right, and was inside it with the doors locked before Gifford tried to wrench open the passenger side. I took my time to get the key in the ignition while he beat upon the hood. Then I was away.

part four

PROUD FLESH

chapter twenty

Not a squashed or swaddled baby — Jarret had done his best to draw a ballet shoe. This boy trusted me. Not only that, his cryptic note indicated he believed in my intelligence (we won't quibble about words right now). My excitement was partly pride, but also fear. He trusted nobody but me. My kids knew there was danger and didn't want to confide in their aunts or uncles, or in Caine. I'd been right to staple that detective to a pallet. I was right to duck away from Philippa's office . . . but on a cold breath I realised this could also mean the kids did not trust Luke.

Dead leaves blustered in front of the car and I nearly bowled an old man at a crossing. I stamped on the brakes, waved an apology to his displeased face and to the critical bystanders, then was off again, tyres squealing. As I'd learnt to do this week, when I reached the ballet school I drove on around the corner. I still had Philippa's beanie, and tugged it on before I left the car. It was much the worse for the whanging I'd given it, but should not attract attention. Though the sun was out, the wind was even cooler now. An arch of black cloud reared up in the south.

The beanie made me feel tougher than I was as I approached the entrance where Madame always had a wrestle with her keys. It was early afternoon and so the door was locked. I strolled along the broken asphalt driveway at the side (so carefree, such a performer!), past the kitchen door, which was also locked, searching for the low trapdoor where stage crew slide in planks, rostra, all the gear of a production. This hall was close to shops (the crucial takeaways), the little den under the stage had an old black and white TV. If you were a kid and decided you must hide, it would serve your basic needs.

As I crossed a patch of long grass and dandelions there was a soft bump from the hall, as if someone had moved inside. I mustn't scare the kids — how to let them realise it was me?

A song. There was one song that would serve, our family song. If anyone heard, they'd think I was stark raving.

My voice was quivery and tuneless, as usual. As I ended the second line of the chorus and stamped my foot three times, the way Tilda, Jarret and I always did for emphasis, the trapdoor creaked open a tad. I glimpsed a grubby hand: the trap eased shut. My heart felt as if would fall apart with fright and relief but I worked at looking casual. The beanie still helped. I sat on the asphalt path, and pushed the trap. There seemed to be a drop of about a metre.

It was like posting myself through a mail slot. I thumped to the floor and the trapdoor closed with a bang. It was dark. There was a short pause, a gasp from the darkest corner, then even in the gloom I recognised the shape that hurled towards me. Tilda!

I wrapped my arms around her and exploded with sobs. Tilda howled too, her firm body hot and shaking as she soaked my shoulder with tears. Jarret approached more slowly.

'You should have stayed away. Mum, you weren't supposed to come here.' His voice was choked.

Then his arms were around me too. I hugged both kids at once, one at a time, then both again. I wished my arms were twice as long to wrap them to me harder. I held them tighter than was possible, stroked my children, kissed them, sniffed them, hugged them again. There was 'Tilda!' and 'Jarret!' and 'Mum!' then 'Ouch! Sorry, it's okay,' from me because of my hand. I rubbed their shoulders, arms, I patted their heads, touched their wonderful faces. My eyes grew more used to the gloom and I saw how grimy both kids were. I'd already noted how unwashed they smelled. As if it mattered. They were here. I was with them. We were three.

There was a battered sofa to sit on, me in the middle and the kids on either side. I didn't think Jarret wanted to be hugged any more, but I was pleased he sat so close. Tilda leaned against me. Even on this lumpy sofa, a steel spring doing its best to pierce my thigh, I felt more physically contented than I had in months. Yes, months. Since — I didn't know, I had to think about that. But I wasn't complete without my kids, without knowing their marvellous shapes filled the right-sized parts of the world, the parts that were Tilda and Jarret. They were my detachable limbs. If that sounds weird, what do I care? It's said that a woman either loves her man completely or devotes herself more fully to her children. If that's right, then I'm for my kids. I would hope some women can do it differently, love the man in their lives as completely as their kids, but for me it had always been the kids. Maybe men sensed this, and that was why I had such pit-bottom luck with romance. Maybe that's why I'd been so unhappy lately (that is, for years) because I'd been hoping I could do it the other way, find a man to whom I could devote myself with a whole heart. Maybe I'd been hoping I would come upon a man who could devote himself with a full heart to me and to the kids. These were strange thoughts to have stirring in my head at such a time.

For a while, we were content to sit in the gloom on the lumpy sofa, side by side by side.

Tilda, of course, was first to chatter. 'Jarret knew you'd work it out, Mum.'

I glanced at Jarret. 'I've figured it out?'

He hiked one leg up on what used to be a cushion but now resembled something chewed by circus animals. 'You figured out where we were, but you probably don't know why we're hiding. We have to stay here, Mum. You have to go.'

'But you drew the ballet shoe.'

'Only so you'd guess, so you wouldn't worry. I knew you'd be worrying, Mum. And, shit, you should!'

This may have been too early after our reunion to give him The Look, but it arrived unsummoned. He gave a lop-sided grin.

'Because Caine is not a good guy,' piped up Tilda. 'Caine has got Aunt Philippa.'

'He — Caine? Has kidnapped Philippa?'

'Shut up, Tilda. I'll explain.' Jarret looked much older than his fifteen years, tense, drawn, like a child in wartime.

Tilda huffed but crossed her arms and leaned back hard on my shoulder. Their relationship was still all give and take — give stick and take no nonsense. How I loved them.

As suits a boy who pretends to occasional monosyllabism, Jarret was succinct as he took me through the points. He'd heard Roger and Philippa arguing about money the day he scrubbed their patio, and noticed how Caine showed particular interest in this aunt and uncle. He'd noticed how Caine showed interest in my bank balance and the value and condition of the house. He too had noticed how swiftly Caine organised to shift us over to his place on Monday afternoon.

'Jarret, all those things could be natural and caring. He's my boyfriend, after all. At least, he was my — okay, go on.'

'Then when we were at his place and you went out, I snooped.'

'Jarret is very cool at snooping,' Tilda said. 'But I watched TV.'

'Shut up,' repeated Jarret. 'Caine had a file of stuff on Auntie Philippa's office, some stuff on Uncle Roger. And other stuff.' He turned dark and silent on it. When a boy turns dark, you wait. He finally added, 'Some stuff was about my father.'

'Well, Jarret . . .' How could I say the words — *Caine's a policeman and his job is to investigate people like your devious, erratic dad?* I couldn't say that to Gifford's son. I also thought it odd that a policeman would have files like that at home. What had happened to discretion and security?

Jarret was my son too, and big on intuition. He batted my arm. 'I've always known my father is a louse. What I didn't know for sure is that Caine's a louse as well, though I suspected it.'

A peculiar feeling coiled inside my stomach. Okay, I hadn't been sure I could trust the ace detective — but he'd said he'd like to marry me, have three more kids with me if the first two turned out okay . . .

'Caine and Gifford want to get money.' Tilda was at her most matter of fact. 'That's what everything's always about.'

'Plus,' Jarret said, and I knew this would be the clincher, 'plus, Mum, after I'd started snooping at Caine's, the phone went and I answered it.'

Tilda was approving. 'He answered in Caine's voice.'

'The person on the phone thought you were Caine?'

'It was the louse!' cried Tilda.

Even in the poor light, I saw how hard this was for Jarret.

'I recognised his voice, Mum. I let him talk. He said Philippa was tucked up out of the way, and Caine better make sure Tilda and me stayed safe as well. And he laughed in a way that meant nobody was safe as far as he was personally concerned.' This was a long sentence, spoken in a way I might do myself. I was impressed and touched. 'He said, all Caine had to do was keep you away, Mum, and it would be okay, and of course Caine knew what to do in the circumstances. And in Caine's voice I said, "You bet, mate," and the louse said . . .' The boy broke off for a moment. 'You've never made a will, have you, Mum? No. So if you . . .' He cleared his throat. 'Well, that means Tilda and me inherit everything. Then if Tilda

— you know — if it's just me left, and I die, the louse would get the lot.'

'But I haven't got anything worth . . .' I took in a shuddering breath and was glad I was already sitting down. Because there was a very goodly inheritance, some of it even here in my capacious bag, far more than the twenty dollars and seven parking tickets I'd started with on Monday morning. As the significance of what Jarret had discovered found its way into my head I felt the blood rush through my body. 'Gifford said this over the phone, to Caine?'

'That's what he meant,' Jarret whispered. 'He said it was all figured out and Caine knew what he had to do.'

'So. That's why you ran.' I pictured my kids on the run. It's a hard thing for a mother to do. I swallowed. 'So you left the first note on . . . which day was it? Tuesday.'

'I snuck in and out fast on Tuesday. And last night too when it was dark.'

'Did you see anyone? Anything?'

Jarret shook his head. 'Lie low, keep quiet. That's the way. See, there's no point in Caine and — *him* — doing anything till they have the three of us together. So they can make sure . . .'

That I died first. They say your head reels at such moments. I don't know what mine did but my eyes stopped working for a moment.

'There's someone else involved,' Jarret added. 'Dad didn't say who, like he was teasing Caine about it.'

A Mister Big. Well, naturally. 'What about Luke? Why didn't you guys tell Luke? Is Luke the Mister Big?'

Even before that thought was fully voiced, the kids both gave me old-fashioned looks. 'We don't want Luke mixed up in this,' they said more or less in unison.

As if a machine had turned on inside my bones I started to shake. 'But why have they kidnapped Philippa? What has it got to do with our kitchen cupboards?'

'Huh?' From Jarret.

'Our cupboard doors were stolen. We got new ones.'

'Last time you blamed us,' Jarret said. Tilda accused me with a downturn of her mouth.

'I'm sorry . . .'

'We didn't mean to break that door,' said Tilda over me, 'but you didn't have to yell.'

For a second or two I rested, then started again. 'You didn't go into the kitchen today? Or on Tuesday?'

The kids glanced at each other as if I'd gone nuts. Of course Jarret hadn't gone into the . . . he'd have felt guilty seeing the mess he thought would still be there and for not tidying up.

It started to come together inside my head. My father had built those cupboards with sweaty curling of his hair and a damp moustache. Mom had slammed around, then retreated to her raggedy cigarettes. Dad must have hidden something in them.

What peculiar behaviour for my father. Why would he do that, if it could somehow be tied up with his grandchildren being murdered — but if Mom and Dad had adopted me, these weren't their genuine grandkids. How dare that pair put my children into this situation with their hidden pasts, concealed money, false birth certificate! However, my head also buzzed with disbelief that so-called-Dad who teased me with boring stories, so-called-Mom who had protected me from the worst behaviour of my older sisters, could have put my kids in danger. This jigsaw did not fit.

Tilda leaned on me again. 'Mum, I'm tired of hiding from the louse. Mum — I'm scared.'

All this talk about the louse — though it was too dark to see the state of Tilda's hair, I stole a look. Some aspects of being a mother never leave, no matter how desperate the situation. 'This is a good hiding place.' My voice quivered. 'I bet you snuck out during ballet, to watch the other classes.'

'Jarret said we should stay hidden but I couldn't help myself.'

Tilda gave the faintest chuckle. She was to be the fairy godmother: I had to keep pretending I didn't know. I had to believe this adventure would end, the danger would be over, that she would appear on stage in a few weeks, a star of comic timing.

'You have a creative spark,' I said, 'and it's crucial to keep it burning.'

'Right,' she said, with a quiver that showed she had hope for the future. Briefly I closed my eyes and simply held her.

'Mum.' Jarret nudged me. 'You'd better go.'

If we drove down to Central immediately, surely we'd reveal the clay feet of the ace detective. Tears filled my heart, my belly. 'We'll all go to the police right now.'

Jarret hesitated, but we agreed to move as fast as possible. The kids shoved their bits and piece into their bags — *Hello Kitty*, Jarret's school bag, the bag with his stuff for the Moynahan Cup. I didn't feel like unmailing myself through the trapdoor so the kids showed me a safe route over the stage props and we scrambled to the narrow stairway that led up to the auditorium.

The door into the hall was closed. We thought it was still too early for lessons, but listened to make sure. Madame would be alarmed if we scampered out into the middle of a tinies' class. We creaked the door open. The hall was empty. As we stepped into it, Jarret and Tilda sighed like travellers near the end of a journey. Tilda tiptoed in her ballet shoes. In the maze of sun from the skylights, her hair was surprisingly glossy though both kids were even grubbier than I had thought after their time beneath the stage. The ballet cardigan had an overlay of grey, and the ballet slippers were also far from pink. Their grimy state would help prove the tale we would soon tell.

I stopped in the middle of the hall. 'Oh, Jarret. I heard about the contender thing. I'm sorry I got it wrong. You should have told me. I am so proud.'

He shrugged *de nada*. My boy.

The front door of the hall rattled.

'Madame!' Tilda said.

'Use the side door,' Jarret whispered.

We scuttled into the small kitchen, unbolted the outside door and threw it open. Tilda screamed. Gifford stood there, pale and sweating though the wind was icy cold.

But Madame would appear any second and sort Gifford out, quick-smart. I grabbed Tilda's hand and we backed into the hall again, to the shafty maze of sun. I wanted to hug Jarret to my side but even at a time like this you don't do that to a boy. I glanced at him, and saw he knew I loved him. We also, both of us, knew love was not much help when a boy was confronted with a louse who would do anything for money and had murder on his mind.

Those blue eyes desperate and exhausted, Gifford entered through the kitchen and propped against the doorway into the hall. 'Oh girl, you've made it difficult.'

'Gifford,' I said, 'before you get carted off to a nasty interview room — which will happen shortly after Madame manages that lock — do the minimum and say sorry to your son.'

'For crying out loud, girl, will you hush?' Gifford said. 'If you could have stayed still for one moment!'

Jarret's face showed a mixture of feelings, one of which was wariness. 'How did you know to find us here?'

Why hadn't I thought to ask that?

Gifford's mouth twitched with grim humour. 'Look in your bag, Suzie.'

I took out his cellphone. It was turned on.

'That's not fair,' Tilda said.

I hurled the damned thing at Gifford. He caught it, turned it off and still blocked the way out through the kitchen.

'It took a long time till you gave a clue where you were hiding. It'll cost me a fortune.' With a sick little laugh Gifford shoved the phone into his pants pocket. The door was still rattling.

'Madame!' I shouted.

'Hush, girl. Sneak out this way with . . .'

'Hurry up, Madame!' I screamed.

'Oh, Jesus!' Gifford said.

How stupid he was being. There was no way Gifford could control a fifteen-year-old boy, a seven-year-old, as well as two grown women one of whom, though small and elderly, could do high kicks.

The door stopped rattling. Tilda broke from me and tried to run past Gifford but he grabbed her. She booted him with no effect.

'Mum's right,' she cried. 'I should wear my proper shoes if I'm not at ballet.'

'Let her go, you fucker!' Jarret yelled.

I heard Madame enter that side door at last — but her gait was heavier than usual, as if she had more feet than one dainty woman should. My children stiffened.

'It's okay,' I said, 'it's just . . .' Before I said *Madame*, I glimpsed a man-in-suit with others, also suited. 'Oh, kids, we're safe. Here's the vicar and . . .'

How wrong I was. Again.

chapter twenty-one

It was no special surprise that on a quiet suburban afternoon at the side of a church hall, in the first drops of rain, three Asian men in suits, holding guns, could easily persuade two children and a woman with only one working opposable thumb into an unmarked white van with no side windows. The shock was that they also, at gunpoint, persuaded Gifford into the van (once again all I can say is these were not Glocks). Was Gifford secretly a good guy? I didn't think so. I thought there was double-crossing going on — or even triple. They searched Gifford for his cellphone but didn't find it. Furious and frightened, he said he dropped it in the hall.

A gun held to Tilda's head encouraged us to keep silent as we drove. Rain pelted the outside of the van. My daughter looked terrified in the gloom, but also outraged. How I loved her. How I loved Jarret for the tension in his young shoulders. How I felt twisted up inside with terror. I tried to catch Gifford's eye, ask what to do. He lowered his head as if there were no way things could have been done differently.

The van bumped to a halt, rain battering its roof. A garage

door rumbled, the van jerked forward and stopped, as did the rain. The rumble came again. The side door of the van thundered open and we were tumbled into the gloom of a closed area with doors leading off it. A storage area.

'We don't want to hurt your children,' said the leading man-in-suit. 'However, many times it happens that for the sake of a higher purpose we must do what we don't like. You comprehend?'

I did, especially when he subtly indicated a heap beside one of the doors. It was yet another guy-in-suit with soft tan skin, the guy who, hands on heart, had slipped me the polite note back in Suite Three. His shirt was no longer laundry-fresh but ruined with a blotch of seeping red. I guessed he hadn't been killed for his bad spelling. I also guessed that he was the one who'd left the business card at the scene where Katherine's body had been dumped, that he may have been a good bad guy who hadn't liked how events had started to develop. I kept myself between this sight and Tilda. Jarret, his face as white as paper, did so too.

At such climax points, villains are meant to put the good guys in separate rooms so they can't swap *what-nexts, what-ifs* and *can-we's*. These villains knew the score. They bustled us through into a short corridor, Gifford was shoved into one small unappealing room, me in the next, with no time to protest. As the door slammed I caught Jarret's look of fear, Tilda's cross and anxious face: those images still flare up in the dark some nights and make my heartbeat stumble.

What next did not take long. A man-in-suit who remained nameless like the cat, came in to see me.

'Where are my kids?' I tried to cry the words but they were only a hoarse whisper.

'These are not comfortable surroundings,' he said. Quite right. No window, a dirty wooden floor, a mattress with holes ripped in it showing its coiled inside. No blankets. One bentwood chair on which he sat, and one wooden crate on which I sank, my breath choked up. Propped against a wall were cupboard doors I recognised, as well as an old bench top. I'd wiped them down for years, not often enough to be a true Cinderella but I'd kept them reasonably clean. The man smiled, an unfriendly Oriental smile.

Shameful to say, I burst into tears. 'This isn't right. Bad guys used to be . . . it's not correct these days. The stereotypes!' I blame my infected hand for this eruption. I'm not normally so fragile.

The Asian man-in-suit showed some concern. 'Carry Bach Flower Remedy with you. Very good.'

I gave a tearful version of The Look and waved my bandage. 'If I have something to eat, I can take more erythromycin.'

'Information from you first. Then we will provide food.' His smile was still devoid of friendliness.

But I knew that the kids and I were intended as the food, for worms or fishes. I wanted to panic, but also to think. At this moment, I couldn't let myself do the first and, as for *think*, my brain throbbed as hard as that damned hand. If only I hadn't been so big on keeping Bernard's windows yoghurt-free this entire situation would be easier . . . it would still be terrible but at least I'd have two operative hands.

The man smiled another of those stereotypically inpenetrable smiles. I wanted to kick him. 'Where is the jade?' he asked.

'Jade? What —'

Oh my heavens. Let me put into a nutshell what he told me. These villains thought I'd had jade concealed in my cupboard doors. I learned that to their minds I was the offspring of villains who had stolen cultural artefacts that belonged to the descendants of imperial Chinese, that they had not wanted to kill anyone, but people kept getting in the way . . .

'You killed Maisie and Katherine for jade? What do you mean, descendants of imperial . . . don't cultural artefacts belong to the nation nowadays?'

'That was our dead colleague's opinion. He represented the

Chinese government. We have other ends. Ends justify the means, and we mean to find that jade.'

'But I don't know what jade! What do you mean?' I seemed to have nothing but questions and this seemed to annoy him. 'The sins of my father should be visited on me and my kids? What about my sisters? They're the real daughters. Why look at me, I'm just adopted.'

The man, still not polite enough to let me know his name, stood up, grabbed hold of a cupboard door and crashed it to the floor. I nearly fainted at the noise. He showed how the panel had been wrenched apart to uncover pockets built to hold something the size of playing cards. He screamed at me. 'We found enough jade for less than half a suit. Where is the rest?'

A suit of cards?

'Like — from the deuce to the seven or the eight?' I asked.

At this point he shrieked invective, as they do if they are villains. 'You have one hour to consider your stubborn foolishness!' He slammed out leaving me alone.

The muscles in my limbs had turned to mush. I dropped to my knees and struggled to upend my bag in case there were peppermints, a crumb of muesli bar, even a furry throat lozenge might be enough to go with another tablet of erythromycin. I found the garlic and echinacea tablets, and swallowed some dry. I found Tilda's sneaker — and Gifford's cellphone. I flew into a tantrum of my own.

'Stupid man! I don't know how to use these damned machines!' I threw it across the room, it skidded and hit a small metal grille at floor level. Of course! There is always a grille through which prisoners can pass notes! I crawled over and saw greasy grey fluff. I smelled stale food, old steam, damp dust.

Where could we be? This building was some kind of decrepit warehouse but we hadn't travelled far from the church hall. I didn't think we could be in the centre of the city. However, this city was so small, and how could I estimate the time we'd been cooped in that van? I hadn't thought to check my watch. Despair washed over me, as I imagine it will be when I begin to have hot flushes. My mother always said, sit tight when you have a hot flush, it always passes. I waited for the passing of despair.

I considered the cupboard doors as I was meant to. I considered the bench top, the scorch of crescent moon where Jarret once set a burnt-out pan. How I had yelled at him. There was the knife mark where he'd tried to cut a pumpkin. He didn't know how much more effective, and enjoyable, it is to hold the heavy vegetable at shoulder height, drop it on the floor and see it split (do this on newspaper). I hadn't told him that. I was a selfish mother and liked to have that fun myself.

My thoughts looped every which way as I sat on that old packing crate. Gifford, prepared to kill each one of us to get his hands on everything (but precisely what was meant by *everything*?), and now he was captured too — or was it a trick? And Caine involved — my heart felt shrivelled. Why the Oriental men-in-suits would fall out with the two Occidental men-in-casuals (that's Gifford and the plain clothes ace detective) I did not know, but the saying is that thieves fall out and so on. And who was that man with the teeth and grey pinstripes, with the gun that wasn't a Glock? Each moment, my thoughts grew more disjointed. If I couldn't convince the villains that I'd no idea where to find the missing cards, they might try torturing my kids. I'd have to torture the villains right back. How could I do that? All that came to mind (please blame my growing fever) was, again, The Song. I began to hum, got carried away, and when I reached the chorus croaked out loud:

There is a rule in Cat Land
Never eat a mouse's bum . . .

At this point, as I've said The Song required, I stamped my foot. The guardian angel of mothers was watching over me — as I stamped, there was a shiver where the skirting board met the dusty grille. I stood up, sang the chorus through a second time and kicked the skirting hard. A small gap showed. I kicked again.

Someone started kicking on the other side. Gifford's side.

Oh for a pair of steel-capped work boots! The best my sneakers did was loosen the panel from the skirting another fraction. I couldn't get enough grip on it with my good hand to make a useful difference. Running a splinter into that hand was less than useful. I swore, and sucked at it.

'Suzie?' Gifford spoke in an urgent muffle. 'Oh, girl, why can't you ever do what you are told?'

I won't tell you what I answered.

'I had your best interests in mind, yours and the boy's. Come on, Suzie, you must know that.'

Even now, his voice was honey and promise. I felt all the turmoil I'd felt years back, the longing to believe him when the evidence was clear as glass. My best interests? Jarret's? Forgive my disbelieving laugh. So that is why one night when I was wait-ressing for Bernard, Gifford skipped off to take part in a poker game and left baby Jarret on his own? That's why, when Gifford was hung over, he flung the crying baby Jarret on the sofa? How Gifford had apologised. How I'd believed that everyone deserved a second chance. How, when he threw the stroller down some stairs with my baby son still strapped into it and used up that second chance, I'd continued to believe those visions behind Gifford's blue Welsh eyes, believed that in his way he loved us. But a third chance? Although I had loved Gifford still, I loved my baby more — as a mother is supposed to, let me shout that! So I walked out. I left Gifford for my baby's sake and, for Gifford's sake, never told a soul what was behind it. Which is why my dad had always been so disapproving.

'What was your vision this time, Gifford?' I asked through the loose panel.

'Not just mine, girl. My vision and Philippa's.'

Gifford and Philippa? There is a phrase that should be used once in every thriller. 'Strange bedfellows,' I said.

'No, no. You and I were good together, Suzie.'

I did not grace this with a reply.

The jigsaw still didn't sit smoothly. According to what his own son had overheard, Gifford had planned to have us killed. But now those dapper men-in-suits had locked him up.

'Roger owes the United States Customs Service one hell of a lot in fines. Philippa saw this as a way to pay them,' Gifford whispered. 'I have my own financial problems.'

He didn't know my sister had been kidnapped. I left the silence to grow longer.

'Suzie? Girl, if it wasn't for me, you wouldn't have got your new kitchen! It was my idea, to see that you got something out of this.'

'You ransacked my house to make sure I was away from home all Monday night.'

'I was looking out for you, girl, believe me.'

'But you were going to have us killed.' God, it was hard to get those words out.

'How did you — no, no. All talk. I persuaded them we didn't need to go to those lengths, girl. What do you think I am? I organised the kitchen for you, girl!'

No reply from me again.

'Listen. Suzie. It was just a way to get my hands on some money. Your boyfriend was supposed to keep you out of it. We didn't figure on you dumping him.'

I thought about that. Philippa, Gifford — and Caine? But Caine took me to the 'm' room . . . he hadn't known it wasn't Philippa . . . Gifford and Caine were only semi-bad guys? 'But why did Maisie Forrest end up in my pantry?'

'Who? What?'

I crouched closer to the gap. 'The dead woman in my pantry. Philippa's colleague.'

There was a silence, then: 'She'd have to be a very tiny woman.'

'Gifford, Philippa's been kidnapped. I saw Roger and Lara with a ransom note. Gifford, you're involved. What's going on!'

'Girl, I'm a prisoner too!'

'How do I know you're not a . . .' What was the animal — ferret — badger — 'mole!'

'Oh shit, oh shit.' His voice was genuinely urgent. 'Look in your bag. My cellphone's there again. Phone your boyfriend — tell him a woman has been killed — you're sure it was Maisie Forrest?'

'Katherine Tiller too,' I said. 'Caine already knows. I told him.'

'Shit. Tell him they've locked me up. Find my phone!'

'You know I can't use those damned machines!'

'Press *send*. Do what I tell you. Your boyfriend's number is programmed in.'

The heaviness since Jarret told me Caine and Gifford were in tandem in this wickedness dragged hard, a hook inside my heart, inside my throat. In this moment I knew the strange uneasiness I'd had about Caine, that mystifying hurt, was that I loved my clean-cut cop. I'd loved him before Monday and still loved him. No matter that he'd turned out to be yet another bad or semi-bad guy. I put my hands over my heart and gave it nurture.

'Suzie,' Gifford whispered through the grille, 'I just wanted what was owed me. You father hinted about the jade but I didn't understand. It was only recently that Philippa found out and — shit, we screwed it up. Look, sweetheart, I ran up my first debts when we were married, I've never got clear since then. Be fair, you share responsibility. Girl, I left that key for your mother's safe deposit box, I thought there might be something useful in there for you. And I organised the kitchen. I got your cop friend to watch out for you. It's not my fault it's all gone wrong on me. Suzie, have you found that phone!'

'I will not call Caine.'

'Dial emergency! Tell them to hurry!'

I'd never heard a human being scream with such rage and frustration. I got the shakes again. I pressed *send*, knew enough to find the very patient operator and said my kids and I were prisoner in an unidentifiable location in this small city but got no further because a herd of footsteps sounded in the corridor outside. I hid the phone in Tilda's sneaker, which I thrust to the bottom of my bag. I hoped I'd turned it off in case it rang — then hoped I hadn't ended the call, because the operator might be able to gather a clue to our location.

'Gifford,' I shouted, much too late, 'where are we?'

Through the wall I heard the door of Gifford's room bang open. The herd of footsteps clattered away and the door did not bang shut. A single set of footsteps returned. My door slammed open.

The same man-in-suit as before said politely that they had given me much leeway over the last few days but the lee was all used up.

I was sweating, shaking. What strengths did I have left? Being obstructive. 'I need to be sure my kids are safe. I have to see them. I need to know about my sister too. I assume you're the people who have kidnapped her as well?'

From the guarded look in his eye, I gathered there was more of the story to come.

On a wisp of thought I commented that the jade he wanted was probably antique. The man inclined his head, a cautious yes.

'Then you've waited centuries to have it. Why not give it one more night?'

In those eyes, purported in old classics of the genre to be inscrutable, was a glimmer of amusement. It goes to show you can't rely on stereotype.

Dinner was surprisingly nice. Veal pot pie. And I was surprisingly ravenous. I choked down another erythromycin but after thirty minutes wished I hadn't. The nausea was not what you'd call post-prandial delight, nor was the double vision. Such terrible tablets. This would have been my chance to use the cellphone again but I had no new details to pass on and was afraid to waste the battery.

After another hour, the man-in-suit returned. I asked if I was going to see my kids. The answer was no. I said I had to use the bathroom. He shook his head.

'Am I expected to sleep here with no blanket, not even a bucket, and be nice to you in the morning?'

He stared at me without emotion.

'Are you waiting for me to say *plese*?'

The guy blinked and shut the door on me. Voices argued in the corridor. Eventually, the light was turned off at a switchboard, I guess, and my door opened. Someone tossed in a plastic bucket and a blanket. I saw a tall silhouette, a man's head and shoulders against dim light from the corridor.

I nearly said his name aloud. I knew now where I'd had that veal pot pie. At Thee Ultimate Café. Faludi's speciality. Faludi, who'd suffered from asthma on Monday. My God — he faked asthma that day because he was freezing Maisie. He must be the Mister Big. This was not a comforting thought to sleep on. I'd seen what the man could do with Bernard's sharpest knife.

The building was so quiet I didn't dare risk trying the phone. I tried to sleep. Thank goodness for the hypnagogic state, a semi-sleep when you're half-conscious of your mind doing the weird and wonderful. It helps time pass. Though maybe it was just some fever dream. Whatever. Somewhere in the night I had an image of Philippa coming to see me a few weeks after Mom died. She'd recovered from her own prostration, but I still found it hard to go far from my house. She wanted something, of course, this time for me to see about those footstools. Nameless tried to smoodge her but Philippa elbowed her reject cat aside. The kids were playing with Jarret's old train set in the hallway. They'd been doing so for weeks. Why care about a tidy house when I had lost my mom so short a time after losing my dad? They'd made little buildings with ten or so shapes of hard yellowy-green plastic that had wire threaded through some of the corners. As Philippa left in an irritated rush she stepped on a small rectangle. She picked it up.

'What this?'

'The kids scrounged them somewhere. Mom said . . .' Those tears that kept leaking made it hard for me to talk, sometimes. 'Said they'd come in useful, I mustn't throw them out.'

'So your daughter keeps them with her toys.' Philippa sounded strange but we all were strange during those weeks. Tilda reached up, slid the little rectangle from her aunt's grip and began to make a roof.

'Can I have just one?' asked Philippa.

Tilda, after cocking her head, chose the smallest piece and held it up.

That unusual greeny stuff must be the jade. My kids had played with imperial Chinese jade? The little toads — for months they had sworn they'd nothing to do with my missing cupboard door. Those jade pieces were at the bottom of my junk basket now, not in the toy box where Philippa might have expected them to be . . . the junk basket had been the only receptacle not ransacked.

If the men-in-suits had found pieces hidden in the cupboard doors and bench top but still didn't have enough for 'half a suit', how many pieces did they think there ought to be? The few pieces in the junk basket wouldn't satisfy these guys. It sounded as if they expected to find dozens, even hundreds.

I woke in the cold, stale dark of the unappealing room, still nauseated, feverish, in pain, terrified and flummoxed. My image of being a spider weaving silver threads over the city had been overly poetic. I had been a marble ricocheting round a bowl and now I had rattled to a standstill.

chapter twenty-two

Breakfast was thick wholemeal toast with mushrooms. Several drops of balsamic vinegar had been added: one would have been enough. It was brought to me by a minion-in-suit who also changed the bucket, a touch of kindness. Perhaps they were softening me up. Much good that would do, since I had nothing to tell them except to ransack my junk basket for another dozen little plaques of jade. It was still dark in the room — nobody had been kind enough to turn the light back on — but I tried the cellphone again. The emergency operator asked if I could pinpoint my location. Good food, I told him, and Faludi. He promised he could do things with this message and warned me to save that battery.

The last time I'd been incarcerated and banged and banged the wall, a Samoyed saved me. This time I banged and kicked, and what did I get? The villains released me from this small stale room, shoved me up a darkened stairwell and into another dingy shabby room. There was my sister, Philippa.

Her prison had a view. High up and narrow, all the window showed was turbulent sky. She sat on an old single bed with a wire wove and mattress, clutching an ancient yellowed pillow. The room also had an old gas stove with legs, something draped in a blue tarpaulin, a bentwood chair, a lidded bucket, another door which I assumed was also locked.

As soon as the door was shut behind me I flung myself at Philippa. The pillow between us, my good hand held her tight, the bandaged one cradled her shoulders, my kidnapped sister. 'Are you all right? Have they hurt you?'

She nodded she was okay, but only briefly met my eyes. I guessed she had some syndrome that happens when you're captured. You lose your will, identify with the bad guys, or plain lose your wits.

'We have to get out! They've got my kids.'

Still she didn't raise her head. 'There's no way. I tried — I hurt my back.'

I released her and examined her more closely. In fact she seemed in fairly good condition for someone who'd been kidnapped several days ago. Her hair was neat and artful. Instead of the usual designer skirt and Italian boots, she wore sneakers and trousers. Trust her to manage to be kidnapped when she was wearing something appropriate, if not as dramatic as she might have liked for any photos when she was rescued . . . I'd always had this liquorice allsort attitude towards both sisters, but especially towards Philippa. Even now, one layer of me was impressed, another envious, one wished I could be like her, a layer knew no matter how I tried I'd only be a pasty imitation. There was misery at how she negated me and a last layer incensed by her very existence and I hoped I would never be like her at all — yes, that last layer was two things and that's exactly what I mean. The sibling frustration! The way Philippa, in a millimetre movement of one nostril, could express how she despised me! It had always disturbed me to my depths. And yet I loved her. The toast. Oh yes, the toast . . . For a moment

I wanted to thrust toast down my sister's throat until she choked. It was because of her that I was here, that the kids were in such danger . . . But as usual, as I looked at her, my heart twanged.

I grabbed the chair and clambered up to check the window. At full stretch, I saw there was no opening mechanism. I glimpsed a parking area where crumpled food wraps skittered in the wind, and nothing else except two bicycles in a metal stand, a giant rubbish bin, a huge pine tree.

Even if I could find a way to break the glass and lever myself up, this window would be tough to scramble through. It would be too difficult for Philippa with her injured back to boost me high enough . . . interesting that I didn't imagine she would do the climbing over broken glass. She'd never been the type. I've told you that she skied, but that had become mainly *après*.

When I peered to the left, I saw that this building was on a typically difficult site for this small city. The room adjoining had an old wooden deck over a dizzying drop. Even so, I jumped down and checked the connecting door — locked, as I had guessed.

I sank on the chair then wrestled in my bag for Tilda's sneaker and thrust the phone towards Philippa. 'Call Roger! Call Lara! Call Bernard!'

Still holding that pillow, she stared at the phone as if dismayed. I waggled it. She still didn't take it.

'I called emergency but I don't know where we are. Philippa!'

She glanced to the side, to the floor. I wished I'd taken more notice of neurolinguistic programming, of hostage syndrome, of — I didn't know what. My bits and pieces brain had let me down.

'At least show me how to use it — okay — okay. Philippa, you and I are in serious danger, and so are my kids. I haven't seen them since yesterday. I think they're locked up somewhere down the hallway, oh God, I hope they're . . .' My eyes blurred. When I focused again Philippa, with a strangely compassionate look, met my eyes at last.

'Suzie, tell them where the jade is.'

'Roger's desperate — he stuck me in a basement to keep me from being kidnapped too, but here I am! All because of some stuff that looks like plastic? Stuff the kids played trains with. You saw them — when did you realise what it was? When did you tell Gifford? Why?' Believe me, I was trying not to scream. 'Why!'

'Just tell me where it is, and we can go.'

'I doubt it.' I buried (that awful expression) my head in my hands. Agony shot through my right arm up to my shoulder. Tears made my vision sparkle as I sat up shielding the bandage.

'Suzie, please understand. The jade is valuable, worth . . .' Philippa gestured to indicate inestimable numbers of big dollars.

'But it's only squares and rectangles. Not even carved.'

'Suzie, it's an imperial burial suit.'

Uh?

'Han Dynasty,' she said.

'That's old. That's ancient. Do you mean — the suit is — for goodness' sake. The Chinese Lego man?'

My sister did the nostril thing then covered her face and trembled, somewhat artificially, I thought and felt a squeak of guilt.

'Suzie . . . let me explain . . .'

I listened. Two thousand years ago. Small plaques of jade, hand-carved, with little holes at each corner for wire of pure gold that bound the pieces into a kind of armour for the body. Jade was thought to preserve the dead, somehow confer immortality. It took probably a decade to make each suit, carve over two thousand shapes of various sizes. Only the imperial family could afford or be entitled to them, or at least the extremely well-to-do and aristo-cratic. The first suit had been discovered in 1972 — that's first as in, the first-discovered — you know what I mean — in a tomb in Hopei Province. Oh, my sister knew these details as if they had been carved into her heart. There were also little jade plugs for all the body orifices . . .

'All? You really mean all?'

'Shut up, Suzie, listen. And *bi* discs, and carved jade shapes called *cong*, though no-one really knows what purpose . . .'

'But how did a burial suit get in my kitchen!' I cried. 'I've guessed Dad put it there, but why? How did he get it?'

Philippa shook her head. Who knew the workings of that man's mind? Or the mind of any botanist?

Two thousand little pieces! There wasn't room for that many in my kitchen unless they were under the floor. All week, I'd been trying to think things through, be logical, but it was like trying to count squabbling cats. 'Philippa, these bad guys have no common sense — if you haven't got the suit, then you don't have any money. Roger can't pay his fines, so how can he pay a ransom?'

She looked at me oddly. 'You — do know quite a bit.' She shifted away from me a little, keeping the pillow between us. 'Roger — pulled out, you see.'

I didn't.

'He was meant to find a buyer for the suit — his contacts in the States. He had one nearly set up, the guy was sending out an agent.' Her hands had become fists, tight on her lap. 'Then on Monday afternoon, Roger pulled out. Without a buyer, Suzie, none of it works.'

'So — my God, Roger is a baddie. And Gifford kidnapped you because of this? He and Caine murdered two women because of it?'

'Caine? Your boyfriend the detective?' Philippa stared as if I'd flipped my lid. 'Murdered two women?'

'Yes. How did Maisie and Katherine find out? They're dead because of it? And the Oriental guys and Faludi are in the act?'

'What's . . . Maisie and Katherine?' My sister backed away along the bed.

I leaned towards her. 'They've been killed. I've seen the bodies.'

Philippa gave that dismissive laugh, that shrug.

This was no good. I had to be practical, climb on something

high enough to break the window and squeeze out. I jumped off the bed, dragged Philippa off too though she protested, and shifted it beneath the window. It was still impossible to reach the glass properly.

'Suzie, this is no help . . .'

I stood the chair on the bed but it toppled before I even tried to climb on it.

'Suzie, for goodness' sake! Pay attention. Just tell me . . .'

The gas stove was affixed to the wall. Maybe I could use whatever was under the tarp. I ripped the tarpaulin off and found another couple of bentwood chairs propped over an old freezer chest. I shoved the chairs off but when I tried to move the chest it budged an inch and then no more. I checked the wall — it was plugged in though not switched on. I yanked the plug and heaved the chest again.

'Suzie, sit and think! Where's the rest of the jade?'

'Forget your back, and help me.' Bit by bit, I strained to shunt the chest.

'Really, Suzie, I'd check if it was empty first,' said Philippa with a *tch*.

Her sarcasm enraged me. I threw open the lid. There was one small purple item at the bottom. A pretty flat-soled shoe.

That nasty sweat that happens at crisis points broke out behind my ears and round my neck. I hoped I wouldn't throw up. My voice came out as a peep. 'You know, Philippa, the police took Roger down to the — oh God, the morgue — on Monday. They can't have known I'd already told Caine it wasn't you. That could well be when Roger changed his mind about a buyer. When he saw the kind of people you were dealing with.'

'Oh yes?' asked Philippa.

'Dead ones,' I squeaked. 'Philippa — do you know Maisie's shoe size?'

'Suzie . . .! All right. We call her Twinkletoes.'

I fetched out the shoe. Muscles seemed to shrink in Philippa's face. The pillow slipped off her lap. Hands claw-like over her mouth, she crumpled back. Her eyes dilated.

A little tune began to play on Gifford's cellphone. My stupid technophobia! But I fiddled. The tune stopped playing. When I said hello, my sister Lara spoke.

'Suzie? Are you with Gifford? This number was my last resort. I've been trying everywhere for you.'

'He's a bad guy!' I cried.

'Rotten through and through. Don't trust him a jot. In fact . . .'

'Philippa's here too.' I clutched the phone tight. 'But I don't know where!'

'Philippa as well? Another mystery solved. Now listen to this. My US colleague came through this morning with some surprising information. It's true, you're not our little sister.'

'Oh God, we haven't time for . . . Forget that, Lara. Listen . . .'

'It's fascinating. Mom and Dad were never married.'

'Lara, please . . .'

'Mom wasn't my mother, but Dad was my dad and Philippa's. Mom was your mother. Suzie, this will take ages to explain, I'll have to draw a diagram. Come to dinner tonight, you and the kids — oh God. Suzie. Please say you've found the kids.'

'Lara, stop! And don't hang up.' I didn't dare think too much about Tilda and Jarret — as long as I was alive, I had to believe they were as well. Though still pale, Philippa had started to come out of her shock.

'Why couldn't we have shared the damn jade suit if it's so valuable!' I cried.

'Jade what?' from Lara. 'Share? Green is not my colour.'

'Real jade! Antique. Worth millions, according to Philippa. It was in my cupboards — at least, the top half of the suitcase was — why do I think it was the top?'

Groggy and ashen, Philippa tried to speak but couldn't. She

looked like a stranded salmon.

'Lara, believe me, we're in danger,' I said. 'We're both kidnapped now. So are the kids. I'm not certain about Gifford. It's because Philippa didn't want to share!'

Sisterly annoyance brought Philippa fully back to life. 'I did so! Suzie, we couldn't let Lara know because she would have tried to take over.'

'Did you hear that?' I asked Lara.

Her response was grim.

'And we couldn't tell you, Suzie, until the deal was complete. We simply couldn't.'

'Why not!'

'Oh Suzie. Isn't it obvious? You're so erratic. You'd have blown the deal at once.'

I think they call this break a pregnant pause.

'I wrote the note,' continued Philippa, her voice beginning to rise. 'I wrote the kidnap note myself. At least, I dictated it . . .'

'Pardon?' I said.

'Shut up,' said Lara on the phone. 'Let her talk.' I held the cellphone towards Philippa so Lara could hear.

'When Roger pulled out, I had to force him . . . I didn't know that Maisie and Katherine . . .' Philippa broke into gasps like a panic attack. In movies, if someone has hysterics you're encouraged to slap them. It's true: your palms itch.

'How much are you getting of this?' I asked Lara.

'Shit a brick,' she said. 'Tell me where you are and I'll get hold of . . .' The phone fizzed and went dead as I'd expected.

Philippa was genuinely trembling. I almost gave her a hug but she pulled a key from her pocket and stumbled to the door in the left-hand wall. As she opened it, my moment of sisterly pity faded fast.

It was a pleasant sitting room. Morning sun came through the French window. There were pink roses in a vase, a sofa bed with mohair blankets, a pile of books and magazines. Another door, half ajar, showed a neat little bathroom. What interested me, once again, was the view. Now they weren't blocked by the huge pine, rooftops showed through a tumble of trees down a steep hill to the harbour. Across the narrow inlet was the rise of Point Howard. We could be very near Thee Ultimate Café.

I rushed to the French window. Locked. And up close the wooden deck outside looked rotten and unsafe. If I broke this window, I'd have to leap an impossible distance to reach the parking lot up to the right.

'How do we get out?' I asked my sister.

Philippa was already trying the handle of a door into the passage. It didn't turn. She answered me in a thin shriek. 'We're locked in — I've been tricked just as badly as you!'

I was seriously tempted, but this was not the time to play *Have not! Have so!*

'We have to go back to the horrid room where they stored Maisie . . .' I paused. My sister blenched whiter than before. 'And you pretend that I won't tell anyone a thing until my children have been brought to us and I've had some time with them.'

'But Suzie, they must be going to kill us too — oh-God-oh-God-oh . . .'

'For the first time in your life,' I said, 'will you shut up.'

It's a measure of how bad things were that Philippa shelved her hysterics. She summoned up her dramatic ability like a pro. In that shabby little room she did exactly right — the bad guys gleaned no notion that she was aware of the multiple betrayals.

'I will bring the children in for ten minutes,' agreed the most suave man-in-suit.

'Fifteen!' I cried.

He regarded me with sorrow. 'Please see yourself as a highly attractive paving stone along our way. Fifteen minutes then, for you all to contemplate the Zen of being stepped on.' He smiled as the door shut on us again. If he was a genuine Chinese, then Gifford was a leprechaun.

In the few moments before the kids arrived a dozen plans rushed through my head and down the cliff. When Tilda and Jarret were pushed in they were carrying their bags — the hopefulness of it cut me in two. They were like sketches of themselves, grey and shadowy. I remember holding them, each with a head on my shoulder.

As soon as the door was locked again I warned the kids to keep quiet and showed them the larger room where we could sit and do that contemplating. Tilda dashed into the little bathroom with a cry.

Philippa sank onto the sofa bed, a hand across her eyes. I hoped she was getting a migraine that would fell a heifer. I hoped it would include nausea five times worse than mine. I hoped disorientating lights would blister the inside of her skull. I hoped she wouldn't recover until a doctor gave her an injection with a cow-sized needle.

She moaned. 'Katherine organised a new filing system for me as my birthday present. That's how she and Maisie found out —'

'Right. Friends should stick with potted cyclamen,' I said.

'Maisie wanted all the money to go on the dogs — Katherine just wanted a medal from the Chinese. It was terrible seeing those two argue over money when they'd been close for such a long time — they'd always been so careful, so efficient — oh, money is an evil . . .'

'Shut up,' I told her again, 'I am trying to think.' It was obvious we couldn't escape from the French window without breaking several legs among us. Nor was there time to smash the small window in the other room and all wriggle out that way.

'But it has to be the little window, Mum,' said Jarret.

I rapped on the bathroom door and dragged Tilda out.

'Look.' I pointed through to the narrow window. 'If we smash it and heave you up, can you run with Jarret as fast and far as possible?'

She looked scared. I still wasn't sure this was the best plan, but plumped her down and made her put both sneakers on at last.

'Philippa,' I asked, 'where are we? I hope you know.'

My sister slid a look at me and pointed upwards. 'This is the café.'

The universe seemed to contract briefly. Thank God! If we could only reach Bernard, we'd all be safe . . .

I felt the daffy expression of joy seep off my face as I realised how wretched Philippa was.

'Bernard,' I said. I should have known. The villain always has a gammy leg.

Philippa cleared her throat. 'Gifford was going to be cleared of debt at last, Bernard was going to build a new Ultimate Café. I was going to restart Suite Three, pay Roger's hundred thousand dollar fines for not checking the blasted fumigation regulations . . .'

Luke was right? The long-horned beetle? I shouldn't have yelled.

'I could have kept my Frances Hodgkins,' my sister continued. 'Your share would have been enough to do something significant with your life at last, Suzie, maybe get some qualifications for that mind you persist in frittering. When Roger saw those blood tests he made me keep it from you, but it doesn't make much difference to me that you're not my real sister. I thought you should have some of the money. Goodness knows, even if we'd shared it equally there would have been plenty . . .'

I longed to hit her.

'But Bernard had his own ideas all along! The greed of him — it's difficult to believe how foul some people are.'

This week I'd learnt more than I wished about life and human nature.

The sound of footsteps came again. We crowded back and shut the connecting door a moment before the small room was unlocked.

The bad guys had Gifford with them. Faludi leaned in the doorway, smiling thinly as bad guys are supposed to. 'To speed things up, Suzie, we toss your ex-husband into the mix. A family conference should include the bad egg, right?' He laughed (as they do), winked at Philippa (a daring touch) and shut the door.

Gifford's hands were cuffed in front of him. He held them up, asking us to help. I put mine behind my back. With her hands, Philippa performed a Scream. The children edged away.

'Oh Jesus, girl — believe me, I am sorry.'

Jarret turned his back.

Gifford wriggled, uncomfortable in those handcuffs, and morally, I guessed, though that was probably a first. His scent was sour. 'Your boyfriend can still save us. Get the cellphone.'

'Batteries!' Philippa hissed and Gifford seemed to shrink.

'Caine's okay?' Tilda asked. 'He's a good guy?'

'No,' I whispered.

Gifford slumped against the wall and laughed, a feeble but unsettling try at nonchalance. 'You'll never know for sure now, girl. Caine might have been working undercover, unofficially. I confess I slipped him the odd piece of information. Don't look at me like that, Suzie. It's a time-honoured custom to play both sides against the middle.'

'As long as it works,' muttered Jarret.

'Caine is so a good guy,' Tilda breathed. She narrowed her eyes at Gifford. 'But you're not.'

'I have my moments,' he replied.

Jarret's reaction was infinitesimal, silent, but complex. So was mine.

All we had was a half-formed plan that changed by the minute. Finally I did not dare risk Tilda outside. Jarret would have more chance for all of us on his own. In Philippa's kidnap haven, I gave my daughter a hug, scooted her back into the bathroom and made her promise she would stay completely silent. She locked the door behind her.

Jarret picked up a dictionary and an encyclopaedia of Eastern archaeology. I grabbed a large book from beside the sofa bed, *Chinese Textiles in the World Market*, and Philippa an incense burner. Back in the small unpleasant room, I closed the connecting door. Jarret and Philippa were the only fully able-bodied (she seemed to have forgotten the pulled muscle in her back), but working together we managed to edge the freezer underneath the window.

'Ready?' I asked.

Jarret braced himself and counted. 'One, two . . .'

'I can't,' gasped Philippa. 'I can't, I can't . . .'

I socked her shoulder hard.

'Three!' cried Jarret.

Philippa threw her most spectacular tantrum and Gifford roared with all the Welsh wind in his lungs. Screaming too, I aimed the *Chinese Textiles* at the dingy window. It was lucky I'd had one-handed practice in Suite Three. Jarret's books hit the window at the same time. The glass shattered. The incense burner took out the rest of the pane. We continued yelling to conceal the crash as long as possible while Jarret sprang onto the freezer and slithered through the jagged hole. I scrambled up too and saw him race towards the bike stand.

'They'll be locked!' I shouted. 'Don't waste time!' But he was on a bicycle and away as if the hounds of hell raced with him.

We kept the hysterics coming.

Heavy footsteps came down the stairs, the door was unlocked, and Faludi and a man-in-suit bullied in.

They stared at the freezer, the broken glass. 'Bloody hell. Where is the boy — the little girl?' Faludi yelled above the row we made. The other guy went for the gun under his jacket but Faludi stopped him. 'Not here!' he ordered.

'Run, Tilda!' I shouted out the window to mislead them. 'Get the police!'

'Fire! Fire! Help!' Gifford bellowed.

I slithered off the freezer. In the hustle, I jerked my elbows into Philippa's ribs by accident. She coughed.

'Run,' she echoed feebly. Then like a frog about to sing she seemed to enlarge. 'Run, Tilda! Run!' And she ran herself, straight at the man-in-suit. Like a minotaur, Gifford barrelled at Faludi.

As the men staggered, I dived for the hall. Gifford and Philippa followed with the men behind them, grabbing. 'Help! Fire! Police!' we cried.

The garage down below would be closed. The only direction was along the corridor and up some stairs. I fell on my right hand but agony propelled me to my feet again, through a doorway and into the kitchen of Thee Ultimate Café.

Bernard's bulk was right in front of me. I plunged into him. He staggered on his artificial leg. But the kitchen was empty. The second man-in-suit was at a table, halfway through a sandwich, but no customers sat having veal pot pie to give us cover while we sauntered out to freedom. The doors were bolted and the closed sign was up. Faludi and the other men thumped up the stairs out of breath and out of temper.

'No guns in view of the street,' Faludi said to Bernard.

Bernard reached to the array of dangerous implements above the bench. He chose the fruit knife.

'Gifford, Gifford. I bent corners for you, boy, and look what happened.'

Gifford backed against the coffee machine and stayed there.

'The kids have escaped.' Faludi was sweating, not nice to see in an assistant chef. 'They'll bring the police.'

A car pulled up outside and three teenagers hopped out to go to the dairy. Philippa waved and tried to run towards the window but a man-in-suit corralled her. The boys took not a crumb of notice. If I'd had the breath, I could have told Philippa: since when did teenage boys look at a middle-aged woman?

Trying to be unnoticeable I shuffled between the tables.

'Suzie, don't even think of it,' Bernard said. 'The window's plate glass, you'd bounce off.'

But we had to stay in full view from the street, and I had to keep them from finding Tilda still downstairs in the bathroom. How long before Jarret could fetch help?

'I used Gifford's cellphone, Bernard. The operator said they'd trace the signals.' Indeed, although they had not done so since I'd first used the phone last night.

Bernard simply laughed, as villains do. 'Get them down below,' he said to Faludi.

'I'm staying here,' I said.

'Me too . . . !' From my years as youngest sibling I knew Philippa was winding up to genuine hysterics.

Gifford pressed further back against the coffee machine, hands still cuffed before him, forehead mutinous.

Faludi and the men-in-suits exchanged disconcerted glances. I checked the time. Jarret might have spun off his bike, had a puncture, hit a truck. And where was that third Asian man-in-suit? My heart pitched like a wild thing.

The teenagers strolled out of the corner store with a bag of nuts and chocolate ice creams. Bernard palmed the fruit knife and began to move towards me. I did not want to be put again in the belly of this building. I was sick to the back teeth of being concealed in the bellies of buildings. I wanted my daughter released from the belly of this building.

I grabbed a salt shaker from the nearest table and hurled it at the plate glass. In the moment of surprise, I ducked under Bernard's arm into the kitchen, snatched a heavy frying pan in both hands (*shit!*), and banged it on the boarded up window. The plywood cracked. Tears of pain poured down my face. I scrambled on to the bench to hit the wood from a better angle. I hadn't known I was so agile. Philippa — my sister! — had worked out what I was up to. She wriggled between Faludi's legs, he grabbed her shirt, but she lunged free, caught hold of another pan, slung it around low and hit up with it. She'd always had a good strong arm at tennis. For a tall man, he creased up small. The two bad suits broke into a language of their own and I bet a translation would scorch ears. The men came for me but I straddled the counter and dropped back into the dining area.

'Go! Go! Go!' Gifford was yelling.

The teenage boys had turned at last. A woman standing well back on the pavement had begun to use her cellphone. Good for her! I gave a bandaged thumbs-up and ducked between the tables, still out of the clutch of the bad suits. I hoped they'd remember not to bring out their not-Glocks in plain daylight, prayed Tilda would stay secure in that small bathroom till the good-suit guys arrived, kept throwing condiments and vases of dried flowers.

A Green Lawn Buddy van pulled up. A small crowd had gathered outside, but Bernard and the bad suits began to laugh as if this were a practice for a clown show. God, this might all look like street theatre. I scooted round till I'd thrown all the condiments — tears almost blinded me by now — but the buddy had begun to rattle the locked door.

Bernard, still laughing as if this were a piece of entertainment, tossed away the fruit knife. He clapped his hands like a prestidigitator, swivelled to the wall magnet and snatched a meat chopper. He caught Philippa and put the chopper to her throat.

The crowd shrieked. But the sturdy Green Lawn Buddy hadn't noticed — which is something I've always wondered: if somebody's making threats but nobody sees — like that tree that's always falling in the forest to entertain philosophers — what really happens? What happened now was that the buddy frowned at the lock and returned to his truck. As I always think, let that tree fall, who cares? He heaved out a weed-eating machine and started bashing the café door.

A police car swerved up and two officers leaped out. Green Lawn Buddy bashed the lock again. The door popped open and he stepped aside. Luke's car squealed to a halt across the road, and Luke and Caine leaped out of it (sorry, that's two lots of leaping but you try writing this down — I'm doing my best in the rush) — I felt a flicker of relief.

There was movement in the stairway. Tilda appeared, hair wet — she'd used the time to wash her hair? — with *Hello Kitty*, Jarret's stuff and my bag. I had no time to scream for her to run back down. Bernard thrust Philippa aside and grabbed my girl.

All of a sudden we were in freeze-frame. My daughter with a chopper at her throat.

A whoosh and skid of bike tyres, a clatter of pedals on the pavement and Jarret hurtled into the café. Luke dived after him and held him back.

Jarret shouted over Luke's sleeve. 'Dad! Stop him!'

Gifford swore and raised his cuffed hands, helpless.

'Dad!' Jarret screamed again. 'She's my sister!'

Tilda looked at me. Her hair dripped on the varnished boards. She glanced at her feet and whimpered. Her head rolled as if she were about to faint. In the next moment she struck her heel at Bernard's gammy knee.

Bernard crumpled with a yell and jerked at Tilda, but the chopper clattered to the floor. Gifford let out a roar and propelled himself towards Bernard. They slipped and fell. Bernard straightened momentarily, snatched the boning knife with an outflung arm, and Tilda was beneath those two large men. Bernard's arm reached up with the knife and brought it down. There was a hideous cry. Bernard raised his arm and stabbed the knife again.

A heartbeat — two —

Covered in blood, Tilda scrambled out and dived at me. Luke and Jarret were beside us a split second before Caine was, checking if the blood was Tilda's, then hugging me and Tilda so tight I had to fight them off so we could breathe. Caine stood aside. I held my daughter, reached for Jarret's hand, and over Tilda's head saw Gifford lying bleeding — so much blood, from his neck and pooling underneath him from a chest wound.

I couldn't see Bernard. He'd disappeared.

Big police feet tramped back and forth in the commotion. The bad suits were all in handcuffs — when had that third guy-in-suit appeared? — and an ambulance siren was screaming up the hill towards the café. Police on walkie-talkies gave descriptions of Bernard. I wondered where the man with the teeth fitted in. Perhaps the agent Philippa mentioned, for the contact Roger nearly set up? The guy hadn't reappeared since he'd run off outside my house.

I left Tilda being hugged by Jarret and Luke, found my bag where Tilda had dropped it and emptied everything out, my wallet, pocket tissues, *Little Black Quasha*, my hairbrush. My mind must have been looping the loop — I wanted a bandage for Gifford. It would have been sensible to use towels from the kitchen, those nice ones with pink checks and crimson edging. His eyelids fluttered. I think he saw me.

The dinky police woman from Monday afternoon moved me and my stuff to one side and cleared the way for the ambulance attendants, the stretcher and oxygen equipment. I felt relief at someone taking charge. I'd not had nausea like this for years. The erythromycin blurred my vision again. I loathed those pills. I stuffed everything back in my bag: the Blu-tack, my perfume, the furry lozenges, those womanly items — a thought socked me and I leaned back with my eyes closed. I'd carted those items around for many weeks now, but when had I last used them?

chapter twenty-three

There are at least eight sides to every story: an up and down, a front and back, a left and right, inside and out. Depending how many people are involved, all that can be repeated a million times and then some. Therefore — the truth? It's a patchwork coat of many colours cobbled together over many years, and people choose whichever patch they like. The truth has ragged side seams and lint in its pockets. It's sure to have a mismatched button. The truth may be out of fashion, best hidden in a storage bag beneath the bed. *Beauty is truth, truth beauty*, the poet said, but truth more often has an unattractive aspect. It was time for the unravelling of the ugly truth, all sides.

Beyond Lara's picture window, the evening sun did nice things to the layers of cloud that often frame the sky of this small city. Luke, Brick and a wiped-out Roger sat in Lara's living room holding glasses of whisky. Tilda and Jarret, side by side on Lara's sofa shared a platter of cold sausages, sliced avocado and tomato, pizza — my sister let the kids sit in her designer living room with greasy fingers! This showed how much she loved us.

Philippa? She had been hours at the police station giving a statement, as had we all. Roger had taken her home, tucked her into bed then come to Lara's house for comfort. He'd explained how he had to pay those enormous fines — and do you know, it was not to do with the Asian long-horned beetle, but a something-or-other kind of beetle, so Luke did sort of have that right . . . Sorry. I will continue. Once Roger had realised it was Katherine in the morgue, he'd been in turmoil, and then he truly thought his wife had been kidnapped.

'Suzie, you wouldn't stay still,' he managed to choke out. 'I had to hide you. I knew you wouldn't believe me — I'm so sorry — you weren't supposed to wake up on your own in Maisie's — Maisie and . . .' His voice as tattered as he looked, Roger broke down.

He meant Katherine Tiller's house of course, but I was not surprised that in his condition he was muddled. I found him a box of tissues and Brick handed him another large whisky. This was not an expensive brand — Brick didn't want to waste one on a man in tears who couldn't use his nose. You remember that Brick cries as well when he's had too much to drink? — oh well, that's Brick. Mind you, tonight, we all leaked tears, each one of us.

Caine arrived as the last rose-coloured cloud turned grey. He took Jarret and me aside. Very gently, he told us Gifford had died two hours after he came out of the operating theatre. I guess my son and I had hoped . . . but we'd also seen what happened at the café. Our hope had been the wisp you cling to until the dreadful words are said.

Jarret met Caine's eyes and nodded. It looked as if Caine wanted to say a lot more to us, but he didn't. I also thought he wanted to hug the boy, but he did not. I thanked Caine, and Brick showed him out. I had questions to ask Caine, something to tell him, too, though the right moment might take a while in coming.

I expected Jarret would want to be on his own but he stayed here with the rest of us — Lara, Brick, Roger, myself, his little sister. I was glad — and glad too that I was with my family. I didn't believe Philippa had ever intended anyone to be hurt. She hadn't been going to steal anything I was aware that I possessed, and maybe she had indeed meant to give me a fair share — Roger might have been able to insist on it. I could forgive her, maybe, in the end. So many *maybes*, *maybe nots*: that's families. Anyway, the jade upper half of the suit (for some reason, we all thought this) had disappeared along with Bernard — so fast the man had moved with that trick knee! Faludi and those Asian-looking dapper men who had been hoping to double-cross Bernard, who had double-crossed Gifford, who had criss-crossed *yah-de-yah*, and so on were all in custody as well, and were, I hoped, feeling abject. The van had been found abandoned near the airport. Bernard was assumed to have left the city.

'The man with teeth?' I asked.

Roger sniffed into his whisky. 'You must mean Hockard. He was my contact with the buyer. I've told the police.'

I glanced at Tilda — this was not the right time to say Hockard hadn't had a Glock and had found out where I lived. Tilda had been sitting with that slice of pizza for an hour now. I doubted she'd eat another bite but she wouldn't let us take it away.

Still staring at her plate, my daughter spoke. 'Maybe Auntie Philippa just needs a rest. Like, we could send her to Fiji.' Her jaw trembled, as did Roger's.

Luke put down his empty whisky glass and stood up — my adorable daughter's father, a man I was proud to once have loved with such angry passion. He kissed Tilda and rattled his car keys in that awkward way that communicates *it's time to go, et cetera*. 'Take care, Tilda. I'll see you tomorrow. Going to school?'

I shook my head. My kids and I would have a long weekend: we needed to be three.

'Okay,' he said. 'What say I pick you guys up here around nine and we'll go somewhere for breakfast. Then we'll go and check your house out. I'll help you tidy your room, Tilda.'

She showed theatrical disgust.

'Stay for dinner, Luke,' Lara offered. 'I'll do some pasta for the rest of us, if anyone's hungry.'

'Lara, that's very kind but no, thank you. I — ah — have a reconciliation dinner planned.' Luke rubbed his healing cheek and glanced at me. In our time, he and I had eaten many reconciliation dinners. They worked. I mean, he and I were friends. We gave due acknowledgement to how much we used to love each other, to how much we loved our child. We gave due credit to how appalling we were for each other too, and that's crucial.

I went to the door, and he took off, our Disney eagle. I had a speck of sympathy for the current woman he was driving to extremes.

When I returned, Brick offered me a whisky. I shook my head. Earlier, Lara had asked her GP to make a house call — a house call! — to check the kids out and also take a look at me. The brisk and kindly woman of my own age had reassured me about the stress, the erythromycin, and its effect on the secret that I carried. Now I had confirmed my secret, I refused to touch a drop of alcohol.

'Suzie, you're exhausted,' my big sister said.

I agreed I would lie down till she had food ready.

Lara came with me to the guest room. 'Our crazy parents,' she said as she spread a rug over me.

Tears seeped out of my eyes. 'I hate this bit in stories. The explanations.'

'Don't be silly, they have to be done.'

As usual, she was right. Lara sat on the foot of the bed and told me what her American sidekick had uncovered. I told her about the family saplings, Mom's letters from the friend who despised Nietzsche. We were pleased we'd each had a share in the discoveries. I stopped snivelling as I saw the internal and external pressures upon families — and also the hero, essentially alone, in every ordinary man and every woman — the pioneering spirit that is resourceful and independent, worming through the good and bad of our society, proving the place of the small and insignificant in the world of the large and the tough . . . sorry, that's getting out of hand, I'll be specific and recap. My mom had been the only child of a millionaire, an electrical magnate. My biological dad's family, the Quinters, had been Boston millionaires as well. Larry Quinter had also been a PhD student of truly abominable electronic music. Against the wishes of both sets of parents, Mom and Larry Quinter lived together in hippy-student-sin at Harvard, and procreated me. Guess what? Next door, arrived an innocent couple from this down-side of the world, a research scientist (the secret life of spleenworts) and his wife with two small children still in diapers. Guess what, again and next? The wife of the botanist — this was her first experience of the big wide world, she'd been a boarding school girl in Oamaru, so it made sense — fell in lust with the abominable music student and he with her. To the wilds of who-knew-where, away they ran. She was never seen again, but is suspected to be working in radio in Montana.

'She left you and Philippa. To leave her children!' I pulled a tissue and blew my nose.

Lara's sniff was one of practicality. 'It wasn't much loss to us, if that's what she was like. And you know what Larry Quinter ended up as — a worldwide joke for trying to combine twelve-tone music with rock'n'roll. Poor Schoenberg — what a legacy. So, your mother and our dad teamed up and stayed together for our sakes — for the sake of we three little girls. They never married because Dad never got divorced. Mom didn't believe in marriage anyway.' Lara blew her nose, this time maybe not so practical, maybe because of a small tear. 'So much for the selfishness meant to be rife in that time of peace rallies and Aquarius. To avoid her angry parents, Mom took my mother's name — she left the States on someone else's passport! — oh God, and I work in Customs. From wealthy

Maria Hurren, Mom turned into modestly well-off Mary Green. This country was a hippie paradise to her. Barefoot in the kitchen, that was Mom's dream and she found it.'

Mom an illegal immigrant, how's that! (And therefore so was I? At least until I'd married Gifford.) As for my biological father — the infamous Larry Quinter, who lost his millions funding his own bad records, to the hilarity of DJs around the world — Lara and I could both remember when he died. It was around the time Mom and Dad had indulged in yet another of their sequences of muffled — and often not-so-muffled — argument.

'Your Aunt Anthonia's been on the phone to me, Suzie, this afternoon,' said Lara. 'She's got a voice like Katharine Hepburn. She was Larry's sister — best friends of Mom's since school, which is how Mom met Larry in the first place. Listen, neither Philippa nor I have any claim to the jade suit. It belongs to you alone — if you can find it. The Quinters, Larry's parents, your grandparents, purchased it legally. Legal for 1973, that is. I doubt the methods and ethics would hold up these days.'

The official government glaze came over Lara's eyes as rules and regulations scrolled in her brain. I wiggled my left palm, fingers standing up like soldiers, and she returned to here and now. 'Mom's parents set private detectives onto her and Dad, refused to give any financial help, and became even more furious when Mom refused to ask for any. So when we left the States, Anthonia smuggled the jade in with their crates. Mom and Dad knew nothing about the suit till the customs inspection was over and they began to unpack in that rented house in Newtown. Remember that? Remember them arguing about how many boxes there should be?'

'I remember everyone being upset we'd had to leave the States, that's all.'

'Some aunt you have, Suzie. She says she saw herself and Mom as sisters, better than sisters. I hope I meet Anthonia next time I get to Boston.'

'Times Square?' I asked Lara. 'Dad shaved his head once, did he? When we still lived in Boston?'

'Mom's father had offices near Times Square. Mom wanted to attend a rally in New York, but her dad's accountant spotted them. They ran.'

That dreadful memory I'd dreamt about heaved up: *sitting on Dad's shoulders, I yanked off the Russian hat to spit on his bald head — Dad yelled — and a bad man chased us.*

I found myself crying again. 'We may never find the jade trousers . . . who cares about the trousers? No wonder I've never fallen in love properly. What an example to grow up with. Mom and Dad lived together only for our sakes, not because they were in love.'

'Unconventional,' Lara agreed. She held my hand. 'Suzie, they loved each other as much as necessary. And they loved us. God knows why. We were unconscionable little brats. At least, you and Philippa were. I was a pompous brat.'

Tilda sidled into the room and up beside me on the bed. 'Jarret's crying. Uncle Brick says to ask, can he give your son a whisky?'

Lara jumped to her feet. 'Not in my house, not my nephew! There's a light beer in the fridge.' She swept out and descended the stairs.

Tilda was in tears herself.

'It's late, sweetheart,' I said. 'Cuddle here and sleep, okay?'

'Can I have my own pyjamas?'

This did not seem unreasonable. *Hello Kitty*, with the few things we'd packed on Monday afternoon — four days since, an aeon — had been left at Thee Ultimate Café. I made her promise to lie down and try to sleep while I asked Brick to fetch us our own night clothes.

I crept downstairs, not trying to be secretive, just feeling beaten. Lara was rattling in the fridge. From the hall I saw Jarret seated between his uncles, both of them so careful with him that it made my heart fill up. Brick was starting to tell Brick Bradford stories about spaceships and determined heroics, while Roger looked like something that our cat would not deign to sniff. Clearly they were both too steeped in whisky to drive across the city for a pair of girl's pyjamas.

Keeping a good distance from the Tibetan gong, I found my bag in the hall and sat on the bottom stair while I used a fresh tissue on my eyes. The cat brooch was still pinned to the bag. Gifford's brooch. The tears flowed faster. I couldn't let Jarret see me like this, nor return upstairs to Tilda. I'd fetch her pyjamas myself. For the first time in many hours I had also thought about poor Nameless.

Lara crossed the hall with a beer for Jarret. Good on her: she wasn't fussing with a glass, just taking the bottle as if the boy was a regular bloke. But she would come the heavy sister if she knew what I was up to. I stole towards her fridge. Though the Chomp was still waiting on my bench our cat deserved a double treat after his period of starvation.

Those damned tree ferns. Tomorrow I'd put this house on the market and move out. This would be the last time I arrived here on my own, those dark wings beating at the night wind. This was when the heroine always thought the adventure was over but someone sprang on her out of nowhere one last time. This was when the audience squealed one last squeak with the fright of it, the fun of it, the thrill. This was when the true hero was revealed as he bounded to her side.

And wouldn't that be nice. But Caine had been told that our relationship was over. He was probably lying on his ark-like bed, a beer in one hand, the TV remote in the other, having a well-deserved rest after this terrible week when he was first dumped then stapled. In any case, if Bernard had not fled the city, his tricky knee would hardly let him leap. My adventure had petered out and I gave thanks. In real life, loose ends usually stay dangling.

As soon as I'd opened the door I hurried round turning on the lights in every room. The sling I'd discarded on Monday was still draped on the kitchen handle. My arm was sore as hell, but before I put the sling on I had better feed the cat.

'Nameless? Kitty-kitty . . .' Isn't it strange how your voice goes to that register whenever you call cats? Just like, when you talk to a baby . . . Oh dear. The end of each real-life adventure had its morning after. This one would also have its night-time feeds.

Still calling Nameless, I unwrapped the cold sausage I'd nicked from Lara's fridge and opened the back door.

Bernard strolled out of the darkness. He must have been waiting in the vegetable patch near the clothesline. Did I say strolled? He mooched, sauntered, a little ungainly on that leg indeed, but truth was, this villain *ambled*. I backed up, hoping to reach the hall and dash across to those very useful students — but in one of his nifty sidesteps, Bernard had me cornered by the kitchen door.

Oh boy, was I tired of this kitchen.

'I will scream,' I said, ashamed of how the threat fluttered in my throat.

'Of course you will,' said Bernard. 'Because I'm going to unwrap your hand and rip each stitch out until you tell me where the rest of the jade is hidden.'

'I don't know!'

'Hah!' was all he said.

Don't faint, I told myself — then thought it would be better for me if I did, as soon as possible.

I twisted to the side but he pinned me with his dishonest, unlovely bulk. He bent my arm and started to unwrap it. He squeezed — the wound hurt horribly — oh God, the thought of pain to come was even worse. My legs were water. I tried to scream but only let out a series of high squeaks — how foolish this must look, me still with the sausage in my other hand, waving it up by Bernard's ear.

There was a chitter and a growl in the darkness outside, and something masked and furry hurtled through the back door. It stuck claws in Bernard's shoulder and savaged at the sausage. Bernard yelled, struck backwards at Nameless, turned awkwardly and slipped, blocking the hall doorway. I lurched away, grabbed the sling, flipped it over his head and figure-eighted it back around the handle. Harder than Tilda had done, I kicked his knee. It felt great. I booted it again then ran like hell for the back yard.

I tripped over the bricks around the clothesline — something large and soft lay under it — tore round the side of the house and over the road. I beat on Beth's door and gasped out what had happened. She and her flatmates poured out and up my front steps. I waited. I heard shouts and thumps.

A band of very happy campers, so to speak, hauled Bernard out to my veranda. While we waited for the police to arrive, they spent a busy, noisy time trussing him with climbing ropes. We left his scratches bleeding. After a while I asked one of the burlier male students to check round the back for me, by the clothesline — the guy wasn't so happy then, when he returned.

I thought I'd better go and see for myself. One horror more or less, what did it matter?

Those activity-mad students brought their strong torches. Bright poached-egg lights flowed over the back lawn, the bricks and, lying on them, a man in a pinstripe suit with wide lapels. He was face up, the gun and holster showing, a crowbar by his side, his eyes and mouth agape. One tooth looked freshly chipped. It seemed Bernard may have killed that American man-in-suit, on the brick-work my dad had laid. Bernard killed the goose that was going to bring the golden egg? Don't ask me to explain villains. I guessed, once again, that greedy thieves fell out.

I stumbled back down the side path and sat on my front steps, endeavouring only to take one lungful in, then slowly out, another in, then out. That was the last loose suit, apart from the missing burial trousers.

Beth appeared and sat beside me. 'I hope you don't mind, I've just fed your cat. He sicked up something horrible so I put down fresh water and opened some Chomp. He's whiskers deep and very happy. Does he always sound like heavy machinery while he's eating?'

I patted her hand to say thanks.

The police arrived. Again Caine turned up with the rest. This time, though, he didn't stay with his colleagues at the crime scene but said he'd take me back to Lara's.

I sat shivering in his passenger seat, a hand up to my eyes. He put the key in the ignition, but didn't turn it.

'I should've been the one who arrived in the nick of time,' he said. 'I should've done High Noon for you.' He rubbed his nose (by now I was peeking). 'Would it have made a difference?'

I bundled my hands on my lap. 'I kind of like the way Nameless came into his own. He got the villain his way.'

How awkward we were.

'Suzie, I hope you've guessed — or Gifford told you, that I . . .' Even in the dark, I saw his blush. 'That I really am a good guy.'

'Yes. He did.'

Caine did that rueful thing with his lower lip and I wished he wouldn't. 'Suzie, I heard Roger's business was being investigated — and that came to nothing — but it led me to the rest of it. I didn't know for sure how much you knew about what your sister and Bernard were up to. I bent rules to keep a check on you.' He cleared his throat. 'The thing is, I wasn't sure if you too, somehow, could be a bad guy.'

I turned that one around a while before I answered. 'You would've covered for me. That's what you planned.'

He did that rueful thing again.

'You took the stickies from the table, about Gifford? You hoped I wouldn't notice. I thought you knew me, Caine.'

He seemed a little bit ashamed.

'But you didn't know they'd stashed poor Maisie in my pantry. Why did they do that!'

Caine coughed as if he wanted to conceal a little grin. 'There was a language problem. It also seems it had something to do with the weekly delivery of meat a day earlier than expected.' He glanced at me in the dark. 'I'll never understand villains.'

And this was the ace detective.

He raised his hand to the ignition.

'Um — so — where is Maisie now?' I asked.

His hand dropped. 'Right now, she's on her way to the — that place you don't like to hear the name of. A squad checked the house tonight, the house where Roger hid you, and opened up the double garage. The place is jointly owned by Maisie Forrest and Katherine Tiller. They've been partners for five years or so, apparently. That's romantic partners, not just to do with Suite Three.'

A few more stereotypes blew apart for me. A hundred thoughts tumbled round but all that came from my mouth was a little moan. How brave those women must have been, how much in love and happy, how pleased to overturn convention and find contentment, and don't misunderstand me — I say it's always hard to stand up for who you are. Another little moan escaped from me — then for those women to have it ended because of someone else's greed and misdirected obsession.

Could any obsession be well directed? Maybe mine, for my kids — oh God. My kids. Now there were three, or would be in a few more muddled months.

For a moment we sat in the brewing darkness.

'Caine, there's something you should know . . .' I still couldn't make myself tell him about the baby. 'I — I know I've messed up.

You've seen my dark side. It's true, as Luke said, I find it hard to trust anyone.'

His hand moved to the ignition again. 'It's okay, Suzie. You and Luke are good together. I understand.'

'No, Luke and I aren't . . . Oh no. Luke is much better as an ex-partner, believe me.'

He gave me a funny look and dropped his hand a second time.

'Um . . . So you have resigned?' I asked.

'Just about.'

'What will you do for a job?' I asked to gain more time.

Caine shrugged. 'Private investigator? Maybe not.'

'I don't suppose,' I said, 'you'd like a sidekick? Well — a partner? In a year or so, that is, I'd have the time.'

He stared at me sideways as if it would hurt to look full on. I did the rueful thing myself and put my good hand on my stomach.

'Lara's GP thought this was about ten weeks,' I said. 'Okay, we took precautions but that tricky Mother Nature has her own ideas, it seems.'

A sound came out as if someone had punched him. His eyes were full of questions. I nodded. He gave a shout, paused, then gasped and swept me to him till I felt nausea again. Two grown-ups in a car, I've mentioned my ideas on that already. I yipped. Caine released me a little, cosseting. Little sliding emotions felt as if ropes were also being loosed around my heart and belly, where the centre of everything lay.

'Are you okay?' he asked, his mouth against my hair.

'Yes, yes . . .' I couldn't bear to let go of him.

But I didn't want to get too sloppy so I added that it had been a week of such surprises as he did not yet dream of, that for instance with this baby I could afford disposable diapers. I leaned on his chunky clean-smelling shoulder. Caine nuzzled my ear and it felt good. I remembered how when Jarret was a baby, I'd snarled about having to use a clothesline in midwinter, fingers white with cold, how wind whipped around me as I was slapped by wet towels and cloth nappies, how when Tilda was a two-year-old, Dad — my crazy unfather, the dad of my heart — had built the brick surround for my outdoor line after he'd finished hurting his thumbs in my kitchen . . .

I had a sudden notion where the trousers might be hidden. It would be so like Dad to ditch elaborate plans halfway for what was easy. That toothy man-in-suit, whatever billionaire private collector he worked for, may have had it figured it out.

We could deal with that tomorrow. I began to laugh a little.

'What is it?' asked Caine against my face.

I let him kiss me. I'd tell him when he'd definitely left the police force, once I didn't have to share him with his job.

It stumbled through my thoughts that this hadn't been a thriller so much as a rite of passage for the early middle-aged. An ugly sister notion said that mutual mistrust was as good a basis as any for a modern relationship.

Don't let me fool you. I was happy. And may I tell you this: how much more precious happiness is, when it's laced around with sadness and self-knowledge.